"Robert L. Duncan is a very good writer. This is adventure writing at its best, with down-to-the-line maneuverings where a few seconds will make all the difference. It will be surprising if this does not come out as a film. It certainly has all the ingredients for a major thriller."

—*The New York Times*

"Robert L. Duncan's *Brimstone* is highly ingenious, highly topical. The hero, Cameron, receives the 18½ minute tape missing from the Nixon tapes. Not only does this constitute an irresistible bait for the reader but links the plot to one of the most notorious political scandals of our time."

—*John Barkham*

"All the elements combine in a thriller as smooth and sinister as the deadly missile at the heart of the Brimstone plan, honing in on its helpless target."

—*West Coast Review of Books*

"Adventure writing at its best...a major thriller!"
-- New York Times

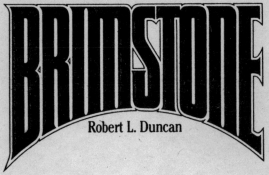

BRIMSTONE

Robert L. Duncan

A TOM DOHERTY ASSOCIATES BOOK
Distributed by Pinnacle Books, New York

BRIMSTONE

A Tor Book. Reprinted by arrangements with William Morrow and Co., Inc.

First Tor printing, January, 1981

ISBN: 0-523-48025-3

Cover illustration by Paul Stinson

Printed in the United States of America

Distributed by Pinnacle Books, 1430 Broadway, New York, N.Y. 10018

Chapter One

Cameron was vaguely disturbed but not surprised at what was emerging from the computer, the chattering pattern of dots which formed the contours of a system of hills and valleys and the profile of what appeared to be a village arranged on an elongated square. The computer printer paused when the sophisticated map was complete and the cursor light on the terminal display winked at him fretfully, as if waiting for the next instruction.

He lighted a cigarette, fascinated, then punched the command into the keyboard.

LIST DATA

Immediately the names of the village streets began to chatter out of the printer in Russian, a language which he could identify but not decipher. He shut down the computer immediately and called Saunders.

"We have another one," he said. "We'd better put our heads together on this."

"Come on up," Saunders said.

Cameron locked the door to his office behind him, glancing up at the electric clock on the wall before he boarded the elevator. It was about eight-thirty; the clock was erratic, always off by a couple of minutes as if time really did not matter in the General Accounting Office Annex. It was going to be a long night.

Saunders was in his office, appearing unruffled as usual, sitting behind his free-form desk with his pipe clenched firmly in his teeth, a single paper in front of him. He disengaged his pipe just in time to catch a sneeze with a linen handkerchief. "I hate the climate here," he said. "It's the goddamned humidity. If it's not that, it's the pollen." He blew his nose. "What's up?"

"I'll be damned if I know," Cameron said, sitting down. "The Defense Intelligence Agency's computer has gone on the blink again."

"What project are you working?"

"I'm making a routine audit of Defense Department financial accounts AA-7016 through QB-8812. I should be getting nothing but expenditures and budgets but I'm picking up Russian maps on account LF-1113."

Saunders grunted, sneezed again before he picked up the telephone. He leaned back in his chair, stared toward the ceiling as he gave the number and waited to be connected. "George," he said. "This is Harley. Look, check out one of your accounts for me, LF-1113. We're picking up a hunk of Russian geography." He grimaced toward Cameron, covering the mouthpiece with his hand. "I'm trying to persuade the GAO to set up a branch in Aspen, Colorado," he said. "Clean air contributes to sharp thinking, that's my argument. As a matter of fact, they should move the whole damn government to the mountains." He turned back to the telephone again. "Shoot." He listened, nodded, a frustrated expression creeping onto his face. "No," he said. "If it's coming through on our terminal, then it's not classified. We sure as hell aren't going to shut down while you boys go through your nut act." He shrugged. "See you Wednesday."

He put down the telephone. "The insanity gets to me once in a while," he said. "You're going to get a dozen of those maps from that account number, all part of a package documenting a Russian nuclear accident back in the late fifties. The damn things have been declassified for a year and a half but he's not sure whether we should have a copy." He sucked at his pipe which had gone dead, proceeded to relight it. "Go ahead and run the damn things."

"Will do," Cameron said.

"By the way, while I have you here, I need to get some information from you," Saunders said. "Have you been the fox in anybody's hen house lately?"

"Are you serious?"

Saunders shrugged again, slid the paper across the desk to him. Cameron recognized the form, an internal audit, a check on the watchdogs, and his name had been typed in at the top. "I went through this six months ago."

"Internal security's putting it to you again," Saunders said. "I raised a little hell about it this afternoon, but it didn't do any good. They picked you by random selection, supposedly." He paused. "How's Annie?"

"How the hell would I know?" Cameron stood up, the old irritation catching him by surprise, not only at his ex-wife and her father but also at the typical Washington paranoia which he tried to avoid but could not. The new audit could indeed be routine, random selection, or it could be a part of the Senator's continuing revenge because Cameron had married his daughter and divorced her. Or the audit could have been generated by a drunken remark made by Annie to one of her high-level friends at a cocktail party. In any event, the result would have to be the same. He would have to call Harvey and see if the results of the last audit could be updated, to save everybody time and trouble.

Saunders leaned back in his chair, rubbed his chin thoughtfully. "Do you look on me as a friend, Willie?" he said. "I don't want you to take what I'm about to say the wrong way."

"That's not in question," Cameron said. "Hell yes, we're friends. What's going on?"

"I've been in government twenty-three years," Saunders said. "And I've developed a sixth sense, especially about my department. I can see budget cuts coming long before they're discussed, and when one of the girls is about to go off the deep end, I sense it before her ass begins to twitch." So, he went on, he functioned as a psychic seismograph, picking up tremors with uncanny sensitivity.

A man named Adamson had been appointed to head a government budget team and he had picked the Defense Projects Section of the General Accounting Office to begin his quest for reductions in government spending. Adamson came in with his crew of accountants and statisticians, making all the right noises, but Saunders was suspicious of him from the first.

"God, I don't know why," Saunders said. "But out of seventy-five employees, he seems to have a special interest in you. Every time something comes up with your name on it, he makes a point of copying it."

"I'll talk to him," Cameron said.

"I don't think so," Saunders said. "There's more."

"All right."

A week ago, Saunders went on, there had been a routine meeting at the Mayflower Room and Cameron's name had come up over dinner, not from Adamson but from one of his accountants who asked if the Cameron in Saunders' section was the son of the late Harry Cameron. Saunders said he believed so, yes, and the accountant expressed the opinion that of all the men around Nixon's Watergate, only Colonel Cameron had come out smelling like a rose. He wanted to know how the Colonel had managed it. "Adamson didn't open his mouth," Saunders said. "But I had the distinct feeling that the accountant was speaking for him."

"I think you're being overly sensitive," Cameron said. "My father was something of a controversial man. He makes good conversation."

"Maybe so," Saunders said. "I hope that's all there is to it. I think you're in for a lot of trouble. What kind, I don't know. But you know the ropes. It wouldn't hurt for you to have a chat with Annie and find out if there's any pressure coming from the Senator. I'll continue to zero in on Adamson to see if you really are his target."

"If there's any pressure building on the section

because of me, you have my resignation. You know that."

Saunders shook his head. "That's no solution, Willie," he said. "We'll let things ride for now."

By the time Cameron reached his office, he found that he was nervous despite his disbelief. He was not sure there was any movement against him at all—Saunders was a man who dramatized everything, invented crises in order to keep his mind and instincts sharpened—and if by any chance Saunders was accurate this time, Cameron did not believe that Annie was behind it. Ah, sweet Annie, he thought, and he sat down behind his desk and flipped the switch to activate the printer and allow it to finish its run. Sweet Annie with the insatiable itch for diversity, and who was she living with now, some liaison officer at the French embassy, some congressional clerk? Always a bedward tilt toward men connected with government and through it all an absolute amorality, not the slightest twinge of guilt.

He felt the familiar pain, not severe, and he picked up the telephone and dialed her number. He was informed by a recording of a change in numbers and he dialed the new one, listening to it ring eight times before she answered it and he deliberately blocked any vague wondering about what she was doing that accounted for the delay in answering. Her voice came on the line slightly breathless. She was always slightly breathless as if she was in a constant hurry, for fear of missing something.

"Hello, darling," she said.

He laughed despite himself. "How do you know who's calling?" he said. "Hell, you could be somebody's wrong number."

"Willie?" she said, delighted. "Is that you?"

"The same. How are you, Annie?"

"I'll tell you in person," she said. "I'll come right over. I have a new album I want you to hear. Shall I bring wine?"

"I don't live in the apartment anymore. I moved into my father's house in Georgetown."

"I'm sorry I didn't come to the funeral," she said. "I thought about it."

"It wasn't pleasant."

"You know me so well," she said. "I have a bad time with things that aren't pleasant. I don't think your father's house is pleasant but I'll come over anyway."

"That's not a good idea," he said. "I just need information, Annie. Is the Senator still on my case?"

"I have no idea, darling. We'll talk about that when I see you."

"You're not going to see me, Annie."

"You're not at home," she said, ignoring his discouragement. "I can tell that. I can hear the computer. Oh, I meant to call you anyway. Two men from the army came to talk to me about you."

"The army?" he said, his interest quickening. "What did they want?"

She laughed lightly, her own private laugh, signaling an advantage as a minor victory. "You see?" she said. "I need to come to your place after all."

"No," he said. "You can tell me now."

"I can but I won't. I'll see you in an hour or so. I know the address."

The telephone went dead and he put it back on

the cradle. He regretted calling her, regretted
exposing himself to even an echo of the pain he
had once felt over her. He could not be sure that
she had any information at all, that indeed the two
army men even existed, for she was a consummate
if non-malicious liar, inventing facts and
situations whenever she needed them for
dramatic impact. Well, he would meet her and
find out what she knew and send her home.

The computer printer had stopped and he
gathered up a print-out of the maps and put it in a
briefcase, then sorted through his library until he
was satisfied he had no better Russian atlas here
than he had at home. Then he left the building and
instead of trying to catch a taxi, decided to walk.

The snow was light and there was scarcely any
wind at all, but before he had gone three blocks he
was chilled to the bone. Off in the distance he
could hear an ambulance or a police car, an
emergency vehicle certainly, and he was aware
that he had not spent a night in Washington in
seven years that he had not heard at least one
siren screaming through the streets.

Washington was an emergency city, despite its
aura of unassailable permanence, and the people
who lived here were perpetually scurrying under
the threat of crisis. He had the fantasy that
someday the weight of all these multiple crises
would become unsupportable and all of the people
would evacuate, leaving those monuments and
memorials as deserted as some gigantic cemetery.

He felt numb with the cold by the time he
reached the house in Georgetown, an old Federal
brick which his father had restored at great cost,
and he could remember the old man standing in

the icy slush on the street, fretfully supervising
the installation of the massive door which had
been copied from one at Monticello. There was an
irony there, the old Washington syndrome, that
his father should have spent so much time and
effort on this house as a perfect site for his retirement only to die in an accident within days after it
was finished.

The moment Cameron let himself into the foyer,
he knew something was awry. There was a light
burning in the library and he knew he had not left
it on. He could not see into the library itself, only
the light spilling out into the sitting room. Something inside him turned cold. Somebody was here,
he knew it, and the thick interior walls of the
house had absorbed the sound of his entrance. He
could hear the whispering rasp of a drawer being
opened in the library. How many people were in
there? One? Two? He lowered his briefcase to the
marble floor, making no noise, and then he opened
the drawer in a small Flemish table in the entryway, slipped his hand inside. His father's pistol
was still there. He pulled it out quietly, the weight
of it reassuring. He stayed motionless a long
moment, listening.

He moved quietly through the sitting room and
just as he reached the door to the library, the light
blinked out. He was so startled that he pulled the
trigger and the pistol went off, bucking against his
hand. The smell of cordite was strong in his
nostrils and he heard the crash of something
breaking in the library. He flattened against the
wall, waiting, but there was no further sound.
Finally, he reached inside the library door, his
hand groping along the wall for the overhead light

switch. The light came on. The library was deserted, the shelves of books gleaming in the light as he moved past the old desk toward the hallway.

Whoever had been here had gone through the kitchen and out the door into the blowing snow in the courtyard. He flipped on the outside flood-lights and pulled back the drapes in the dining alcove, but the glaring lights reflected against a blinding screen of snow and he could see nothing.

He closed the back door, put the dead bolt into place, drew the drapes, then went back into the library and poured himself half a glass of bourbon from a decanter on the sideboard. He picked up the telephone, dialed the special number he had been instructed to call, reported the break-in. Then he surveyed the damage. The bullet he had fired had struck a lamp which his father had brought back from China, a porcelain monstrosity which Cameron had never liked anyway. The pieces were strewn along the top of the teak table and onto the Persian carpet.

Curious, for that was the only damage in the room and nothing else was out of place. The carved desk sat intact. All of the drawers were closed, no sign it had been rifled. And then his eye happened to catch on the lower bookshelf where he kept the large volumes in his library. There was a book of European art he had bought in Paris which had occupied the place at the far left side of the case, the last book on the shelf, but it had now been juxtaposed with a volume of Oriental prints.

He sat down in a chair facing the wall of books, his drink in his hand, studying the arrangement on the shelves. His work called for him to be meticulous, nothing out of order, and the books had been alphabetized, but they were in order no longer. Here and there a volume was out of place, not a wholesale disruption, just a scattered pattern of books drawn out and put back in an improper order. The intruder had been looking for something. He had no idea what.

The drink calmed him. He went upstairs, turning on all the lights in the bedrooms, and was cheered by the fact that nothing was disturbed up here. He heard the door chimes and went downstairs to admit a tall lean man in a gray topcoat who identified himself as Wicker, showed identification from the Documents Security Section of the GAO, and stood in the entryway, brushing the snow off his coat while his eyes examined Cameron.

"Are you all right, Mr. Cameron?" Wicker said.

"I'm fine," Cameron said. "It's just that it happened so quickly, so unexpectedly."

"It can be damned unsettling." Wicker moved into the sitting room, looking around while Cameron filled him in on what had happened, the light in the library, the exit through the kitchen door. "As far as I can tell, there's nothing missing," Cameron said. "A few books are out of place in the library."

"I'll have a look around," Wicker said.

"Can I offer you a drink?"

"A brandy would be appreciated."

There was something comforting about having Wicker here, Cameron decided as he poured the drink. He could hear him in the kitchen, opening the back door, going out into the courtyard briefly before he reentered, closing the door behind him.

He came back into the library, looked at the shattered lamp, then sat down in a wing-backed chair and accepted the brandy glass which Cameron offered him, cradling it in his hands. "He's cleared away, whoever he was," he said, sipping the brandy, his voice palliative. "Now, the question is, what was he after? Do you keep documents in the house? Do you have a safe?"

"I sometimes bring work home overnight. I don't have a safe."

"Classified documents?"

"Print-outs," Cameron said. "I run audits on government projects. Hardly the kind of thing to attract a thief."

"You never can tell," Wicker said. "I've been in security twenty years and I've seen some strange things in my time. I had a case once in which a young black man was trying to sell a public directory of the State Department to the Russians." He sipped the brandy, the light reflecting off the round steel frames of his glasses. "It's possible, of course, probable, that what happened here was not document related at all. This is a fine house, full of items which could be sold for a good price."

"Then why didn't he steal anything?"

"Because you interrupted him just as he was getting started."

"I don't believe that. He went through the books on the shelves. How did he get in?"

"I checked your lock before I rang the bell," Wicker said. "It's an old one, fairly easy for an experienced man to get past. I would guess your intruder picked the lock, let himself in, started in the library, just as you came home. You shook him up, that's for sure, when you fired the shot, and he took off out the back door."

"Did you find his tracks in the courtyard?"

"The wind's too high for that," Wicker said. "Along the brick walk and then over the wall. That's the way I figure it." He finished the brandy, set the glass on the table. "You can always call the District police if you like, Mr. Cameron, but I don't think they will do you much good. Your intruder won't be back, you can count on that, and as you say, there's nothing missing. But I would change the locks, if I were you."

And there it was, Cameron realized, the reason why the longer Wicker talked, the more uncomfortable he himself became. For Wicker was just going through the motions and from some moment in his investigation the doubt had set in and he was going to pass this off. "You haven't explained why he went through the books," Cameron said. "An ordinary thief wouldn't take time for the goddamned books."

"I have no explanation."

"But you aren't even curious."

"Do you mind if I smoke?" Wicker removed a pack of cigarettes from an inside pocket, proceeded to light one, waving out the match and dropping it into a silver tray. "It's been a long day," he said wearily. "I like to be politic in my job, Mr. Cameron, sensitive to people, because by the time I'm called in, the person is generally upset. Have you fired that pistol of yours before?"

"No. But I don't see the point."

"Body chemistry is the point. Metabolism is the point. You come home, find an intruder, fire the pistol and your adrenaline starts pumping. You need some way to dissipate it, some resolution and there isn't any." He stubbed out the cigarette, stood up. "If you say someone has gone through your bookcase, then I won't dispute it, Mr. Cameron. Are you a collector of rare books? Does anyone have reason to think you might use them as a hiding place?"

"No to both questions."

"You're single, I take it. Who cleans your house for you?"

"I have a cleaning woman."

"With your same penchant for orderliness?" Wicker smiled. "I suggest that you go through your house with a fine-tooth comb, Mr. Cameron. If you find anything missing, anything further out of place, give me a ring. Talk to your cleaning lady about the books. And above all, get some good locks on your doors."

Cameron saw Wicker out, watching him hunch up in his bulky topcoat as he made his way toward his car through the heavy snow. Cameron closed the door, locked it, went back into the sitting room, and kindled a fire in the small fireplace. It was entirely possible Wicker was right and he was making too much of it, carrying the paranoia Saunders had planted during the afternoon. Someone had been here right enough, a common thief, scared away. He made a note to question Mrs. Norquist about the books tomorrow. She was a darting, thorough little Scandinavian woman with a ferret-like disposition and an absolute intolerance for dust. It was entirely possible she had decided to tackle the bookcase and then replaced the books in approximately the right order.

He retrieved the briefcase from the entry hall and after he had mixed himself another drink, he settled down in front of the fireplace. He was always distracted by his work, by following the fiscal track of government projects which often led in wondrous directions. He put on his reading glasses and located the first page of the computer print-out, marked LF-1113. This was a special research account for the Defense Intelligence Agency and he could count on the papers to make little sense at all. This section of the agency seemed to be a catch-all designed to handle a lot of non-priority items. He was amazed at the amounts of money funneled out through LF-1113, but it was not his job to judge the policies of the spending of the money but only to include an account of that disbursement in his report to Congress.

It amused him to note that even with the change in administrations, from Lyndon Johnson's push toward social programs, to Nixon's imperial presidency, to Ford's caretaker government, and finally to Carter's version of a people's republic, the budget for LF-1113 remained constant at $47 million a year. He pictured in his mind a group of hoary-haired researchers squirreled away in a Pentagon annex, retired historians perhaps, performing a footnoted overkill to research problems to keep the funding alive.

The whole computer system fascinated him, the sophistication of an elaborate technology which could so easily go awry. There was so much information, so many pieces of trivia collected by intelligence agencies, that to keep the data on paper had become impossible. So now there were literally thousands of computer specialists in

Washington who did nothing but transfer words and numbers from paper to the data banks of the computers where the material was supposed to be immediately accessible to officials authorized to have it.

But there was no such thing as a perfect computer system and the Defense Intelligence Agency computers seemed to be especially quixotic. The LF-1113 file was a good case in point, a perfect example, for all of the expenditures of this subsection had been put into the computer and when GAO requested an audit, the DIA computer was supposed to feed the fiscal facts into the GAO computer. But the DIA computer went occasionally wild, spewing out not only the financial data but material stored in adjacent files.

Looking at the material the DIA computer had dumped on him this time, Cameron could pinpoint the source of this research immediately, a bureaucratic comedy of errors which short-circuited any claims the DIA might make to keep this secret. In November of 1976, a Soviet scientist named Dr. Zhores A. Medvedev had written an article for the British magazine *New Scientist* about two nuclear accidents on the eastern slope of the Ural Mountains in the city of Kyshtym where the Russians had constructed their major nuclear facilities. The accidents had occurred between 1958 and 1961 with hundreds of people killed and thousands more injured when buried nuclear wastes had exploded. More accidents occurred when Soviet scientists exploded a twenty-megaton device over a specially constructed village stocked with sheep and goats to test the effects of the bomb.

A year after Medvedev's article, the CIA had released documents describing a number of Soviet accidents and had been sharply criticized by Ralph Nader for the delay. He suggested that the CIA had sat on the information rather than stir up people against the possible harmful effects of nuclear power in the United States. Incredible, Cameron thought with some amusement, that now, years later, with the research into these accidents already completed and made public, the DIA was covering the same ground on its own.

He flipped through the maps made by the computer and on a separate pad listed the Russian cities covered by the research team, hoping to catch them in a spelling error at the least. Asbest, Nizhniy, Tavda, Arnshe, Novaya Lyallya, Droitsk, Beloretsk, Kartally, Bayanovski, Tagil, Ufa, Satka. He went into the library, moving past the smashed lamp, running his hand along the shelf until he located the Russian atlas. He carried it back to the sitting room but he found it difficult to concentrate. The wind was moaning against the house. He still felt a residual frustration from the intruder, a mild outrage that no place was safe anymore and that the authorities, whether District police or Federal Security, could not be counted on to do any more than commiserate with him and advise him to buy better locks for his house.

He thumbed through the atlas, realizing that what he was doing was bizarre. At the University of California, he had been a crusader for government reform and now here he sat, poring over reports which had cost the DIA a fortune, able to do no more than needle the Pentagon bureaucrats over inconsequential matters when once he would have stormed against a wasteful system. But then again, he was older now and aware that the system could not be changed, and perhaps this form of protest was better than nothing.

He ran his finger down the irregular line of the Ural Mountains, locating the cities, the names written in English characters, fortunately, and he located two errors right away. The DIA boys had added an extra "l" to Novaya Lyalya and put the wrong suffix on Bayanovka. But something struck him as odd, for one of the cities he could not locate at all, Arnshe, and he flipped back in the atlas to the list of alphabetized cities. Still he could not find it.

He picked up the print-out and folded the sheets awkwardly until he found the map for Arnshe and placed it on the table to study it. Apparently, Arnshe was a town of 2,461 people, relatively cohesive in that the streets were few and close together. The map showed concentric circles superimposed and centered over the intersection of the principal street and a road which, from the configuration, appeared to wind up into the mountains to the east of the town.

It disturbed him that he was unable to locate the name of the town in any Russian listing, but when he consulted the print-out accompanying the map, the reason began to come clear. Evidently, this was the deserted town the Russians had used in one of their nuclear experiments with a population of sheep and goats, and there was a kill projection in the data which explained the concentric rings.

POPULATION: 2461
ESTIMATED CASUALTY TOTAL: 2461
                              PRIMARY: 1592: WITHIN 1 HOUR
                         SECONDARY: 615: WITHIN 3 HOURS
                           TERTIARY: 254: WITHIN 6 HOURS

With ground zero immediately above the intersection, using sheep and goats, then either the
Russians or the DIA had estimated a clean sweep.
Further data showed that warning signs had been
posted at five kilometers on all access roads,
advising motorists not to stop in the contaminated
zone.

It was no wonder the name Arnshe did not
appear in his atlas. It was possible the Russians
had given this name to an experimental village
which had never really been a town at all. It had
been blown away, obliterated in one test of the
new technology. And if the print-out was correct,
they had been thorough, for there were military
hardware symbols in the legend to indicate that
Russian army equipment had been placed in that
town to test the effects of the nuclear blast.

He was about to turn his attention to the budget
columns on a separate print-out when he heard
the door chimes. His first thought was that Wicker
had returned, but the clock on the mantel above
the fireplace showed one o'clock. Too late for
Wicker. When he turned on the outside light and
looked through the peephole, he could see Annie
peering back at him, her face distorted by the fish-
eye lens. With a feeling of slight dread, he opened
the door and let her in. She was a small woman
engulfed by a massive sable coat which still
carried snow on it and with a flourish she shed it

in a heap and revealed the fact that she was wearing nothing but a short, lacy nightgown beneath it.

Her bright eyes were examining his face, looking for either shock or surprise because she fed on both, but he allowed neither to show. "I forgot you were coming," he said.

She moved past him into the sitting room. "I hope you don't have company, darling. And I didn't bring any wine. But then, I'm not thirsty and you don't care for it, so it would be a waste."

In the sitting room, she curled up in a wing-backed chair, smiling at him, and for a moment he felt a pang of desire, and irritation that she had purposely provoked it. She knew he could see her breasts beneath the lace and she posed herself reflexively, giving it no thought, so that her fine golden hair would be backlighted by the fire.

"This is only partially for your benefit, darling," she said happily. "Actually, I had decided not to come and went to bed and then decided to come on the spur of the moment. But then, I want you to see what you're missing."

"I'll give you that," he said. "You were a great piece of ass."

"Touché," she said, smiling. "I've touched you. You never get crude like that until you're wounded. But I don't take that description as a slam. I was a great piece of ass. I still am a great piece of ass."

"I've had a long hard day, Annie," he said. "What do you want?"

"I want to come back to you."

"What's the percentage?" he said. "What's the point?"

"We used to have interesting conversations."

He looked at her sober face and realized she was quite serious. He laughed aloud and freshened his drink.

"We did. You have to admit that."

"The years with you were not only enough, Annie, they were too much." He sipped the bourbon. "Besides, what happened to the British attaché, Arnold?"

"Roger," she said. "Poor Roger. I spent a couple of months with him and then suggested he find somebody who knew the words to 'Rule Britannia.'"

It was good to have her here and he had passed his own test. He looked at her as she shifted to reveal the slightest hint of inner thigh, shaking her head to clear the mane of golden hair from her face, and he realized that all of the anger and the possessiveness he had once felt so keenly had burned away. He was able to see her dispassionately, a self-indulgent girl who despite her thirty years had never grown up.

"Why are you looking at me that way?" she said.

"What way?"

"It's what I call your measuring look."

"That's about right, babe," he said. "We had some interesting times, I'll admit that. But my desire to live in a volcano is gone."

"All right," she said with a sigh, hugging her knees. "But we can still talk, can't we?"

"Sure," he said, and now he knew why she was here. At times during their marriage she would reach the point where she was unable to maintain her façade and she would sit for hours, her legs doubled up, her arms clasping her knees, and the words would tumble out of her with a spontaneous honesty, and then she would weep and he would be drawn into that openness of hers and mistake it for permanent change when it was no more than a temporary catharsis, a release of excess emotion.

"Do you know how old my father is?" she said. The old theme, yes, her father the Senator, the reference point around which her neuroses gyrated, the unattainable and flamboyant man with silver hair and the mercurial cunning of a southern fox who had become a power in the Capitol, bringing his jowls and his shaggy condemning eyebrows to battle in committees, and his fierce eyes to bear on his daughter who outraged him and broke every one of his verities, her unknowing form of silent warfare. And sitting here, she worried about her father's age, that irrevocable creep toward physical debility and senility and death, about what she would do once he was gone and how she could make things up to him.

"The things he's had to put up with," she said, almost to herself, and she began to talk about the men in her life and the outrageous things she had done and how she was ready now to settle down, to start being ordinary again.

He smiled slightly. "When have you ever been ordinary?"

"Part of the time we were married."

"Which part?"

"Why do you insist on badgering me?"

"I'm not badgering you," he said. "But it's no wonder your father was after me for such a long time. You make him believe that it's the men in your life that screw you up."

"He still doesn't like you. Sometimes, I encourage that because we get along so much better when he has someone else to blame for my sins."

"I want him off my back," he said. He changed the subject. "You said two army men came to see you about me."

"I really don't think it was important, darling," she said. "I really was just using that as an excuse to come over here."

"You didn't make it up, then? There really were two army men?"

"Yes. Totally unimportant, believe me."

"Let me be the judge of that," he said. He told her about Saunders' suspicions, the intruder who had been here tonight. "You can consider me more than slightly paranoid," he said. "Who were the men? What branch of the army?"

"I'm no good at names. One was a Captain, I think, and the other was a Major. I'm sure of that much."

"Pentagon?"

"I don't know."

"What did they ask you?"

"They wanted to know if your father called me from Las Vegas the day he was killed. They wanted to know if he had left me anything, if his will had included me, that sort of thing. I told them no. They asked if I had seen you lately, if your father left a large estate, if I knew how much money you had. I told them that I was independent, that there was no alimony, that you were presumably a hard-working public servant, that if they wanted to know about your finances they would have to ask you, and that I considered the army to be the asshole of the services."

"So you said that?" he said, smiling.

"It didn't please them," she said, moving again in the chair, looking directly at him, eyes wide, serious. "We are going to make love, aren't we?"

"Yes."

"Then I would like to have a small glass of wine."

He brought her one and she made room for him in the chair and held the glass by the stem, between thumb and forefinger, holding it up to catch the reflection of the firelight. "I am the way I am, darling. I'm not likely to change."

He was touched by her attempt at warning. "You don't have to protect me from you," he said. She drank her wine and extended the glass to him to be placed on the end table. He placed his fingers lightly against her throat, her skin incredibly white, and he felt the pulse of her heart and the tension in her tendons. She held her head back, her eyelids closed and fluttering slightly as if she was about to be sacrificed. "You can let go," he said quietly.

He traced the line of her neck with his fingertips down to her shoulders and her breasts and she was trembling so that when his mouth met hers it was not so much a kiss as it was an inner explosion, feverish, and he gathered her up, this slight and vulnerable woman whose arms were wrapped so desperately around his neck, and he put her down in front of the fireplace and lay beside her. He drew her to him with great care and held her tenderly, tucking her head beneath his chin. Slowly, she relaxed against him. He listened to the crackling of the fire, smelled the pungent odor of the pine logs, felt the warmth of her fragile body. It was good to be alive, even in his father's house, with this woman. His arm tightened around her and briefly he felt the old possessiveness. His mouth sought hers and he kissed her. He brought himself up short. This was Annie and nothing had changed and he had no desire to be one in a long line of men.

"Ah," she said, when she at last had breath to speak. "You can be touched, darling. You can be reached." She ran her fingertips along the outline of his lips. "I reached you again."

"That was never the problem, Annie." The feelings were gone. He sat up, fumbling for a cigarette, lighted one for her. "There was never a time when I couldn't be reached. And now I can be reached but I'm not susceptible. Do you know the difference?"

"I will like living with you again," she said. "This time it's going to be different."

"No."

"No what?"

"We're not going to live together again," he said.

She was quiet a moment, inhaling on the cigarette, her face turned toward the fire. "Do you mind if I spend the night?"

"No."

"I froze my ass off getting here, just for the effect. Was it worth it?"

"It was a marvelous effect."

She sighed slightly. "Good." She stood up, slightly unsteady, looking in the fire. She was a beautiful woman, he decided, and she always had been, the whitest skin he had ever seen. He reached out and touched her leg, surprised to find it warm.

"The bedroom's at the top of the stairs," he said.

"You're not coming up?"

"In a little while."

He watched her disappear up the staircase while he sat and finished his cigarette and became aware of a change he had gone through since the last time he had been with Annie. For then he had been obsessed with permanence, with correcting the problems between them, with seeking a final resolution as staunchly immutable as the brick fireplace. His father had always been in pursuit of permanence as well, projecting his plans into this house, the future, considering marriage again, travel, the accumulation of experience, and now his father was thirty days dead and in the ground at Arlington and that permanence had been illusory after all. His own preoccupation with permanence, with security, had died with his father.

He would like to see Annie from time to time. He would take her for what she was. But there was no way he would go back to the kind of life they had had before.

He stood up, closed the glass door on the fireplace, thinking about the intruder again. Something was eluding him, some combination of facts he could not put together. And then he caught the glimpse of a possibility. Suppose the intruder here tonight had not selected this house at random after all. Suppose this was not connected with the Senator's revenge in any way. Suppose that the search was not for articles of value which could be pawned or sold. Suppose that the two military

men who had questioned Annie had been looking
for something specific, something his father had
which the army wanted. Was it possible they had
searched through this house and that he had
interrupted not *before* the fact but *afterward*, just
as the search was being finished?

The paranoia again, the interpretation of possi-
bilities against insufficient data. He yawned,
tired. Two-thirty and he would have to be up again
at seven. He turned off the lights and went
upstairs to bed.

Chapter Two

The next morning at the office, Cameron put in a call to Harv and listened to the secretary's usual protective announcement that Harv was snowed under and would try to get back to him before noon, and then Cameron devoted himself to the computer, feeling more cheerful than he had in weeks. The snow had stopped and the sun had come out and the city was a dazzling white. From his window he could see a line of protesters carrying placards in the street far below, men in plaid jackets tramping a trail through the packed snow. He could not read the placards they carried and had no idea what they were protesting, but their presence cheered him nonetheless.

There were always protesters marching in Washington—against farm prices, low wages, bad decisions, something; it was a sign of normalcy. He had been taking himself much too seriously— he could see that—and he expressed himself by writing a memo to those faceless men behind DIA file LF-1113 in mock seriousness. He pointed out the misspelling of the two Russian names and asked for clarification on the Russian town they had included for which he could find no listing.

Intrigued by the missing city, he put the memo

aside and decided to track it down so he could
include the data in his memo. He sat in front of the
computer terminal and blocked out a flow chart
by which he could hope to get the information. He
had a special fondness for this computer and he
could understand the computer operators who
gave names to their machines and came to regard
them with an anthropomorphic intimacy. For the
keyboard and the display screen in front of him
seemed indeed to reflect a massive intelligence
hidden somewhere in a network of data banks in
this building and in other agencies stretched
across the District. It was as if all the facts, all the
discrete data in the world were recorded here
someplace, stored, requiring only the skill of an
operator to coax the machine to put any required
sequences together and spell them out.

He searched out the State Department access
code, typed it into the keyboard, asked for file
contents, and then addressed the proper memory.
The display screen complied immediately. READY.
And so he entered the name ARNSHE and asked the
computer to search for any record of such a town
on the east slope of the Ural Mountains, and then
he waited while the operating lights blinked,
assuring him that the computer was working on
his problem. Then the words washed onto the
screen.

ARNSHE DOES NOT APPEAR IN ANY
RUSSIAN RECORD OF VILLAGES, TOWNS,
CITIES, PRINCIPALITIES AS OF 1910-1980.
READY.

Very well, he thought, and he broadened the

question and asked for a reply without limiting the date.

> ARNSHE DOES NOT APPEAR IN ANY RUS-
> SIAN HISTORICAL OR GEOGRAPHICAL
> ATLAS.
> READY.

He was fascinated now, puzzled. The secret to coaxing information from the computer always lay in the accuracy of the question, the precise wording. He took all the information he could find on the Arnshe print-out, the configuration of the town, the population, and then asked the computer to compare those characteristics with all the Russian towns on the east slope of the Urals and to give him those which most closely resembled Arnshe.

He lighted a cigarette and waited. In a few moments the computer began to spill out names, the lines scrolling on the screen, and he slowed it down, examining them one at a time, a dozen of them, similar only in isolated characteristics, in approximate population or in the resemblance of some fraction of the town plat. But none of the towns the computer gave him were close enough to the actual configuration of Arnshe to interest him further.

And finally, on a hunch, he limited himself to the altitude of the peak just east of the town, changing the meters into feet, 6,376. He asked the computer to give him all the peaks in the Ural Mountains that came within one hundred feet of that figure. The answer came back almost immediately.

THE MIDDLE URALS ARE AN 80-M. BROAD
PLATEAU (1000-2000FT). MAXIMUM
HEIGHT PEAKS IN 5000-5558FT. RANGE.
HIGHEST PEAK IS TELPOS IZ. DO YOU
WISH COORDINATES?

He responded in the negative. Intrigued, he
leaned back in his chair as Connie came into the
office, carrying a tray of boxed tapes which had
arrived in the mail. She put them down on a work
table and handed him the clipboard for his
signature on the receipt. Then she came over to
glance at the computer, which she always did,
interested in everything taking place in the
section. She was a striking woman, in her late
twenties, he supposed, and she had become something of a fixture in the section, a subject of sexual
speculation for the men over drinks before the
commute toward home, but none of them had ever
had any success with her. As Annie was
ephemeral, Connie was solid, perpetually curious,
eternally good humored. He welcomed the break.

"You must be working a thin-ice account," she
said. "You're frowning."

"I'm always frowning."

"Sometimes more than others." She filled two
Styrofoam cups from his automatic pot, put one in
front of him. "I brought you some time killers, the
supplemental financial tapes that just came in
from the West Coast." She sat down across from
him, crossing her legs, and he felt as if she was
studying him as she studied everything that
puzzled her. "What's troubling you?"

"The DIA has misplaced a whole Russian town,"
he said, thinking aloud. "They collected a hell of a

lot of data on a place which doesn't appear to exist." He sipped the coffee. "It's not important. It's a game I play with the intrepid men of LF-1113. Their imaginary town could be an extrapolation, a projection. But I'm curious to know why they're doing it."

"Who knows why anybody does anything in Washington?" she said.

He saw that she was smiling at him and he realized that for the first time he had been staring at her legs. Attractive. It embarrassed him. "How old are you, Connie?" he said.

"Twenty-nine."

"Where do you come from?"

"Omaha," she said. "I'm flattered."

"At what?"

"You're collecting personal data, right?"

He grinned. "There's a reception tonight, a GAO affair," he said. "It's formal and it's generally very dull but I'd like to take you with me."

"I'd love to go." She wrote her address on a piece of paper, very direct, no indecision. He liked that. She handed it to him. "Do you know how to find it?"

"I'll manage."

"The telephone number is there if anything comes up."

"Nothing will. I'll pick you up at a quarter to eight."

Very good legs, he thought as he watched her leave the office and in some way he had Annie to thank for a new sense of freedom. Well, that was tonight, but presently he was facing a problem and he turned back to the computer, certain that he should back away from this one. For he had

moved into an area which LF-1113 meant to keep
concealed. This single map was one of their covert
information caches, put into the computer with a
mass of trivia which served as a cover. Very well,
he would let it rest.

He destroyed the memo he was drafting for the
boys at LF-1113 and put the bulk of the print-outs
into a large folder, concentrating his attention on
the financial data which occupied another print-
out. It was a routine comparison of their fiscal
outlay as compared with the budget projections.
The telephone rang and he picked it up to find
Harv on the line, his voice querulous, tentative, as
if he took personal umbrage at what happened to
his clients and at the same time held it against
them.

"Lunch," Harv said. "And you had better count
on a couple of hours."

"What's happening?"

"I've talked to your internal auditing people.
Don't any of your people trust each other
anymore? I'll need whatever figures you have on
the preliminary settlement of your father's
estate."

Cameron agreed to meet him at the Carlton. He
rummaged through the desk until he found the
folder containing the correspondence from his
father's lawyers, a rather loose detailing of assets
which, at the end, would not amount to a great
deal of money. He had not been close to his father
in years but he was aware of the Colonel's reputation as a profligate, his taste for showy, glittering women and the passion for remodeling the
Georgetown house, both expensive hobbies. There
was no specific mention in the letters about the

extent of the eventual settlement, but there was a mortgage on the house and sufficient debts to consume whatever cash his father had left behind.

Saunders stuck his head in the door. "Are you at a place where you can take a break?"

"Sure," Cameron said, and he followed Saunders down the antiseptic hallway which for some reason had been painted a hospital-green. Saunders was in one of his fretting moods which meant he had something on his mind and he was obviously irritated by the people who stopped him, asking technical questions, regarding him as fair game outside the protection of his office. Once they reached the elevator and the doors closed, he leaned against the wall, looking at Cameron over the tops of his glasses. "You've turned into a god-damned snowball," he said.

"What are you talking about?"

The elevator stopped on the top floor and Saunders led the way toward a controversial dining room (non-egalitarian, restricted to top men) which was deserted at this time of day. He picked a table next to a panoramic window which looked out at the distant Capitol dome, signaled a white-jacketed black waiter and asked for a cup of coffee.

"A snowball?" Cameron said, smiling.

"A snowball effect," Saunders said, quite seriously. "Those who start generating and collecting controversy continue to accumulate it. What happened at your house last night?"

"I got home to find a burglar there."

"A burglar?"

"Yes. That's what you're referring to, isn't it?"

Saunders grimaced, nodding at the waiter who

served the coffee and then retreated. "Sometimes I actually hate the bureaucracy which I am paid to help sustain," he said. He tasted the coffee, grim again. "You would think that in a multi-million-dollar building, the culinary experts would know how to make coffee that tastes like coffee."

"What do you know about my intruder?" Cameron said. "Did Wicker file a report?"

"Oh, he filed a report all right, a minor classic, and he also sent a copy of it to medical."

Cameron shook his head, knowing instantly the significance of the double filing. For if anything occurred in the course of an internal security investigation which revealed medical problems which could interfere with the efficiency of an employee, the investigator was required to report it to medical. "Have you seen the report?" he said.

"Yes, I've seen it," Saunders said. "You'll get a copy in due course. He reports everything you told him and then demolishes it by refusing to corroborate any of it. He found no evidence of a break-in, nothing in the courtyard to indicate anybody had run out into the snow. He reports that you found nothing missing. He reports that you had been drinking heavily, that you had fired a pistol into a lamp in your study, the bullet lodging in the wall. He reports that you complained about some of the books on your library shelves being out of place. Now, is all that accurate so far?"

"Partially."

"What does that mean? Did he leave anything out?"

"Only the shadings. I had a drink after I chased the man out of my house. That's not exactly heavy drinking. I fired the pistol and the bullet hit a lamp. That's not quite the same as if I had intentionally demolished it. The wind was so strong it obliterated any tracks in the courtyard. I don't have to defend this. We're into a subjective interpretation here."

"Then let's get into objective, hard facts," Saunders said. "You don't have a pistol registered to your name in the District of Columbia."

"It belonged to my father."

"Nevertheless, it isn't registered."

"True."

"And during the whole incident, you left a briefcase full of classified material unprotected, sitting in the foyer, against specific security regulations."

"I put it down when I discovered the man in the library. Is that all?"

"No," Saunders said, becoming more reflective now, quieter, his eyes following a flight of black starlings to the snow-covered rim of the roof. "We also have a complaint from DIA that you are misusing computer access codes to obtain unauthorized material."

"They're trying to cover their collective asses," Cameron said. He told Saunders about the map of the Russian town that didn't exist. "I didn't mess up. They did when they transmitted the material."

"You needled them on the last run-through." Saunders shrugged. "Adamson's putting pressure on me to terminate you, Willie."

"That's bad, then," Cameron said, feeling oppressed, a little short of breath.

"That bad. Adamson used to work for the Senator. They're close friends. Don't underestimate his ability to carry a grudge," Saunders

said. "They have you on the record as emotionally
unstable. Now, they may not be able to dump you
that easily but you can count on continual
harassment until you decide to leave." He
removed his glasses, cleaned the lenses with a
tissue between thumb and forefinger. "I want you
to do me a favor and spare me the aggravation of
seeing you pinned without being able to do a thing
about it. I want to assign you to defense cost overruns with aerospace contractors on the West
Coast."

"Starting when?"

"I'll announce it this afternoon. You can leave
anytime. In the meantime, you go home."

"How long would this assignment take?"

"Six months. A year."

"No," Cameron said.

Saunders arched his eyebrows, replaced the
glasses on the thin bridge of his nose. "You don't
get extra points for stubbornness. There's no such
thing as a revered martyr here. If you get thrown
out of the GAO, you're out, period, as far as the
government is concerned."

"I'm no martyr," Cameron said. "But I'm not
going to be stampeded. I'm not ready to go anywhere, that's the long and short of it."

"All right," Saunders said, resigned. "There's no
formal charge yet. They're just laying the ground-
work. I'll go to bat for you but I want some
guarantees from you."

"What kind of guarantees?"

"First, you send all the material back to
LF-1113, every scrap, and you sign a certificate of
their balance. Obviously, that's a blind fund
anyway."

"All right."

"I'll assign the DIA to Carruthers. He's ex-military and the DIA will be more inclined to accept him. Next, you'll schedule a full physical examination within the next week and get a doctor on record that you're in fine shape, no evidences of alcoholism. Ignore the security report but see if you can find your father's records on the pistol. Then have it registered in your name. At the same time, notify the D.C. police of the break-in and let them know it's for the record, that Wicker was our investigating officer. Then take something home to work on, anything, but just keep a low profile for the rest of the day and I'll inform anyone who asks that I have you on assignment."

Cameron was touched. "Why are you doing this?" he said.

"I'm as stubborn as you are. I'll back you all the way."

"I appreciate that," Cameron said.

He went back to his office and had the DIA packet sealed and dispatched by messenger, then he took a cursory glance at the cardboard boxes Connie had left in the tray. They were all cassette tapes from various reporting government agencies on the West Coast. This had become the age of the minicomputer and the examining auditors simply dumped their findings onto tapes to be mailed back to Washington office. He would take these home with him and examine them and then feed a summation into the central computer.

He packed the tapes in his briefcase and put a Xerox copy of Connie's log sheet in with them. He folded the letters from his father's attorneys and put them in his pocket.

It was cold outside. The sky, brilliantly clear earlier, was now overcast again and he would not be surprised if another storm struck by nightfall. In front of the decrepit Pension Building across the street, he saw two massive farm tractors parked, and a group of men in brightly colored caps and heavy coats was standing in front of the steps, carrying placards which protested farm prices. He was tempted to tell them they were demonstrating in the wrong place but he would have to tell them there was no right place, that all of these buildings were filled with people just like him, and that policy was not set by the President or Congress but in the filtering bureaucracy which questioned some actions and let others pass.

He moved on, facing the unpleasant fact that he had agreed to certify the LF-1113 budget with no examination, that he himself had established a policy which said, in effect, that the DIA could force the automatic passage of an unexamined budget by bringing personal pressure to bear.

The Carlton was mobbed but Harv with his usual efficiency had already claimed a table in the old dining room and he glanced at his pocket watch as Cameron approached. "You're late," he said. "Sit down, William."

The waiter approached. Cameron found that he had no appetite. "It's been a hard morning," he said. He settled for soup. "What do you have for me, Harv?"

"That's not really the question," Harv said. "I hear that you're leaving."

"Where do you hear that?"

"I talked to your Mr. Adamson and he was under the impression that the matter was being resolved by transfer. If you're in a different office, you're out of his immediate jurisdiction and he will simply make another random audit here."

"That isn't usual procedure."

"Who can say what usual procedure is in Washington?" Harv said. "Where would they get the idea you're transferring if you're not?"

"That's their plan," Cameron said. He filled Harv in on the pressure against him, and Harv listened with no change in expression. "So I've decided to stay and see this through," Cameron concluded. "We survived one audit this year. There's no reason why we shouldn't take another."

"I need those letters from your father's attorneys," Harv said evenly and Cameron gave them to him, directing himself to the soup while Harv read through them and for the first time Cameron detected a slight doubt on Harv's face, a furrow between his eyes.

"What's wrong?" Cameron said.

"I'm not sure anything is. But we're going to have a rather large discrepancy to explain."

"What kind of discrepancy?"

"I think your father meant well but he obviously didn't know anything about the tax laws." He picked at the salad in front of him as if grading the lettuce. "Eighty-seven thousand three hundred fourteen dollars and fifty-six cents," he said. "Does that mean anything to you?"

"No. Should it?"

"Probably not," Harv said. "But that amount was transferred to your account at the Hanover

Trust Bank as of three o'clock yesterday afternoon."

"Are you sure?"

"Hanover Trust is not a charitable institution,"
Harv said with a slight smile, his jaws grinding
mechanically on the salad. "I called the bank this
morning after I talked to you and I had a friend get
me your current balance figure. The deposit
startled me and I asked my friend to check it and
he backtracked to discover it had been transferred
from Credit Suisse in Geneva, from a blind and
numbered account, its secrecy protected under
Swiss law." He discarded a shred of lettuce,
separating it from the body of the salad with his
fork. "The romaine is gritty. Not up to their usual
standards here."

"The money must have come from my father."

"I've run into this kind of thing before. A husband establishes a trust for his wife in a Swiss
bank and then when something happens to him,
the money is automatically transferred, generally
in cash, with the husband hoping to avoid probate
and taxes. Sometimes it works, sometimes it
doesn't." The fork speared a fresh leaf, carried it
to the thin, even incisors. "Your father's lawyers
know nothing about it. Ordinarily, we would just
file an amended estimate with Internal Revenue
and nothing would come of it."

"But," Cameron said. "I hear a qualification."

"A rather large one." And as Harv talked,
Cameron felt a quiver of apprehension, for this
man, sitting across from him, methodically consuming his lunch, was outlining a potential
disaster in the same flat voice he would use to discuss the weather or the traffic. "Given sufficient

time, it might be possible to establish your
father's Swiss account as the source of this
money. With the tax people, the circumstances
would be *prima facie* evidence which they would
be inclined to accept, especially on our
declaration and payment of taxes."

But Cameron's position had to be taken into
account, Harv went on. Cameron was in a
sensitive position, responsible for certifying many
very large government accounts and traditionally
the employees of GAO had to maintain a reputation more spotless than that of Caesar's wife, for
the opportunities for extortion and the temptation
to accept bribes were considered particularly
great. "If you go through another audit, the
money's bound to surface. They can make the
assumption that the money was the result of an
illegal transaction. You're in this business,
William, so I don't need to give you a lecture.
What would you think if you suddenly uncovered
an amount of money this large in somebody's
personal account, money transferred from a blind
source?"

Cameron leaned back in his chair. His irritation
at Harv faded, for Harv was simply the bearer of
bad news. He signaled the waiter and ordered a
bourbon and water. He knew how the section
worked and if Adamson got wind of this discrepancy now, this sudden bequest, it would be
sufficient grounds to call for his immediate sus-
pension. He was required by regulation to report
this to Saunders himself and put a clarification in
the works, but he could not bring himself to do it.
"What do you suggest?" he said to Harv.

Harv was at the coffee stage of his meal now.

Carefully, he stirred in the cream, added sugar. "Considering your circumstance," he said, "I would take the transfer. That would forestall any immediate audit. Then, I would file an immediate declaration with the IRS, explain the situation in writing and ask them to file with Swiss authorities for disclosure. You would be stating your case through indirection and by asking the IRS to investigate, you could then claim, justifiably, that you believed the transfer of funds to be a routine one, the settling of your father's estate, and that you saw no need to file a supplemental report with the GAO until you had their findings."

Ah, the labyrinth again, the twisting path of law and a governmental logic which was not logical at all. All foolishness. He finished his drink and ordered another, remembering Saunders' injunction about alcohol and disregarding it, aware that Harv was slipping the pocket watch out of his vest, sliding his eyes down to the golden face. The time allotted for the luncheon had clearly expired.

"I'll give it some thought," Cameron said.

"Just give me a ring and I'll file with the IRS." He beckoned the waiter, examined the check with a sharp eye and then signed it. "It's always good to see you, William. Let me know what you decide."

Cameron stayed where he was. He finished his second drink and ordered a third, beginning to feel comfortable for the first time today. His eyes fell on a woman in a distant booth, in the act of laughing, head tossed back, perfect lips pulled away from even teeth.

A quite normal world after all, and he had been going about this from the wrong direction, dealing with the peripheral issues which would vanish once he had solved the central problem. He would have to deal with the Senator directly.

He had encountered the Senator the last time during the divorce proceedings when the old man had called him a "son of a bitch" outside the courtroom for subjecting Annie to such pain. He had never disillusioned the old man by telling him the truth about his daughter. But now a confrontation was mandatory. He would see the Senator and talk out the situation with Annie to back him up. Once the Senator understood, he was bound to remove the pressure.

He went to the hotel lobby and the row of telephones, and as he was about to dial Annie's number, he saw a dark man in an army officer's uniform standing at the hotel desk, staring in his direction, and he had the feeling he was being watched. He pushed the feeling away from him and dialed the number.

The telephone was answered with a recording of Annie's voice. "I'm never home," she said. "And if you knew me well you wouldn't expect to find me here. I'll be at Sinbad's Retreat after ten o'clock. When you hear the tone, don't leave a message because I can't stand recordings."

He looked up at the Senator's number. He glanced toward the hotel desk. The army officer was no longer there. He rang the Senator's office and when a secretary answered, identified himself.

"This is William Cameron with the GAO," he said. "It's quite important that I speak to the Senator."

"Did you say the GAO?"

"That's correct."

"Is it concerning the GAO reception tonight, sir? The Senator is running about an hour late and wonders if the service awards can be delayed until nine o'clock."

"I'm calling on a personal matter," he said. "I suggest you call the office of Harley Saunders."

Ah, no need to track the Senator, no necessity for making appointments. In many ways, Washington was a small community and he should have known that the Senator, head of the Appropriations Committee, would be there tonight. It would work much better this way, an informal meeting in neutral territory.

He took a taxi, went home to the house in Georgetown.

2

He enjoyed his work and he had discovered in his years in Washington that he was one of the few who did, for at cocktail parties and dinners and informal meetings of the section staff, there was an underlying state of discontent as if whatever a man was doing now was only temporary, a way station to higher position and greater responsibility and money. His father had been caught in the same tide, and his father had been a Captain who had spent all his time planning an ascendancy which would eventually see him assigned to the White House with the rank of Colonel. It was there that his discontent had reached a final flowering.

For he had been close enough to the center of power to see Nixon and Haldeman and Ehrlich-

man and to speak to them, to observe that they
were in effect no brighter than he himself was,
and yet through circumstance, through mere
chance, they were running the country and he was
assigned to transportation and accommodation,
following orders in the hope that one day he would
become another General Haig, move from the
eagle of the Colonel to the stars of the General.

It was all vanity, of course, a part of the game,
for his father had neither the background nor the
political acumen to rise any higher than he did.
Cameron had never been caught in the same kind
of ambitious discontent. On looking back, he could
see that he had been most satisfied in his entry-
level job at GAO, setting up financial programs for
the computer. There had been a simple order to
his life then that was lacking now. He had not been
called on for subjective judgments. There was a
cold clarity to mathematical functions, a comfort
in certainties.

Now, prowling around his library, he was
uneasy. Mrs. Norquist had removed the pieces of
the lamp, the Persian carpet was pristine, but
there was the bullet hole in the oak paneling to
remind him of last night. And there was her one-
word answer on the note he had left asking her if
she had touched the books yesterday. No.

He uncovered the computer terminal on the
refectory table and removed the cassette tapes
from the briefcase, checking them off against the
log Connie had prepared. There were perhaps two
dozen of them, routine, and he stacked them next
to the computer terminal.

One of the tapes mystified him temporarily. It
was in a regulation mailing carton but in the

upper left-hand corner was the designation
number of an agency he had not seen before,
GAFX/734, postmarked Las Vegas, Nevada, and
the mailing label had been marked for his
personal attention. He opened the mailer and
realized that the cassette was not one of those
designed for computer use. He was curious. He
searched around until he found a cassette player,
inserted the cassette and sat down to listen.

The recording was poor quality, the tape hissed,
but he could tell that it was a conversation
between two men in a large-sized room which cast
a muffled hollowness on the voices, and there
were background sounds which obliterated an
occasional word, the rattling of coffee cups
against porcelain saucers, the scraping of chairs,
the shuffling of feet.

He was intrigued. The mailer had been marked
with his name, for his special attention, and it was
obviously meant that the tape should have some
significance to him. He took the time to pour a
drink and laid out a yellow legal pad on the table
and supply of pencils, preparing to transcribe the
conversation. For the moment, he would label the
first speaker as "A," the second as "B." He ran the
tape back to the start, pressed the *play* button and
began to write.

A: Come on in.
B: Thank you, sir. I realize that
A: Uh huh. There's never a good time
B: The newspaper stories
A: Never, uh, trust what you . . .I'm thinking that
B: I wouldn't have requested this time but
A: There are things that can't wait. Shit, that's

B: life here, right here
B: Did you get the position
A: I think I had a summary paper. Well, but was this included in the NSC summary? I
B: No, I don't believe so, sir. This hasn't gone through the Joint Chiefs or the NSC. Clyde was supposed to bring the position papers directly to you, if you'll remember
A: Clyde's daughter, yes, how is
B: I have no recent report but she
A: A real tragedy. Suppose you fill me in, uh, not the details, general principle. Uh, how close
B: Are we?
A: Yes.
B: A year, sir. Maybe eighteen months
A: Until it is operative, correct?
B: The threshold of operability, sir, yes, the best estimates
A: I never trust best estimates, but

The pencil lead broke and Cameron turned off the recorder briefly. The conversation was incredible, like dialogue from a Pinter play. He picked up another pencil, turned the recorder on again.

B: A personal guarantee, sir. It is
A: Then it's more than an estimate. It's your
B: I have a copy of
A: The position paper?
B: Yes.

There followed minutes of extraneous noises, the sound of a chair being moved, the rustle of paper. Obviously, A was reading. When he spoke again, his voice was so tentative, his thoughts so rambling, that Cameron had to move the tape back and forth to record the words.

A: I have never, uh, I have always been opposed to, uh, but this is a violent world. These projections you have, I, uh, are we talking hypothetical or actual?

B: What?

A: I mean there has to be a line drawn. So is this just theoretical or

B: Either, sir. I mean

A: I understand. A terrible business, but

B: There are precedents, sir, if

A: Don't tell me about precedents because I know there are precedents and they don't mean ... I mean, to justify something. What do you want from me?

B: Permission to proceed, to examine alternatives and

A: We never know what's down the road. If I had certain things to do over, well ... You are projecting casualties here. I

B: Not necessarily, no, sir.

A: The position paper says you plan to use a hundred and ten men of which you would lose

B: Not lose, necessarily, no

A: But your projection calls for a casualty rate of fifty percent, and

B: Of course, in a study of this sort we would hope for an optimum survival rate. With improved technology

A: No guarantees, then. I hope to hell you know what

B: Always a risk, but

A: This name, BRIMSTONE, uh, ominous sounding. It's

B: That's our in-house designation only and

A: How are you currently funded?

B: Under a blind defense account number, fully

> funded under FY seventy-two

A: Forty million

B: More or less, yes, with auxiliary split account.

There was another pause, more paper shuffling.

A: The public would never understand, uh, BRIM-STONE, not good connotations. You can never, uh, even a hint of a study like this, under-estimate public opinion. Always some bastard to misinterpret. That's the story of my . . . after Vietnam, uh, always somebody . . . And this will increase our defense capabilities by

B: Not just increase. Revolutionize

The conversation was interrupted by the ringing of a telephone and a word was obscured. Cameron attempted to pick it out, replaying the section, but he could not. He let the tape continue.

A: Yes. Ten minutes. [*Sound of telephone being replaced*] I must tell you, I have great doubts, but . . . the location, uh, the area

B: Remote

A: The arrangements, uh, complicated. They seem very

B: The scientific measurements

A: I see. Necessary. Then the arrangements

B: They're tentative. We have lists

A: I can remember one trip down South. I was quite young, and, uh . . . this business, politics . . . I've sometimes thought . . . I could have stayed in New York where all the hassles . . . predictable. Do you come from a large city?

B: Nebraska. A small town, population of twenty-

three hundred and fifty-six, but then, California

A: California has changed. [A buzzer] [Yes] All
right.

B: I take it you want us to continue, sir.

A: With conditions, uh, strong conditions

B: Yes, any

A: You stay on track, make the arrangements.
Then one year from today, at the outside, you
show me a guarantee, no casualties

B: I don't know, sir, if

A: That's the condition and

B: And at that time the final go-ahead. Yes. I
appreciate your taking the time to see me
now.

A: The business of the country has to go on.
Stay

B: I'll keep in touch, sir.

And there the tape ended. When the cassette
player clicked off, he took out a cigarette. He had
not gotten all the words onto paper, they were not
precisely correct, but he had the essence of the
conversation and it made no sense at all. Two
government men talking about a project he had
never heard of and for the life of him he could not
understand why this had been sent to him.

On impulse, he dialed an access number to the
central computer and placed the telephone on the
interface, giving him a tie-in. He asked a simple
direction of the computer, to search the
accumulative memories of all government agencies and to let him know all government projects
in the past forty years which had carried the name
BRIMSTONE. In less than a minute the display
flashed on the screen.

THERE ARE NO UNITED STATES GOVERN-
MENT PROJECTS/UNDER DESIGNATION
"BRIMSTONE" FROM 1/1/40 THROUGH
THIS DATE.
READY.

That was that. In all probability, BRIMSTONE had
been one of those thousands of government operations which had been formulated, considered,
explored, and then abandoned before any action
was taken. He would have to call Purdy in Las
Vegas and ask him what in the hell the tape was
supposed to mean. But not now. It was getting
late. He had lost track of time and he was due to
pick up Connie at a quarter to eight.

Chapter Three

Over the years there had been frequent changes in the government functions Cameron attended, and they generally reflected the attitude of the man who sat in the White House, ranging from the beautiful-people image of the Kennedys to the strained pomp of the Nixons. But the section's annual reception-dinner honoring people who were retiring seemed unchanged.

For as long as Cameron had been with the section, the affair had been held in a hotel ballroom, well catered, black tie, a formal affair which was like the celebration of a family sacrament with the presentation of hand-lettered scrolls and engraved plaques and gold watches, depending on the position of the retiree.

But as Cameron entered the ballroom with Connie beside him, radiant in a formal gown, he was aware that what had once been the ritual of an extended surrogate family had become a political arena, a forum for exchanging inside information, and there were a half dozen Senators and Congressmen here tonight, scattered through the crowd, and they were not here to pay tribute to departing personnel as much as they were here in recognition of the growing power of the section.

"It's the age of the accountants," he said aloud.

"Beg your pardon?" Connie said.

"Do you recognize Adamson?"

She peered through the swarm of people. "There, standing by the head table, the bald man." Yes, bald, with a head that shone as if it were waxed, Adamson, a svelte man in a tailored dinner suit, not one hair on that shining dome, wearing heavy tortoise-rimmed glasses, and even from this distance Cameron could see an affected smile on his face as he chatted with a Senator. The true autocracy today, he thought, the watchdog of the watchdogs, and Adamson looked to be a man who would play the role to the hilt. From what Cameron knew of him, Adamson was an ivy league CPA who had been plucked out of a lucrative practice in New York City in an attempt to make the GAO razor sharp.

"I'd like a drink," Connie said. "If we can get past the Marines."

"No problem," he said, and he led the way through a platoon of Marines in dress uniforms, playing violins as they strolled through the crowds. At the long bar, he established a position and then looked back to Connie. "What do you drink?" he said.

"At this time of night, I'm not particular. Bourbon is fine."

He collected two bourbons in plastic glasses and led the way to the far side of the ballroom, away from the congested center. Chairs had been placed along the wall flanking a dance floor which would come alive later in the evening, after the dinner and the speeches.

"The poor bastards," Connie said. "Why do they do it?"

"Which poor bastards?"

She nodded toward the six honorees and their wives who were being positioned at the head of the line near the buffet tables, flashbulbs popping as staff photographers urged smiles. "There's a Mr. Jensen who's been with the government forty-one years," she said. "Forty-one years of one desk after another to end up with a drink and a watch and nothing to fill his time."

"He went with the government a year before I was born," Cameron said. "I know him. He always liked the routine." He sipped the drink. The bourbon was first-rate now, but by the end of the evening the bartenders would have switched to a cheaper brand.

"Do you?" she said.

"What?"

"Like routine."

"I could use some, along about now," he said. "Ordinarily, all of the people in the section with lesser ratings would have touched base with me, but it appears we're out of favor. If you want to get ahead with the GAO, you've picked the wrong escort tonight."

"I have no desire to get ahead with the GAO," she said with a smile.

He was getting nervous again, despite his attempts to keep himself calm. Adamson was talking with Saunders and he wondered if they were talking about him. He looked at Connie. "I'm lousy company tonight," he said. "I'm sorry about that."

"I don't blame you. I understand. Why are they

out to get you?"

"You know about that?"

"Everybody in the section knows about it."

"It's much too long a story for here and now. What are you doing in Washington? How did you come to work at the GAO?"

But no sooner had she begun to tell him than he knew Senator Beckwith was coming into the room and he did not see the entrance as much as he felt it, the rustle at the far side of the room, the presence of power. He kept his eyes on Connie's face as she talked but his mind was on the Senator. There was an art, predicated on proper timing, to dealing with powerful men, and here tonight, with the Senator very much aware of his influence upon the room, and filled with self-importance, the timing was wrong. Nevertheless, it would have to be settled here tonight. Tomorrow might be too late.

"You're not listening," Connie said tolerantly. "What can I do to help you?"

"You're doing it," he said. "Just put up with me."

"Certainly," she said. "And now I think we should go through the buffet line."

He found, once he had reached the table, that he had no appetite. He picked at his food and finally caught the attention of a waiter and asked for another drink. He sat through the dinner and the presentation of the retirement awards with a growing weariness and by the time the Senator was introduced to make his remarks on the importance of economy in government, Cameron's sense of awe had passed and he could see the Senator for what he was, a tired old man who was hanging on to power with a death grip. When the speech was over, Cameron watched the section officials gathered around the Senator. The small orchestra was beginning to play on a raised stand flanking the dance floor.

"I have to see the Senator," he said to Connie. "I should be back in a few minutes."

She nodded and he made his way through the tables. Saunders was speaking with the Senator, hunched forward as if in deference, and his face darkened perceptibly as he saw Cameron approaching but to his credit there was nothing more than that to mark his uneasiness.

"Good evening, Senator Beckwith," Cameron said, and the Senator turned slightly. "I want to talk with you, Senator."

"I don't think we have anything to talk about, Cameron."

"We can have this discussion here or we can have it in private," Cameron said, firmly. "But we are going to have it."

The Senator considered a moment, then shook Saunders' hand. "We'll be talking, Harley."

The Senator led the way behind the buffet tables to a door opening into a section of the lobby which was all but deserted and then waved Cameron ahead of him toward a blue velvet couch positioned beneath a painting of George Washington. The Senator remained standing, unwrapped a cigar, clipped off the end, rolled it in the flame of a gold lighter, every movement precise, a practiced ritual. As he clenched the cigar in his teeth, he rolled his eyes slightly toward Cameron. "What do you want?"

"I want you to stop the harassment."

The Senator waved the cigar slightly, dismissingly. "I want you out of Washington and I'm not without power in this city."

"You continue to blame me for Annie, Senator. That's a mistake. You must know that Annie was the way she is long before I met her. You must know that she has gone to bed with enough men to fill the United States Senate."

The Senator glanced at him sharply, those pale and rheumy eyes filled with an almost unbearable pain, and Cameron could tell that for a long instant the Senator knew that Cameron was telling the truth. He drew himself up to his full height. "And you, sir, are a lying son of a bitch." Abruptly, he turned away and walked back toward the ballroom. Cameron lighted a cigarette, waiting for the anger to subside.

In the ballroom, the orchestra was playing a waltz because the section head enjoyed old-fashioned music. Cameron found Connie near the small dance floor. She put her hand on his arm, concerned. "Are you all right?" she said.

"No," he said. "I'm not all right."

"We'd better go someplace else," she said instantly. "I think the hotel has a bar."

The bar was dark, cavelike, the booths lighted by candles; it was decorated in a pirate motif and the waitresses wore Jolly Roger caps. He ordered a double, aware of the concern on Connie's face and the fact that she was giving him room to talk. "Have you ever been married?" he said.

"I lived with a man for a year and a half. We didn't go the marriage route."

"What broke it up?"

"I don't know," she said. "He was a climber in

the State Department and he always wanted more than he had. It was very complicated. But we decided we didn't want to live together anymore."

"Amicably?"

"No. Bitter brawls. A bad business."

"Always a bad business."

Cameron began to talk, pausing only long enough for the waitress to serve the drinks, no filter on his mind now, nothing to screen the relevant from the irrelevant. He told her what had happened and then expanded into his marriage to Annie, the procession of men—not all government connected—random men, confrontations, denials; finally, confessions without tears, choices, preferences, a negotiated balance, then concealment and pretense until the time came when he refused to tolerate it any longer.

"I don't know why I'm telling you all this," he said.

She ran her index finger around the rim of her glass, a thoughtful expression on her face. Beautiful by candlelight, he thought, illogically, a stranger, somebody he knew only from encounters at the office. "I think you're a kind and decent man," she said. "I also think you're in an impossible situation. Everybody knows about the crazy lady you were married to. There's absolutely nothing you can do about what she does, one way or the other. So if the pressure is on you to transfer and that will solve anything, then leave. I guess what I'm saying is that the only thing you can do is to protect yourself, as best you can."

It was possible that if he went to California, the situation would resolve itself. But he did not believe it. The country was too small for that, the continent had become compressed and Annie had included him in the battle, made him the center of it. Relocation would not change that.

"You're right, of course," he said. "But I can't let this pass. I have to do something about it. What time is it?"

"A little after eleven."

Eleven o'clock and he remembered the recording on Annie's telephone. She would be at Sinbad's Retreat now, and he knew what that was, a new sex club, one of a franchised chain, the final liberation from the old values. Quite suddenly, he realized that his drinking tonight was inappropriate, for there were hard decisions to be made and he could not afford to be muddleheaded.

For the first time, he noticed the miniature flagpole on the table, the small banner with the skull and crossbones on it, clever, and he pulled the string and raised his flag to the top of the staff. When the waitress appeared, he ordered a cup of black coffee and then pinched the bridge of his nose, trying to dispel the fatigue, the incipient headache.

The coffee was hot, bitter, black. He drank it in silence. "It's going to be a long night," he said, standing up. "I'll drop you by your place."

"I can get home by myself," she said.

"I know you can." He paid the bill and led her out into the snow-filled night. What the coffee had not accomplished, the chill wind did and he was suddenly quite sober. He raised a hand to signal a taxi and helped Connie in, knowing as he climbed in beside her that what he was doing was more than a demonstration of chivalry. Under normal circumstances, given enough time, they would have become close friends, lovers perhaps, but he could see little chance of normalcy ahead of him.

The taxi reached her apartment house and he saw her to her door.

"This isn't what I had planned for tonight," he said. "I enjoy your company and instead I have to climb back in that taxi and spend the night tracking Annie."

"I know," she said. "I wish you luck." She leaned forward, kissed him lightly. "I'll see you tomorrow."

He waited until she was inside, then reluctantly he went back to the taxi, turning his mind to the unpleasant business ahead of him.

"Do you know a place called Sinbad's Retreat?" Cameron said through the protective screen that separated the front seat from the back.

"That's going to cost you double fare. It's out of the District."

"That's all right."

The taxi lurched off through the snow and he leaned back against the seat and counted the money in his wallet. A hundred in twenties, a couple of tens and fives, a few ones. He would make do. He would find Annie, take her down to see her father in Alexandria tonight, force her to tell the truth. He would not try to resolve what was going on between her and her father; that was beyond his understanding as well as his control.

"You know what Sinbad's Retreat is?" the driver said.

"Yes."

"It's none of my business, buddy, but they're not going to let you in by yourself. They have a rule against stags."

"I'll manage."

"That's up to you."

He rode for an hour and the city faded and he could see the deep woods in the snowy glare of the headlights. Finally, the taxi turned up a narrow lane and he saw the country lodge settled in the trees against the bank of a hill, an almost idyllic setting. The taxi drew to a stop in the parking lot dotted with isolated cars half covered with snow. The driver shut off the meter.

"Wait twenty minutes for me," Cameron said, "and I'll pay triple fare."

He could see the driver shrug through the wire mesh. "In advance."

Cameron folded three of the twenties and pushed them through the slot in the screen.

"Twenty minutes," the driver repeated.

He crossed the parking lot to the front entrance and was surprised to find that the door was not locked. It opened into an elegantly furnished foyer, a small reception room where he was greeted by a man in black tie. "Good evening, sir," the man said pleasantly.

"You're a hell of a long way out." Cameron forced a smile as he went through the process of removing his coat, brushing the snow off it.

"I'm afraid you've wasted your time, sir," the man said. "We have a club rule against singles."

"I understand that," Cameron said. "My wife's already here. I was supposed to come with her, but I got held up. Let me talk to your manager, please."

The man spoke into a telephone and then opened a door to the right of the foyer, pausing to let Cameron enter first. The office was as elegant as the foyer. The manager, a small man in an expensive silk suit, introduced himself as Raphael. He asked Cameron to sit down in a wing chair by a coffee table and then sat down himself.

"I'm the last one to ask you to break any of your rules," Cameron said, maintaining his smile. "I work for the General Accounting Office and I know the value of regulations." He went on talking, falling easily into the patter, all the right gestures, never losing his eye contact with Raphael, for in his years with the GAO, Cameron had learned how to put a man at his ease, and Raphael was buying the story. "My wife's been here quite often and she assures me that you have excellent security, but I'll be frank with you, Raphael, as much as I appreciate what you're doing here, let's say that I'm in a sensitive position."

"We like to think of ourselves as a life-style private club," Raphael said. "And we pride ourselves on the fact that we respect the privacy of our members."

And Cameron could tell that Raphael was balancing the risk against the overhead, influenced by the dearth of cars in the parking lot, the terrible weather, and finally he nodded and the rule had been bypassed. Cameron felt pressured by the time limit on the taxi outside; it would be impossible to get another one to come out here on a night like this and he feigned attention while Raphael described the physical layout of the club, the steam rooms and the Jacuzzis, the relaxation room and the pinball room, and of course all liquor and food was complimentary and Cameron removed his

American Express card, keeping an eye on the
clock, three minutes for the formality of a young
and dazzling girl to take his card and run it
through a machine, and thirty seconds to sign the
statement, quasi-legal, that the nature of the club
had been explained to him, that he was above
twenty-one years of age, and represented no law-
enforcement agency.

And then he went through the door into the
main lounge, semi-dark, the disco music blaring,
strobe lights synchronized with the music, the
small dance floor spotted with couples, and with a
start he realized that some of the couples were
naked.

The ultimate liberation, yes, the final expression
of freedom from the old standards, the ultimate
private act made public, and he accepted a drink
from a hostess carrying a tray, and wandered into
another room where a fully dressed couple was
sitting on a sofa, arguing politics, voices strident,
while they watched a couple screwing joylessly on
some pillows on the floor, a dark-skinned man,
middle-aged, pumping away at a girl who lay
flaccid and passive beneath him. Cameron felt
nothing. The ultimate liberation appeared to have
transformed sex into something totally non-
sexual, an exercise in hydraulics.

Raphael was losing money tonight, no crowds,
more couples in the Jacuzzi pool but they did not
appear to be enjoying themselves.

He went into the steam room and there she was,
naked, sitting on a wooden bench, her hair
hanging down around her face, eyes half closed,
only partially aware, looking more like a girl than
a woman, no sensuality here. There was a fat man

in another part of the steam room. Cameron
ignored his presence, sat down on the wooden
bench beside Annie, and his anger turned into a
deep-seated pain. She stirred slightly, looked at
him, only half-seeing him. She was spaced out on
something.

"Willie," she said. "Hello."

"Oh hell, Annie," he said despairingly. "So this
is what it comes to."

"Hang loose, darling. The steam is good for your
pores."

The fat man was asleep now, head lolled
forward on a cushion of immense jowls, a light
and rasping snore. Cameron thought of a whole
pattern of confrontations in unlikely places, and
how he had loved this woman once. "I talked with
your father tonight," he said. "What in the hell
have you been telling him?"

A sigh, a slight heave of her damp breasts, a
stirring in her eyes as if she was trying to bring
into focus something which would always be too
far away. "I don't know," she said. "I don't know
why I do things."

"You're going to have to undo this one, Annie,
whether you understand it or not. Do you know
what I'm saying?"

"No." She closed her eyes.

He touched her arm. The skin was cold. "This is
serious, Annie. You're not going to flake out."

The eyes opened. She said nothing.

He felt the tyranny of the helpless. There was
seduction in that. If he accepted her helplessness
now, they would both be lost.

"You're angry with me," Annie said. "I don't
want you to be angry."

"I'm not angry," he said. "Frustrated maybe, because I've never known why it had to be like this." He put his hand on her cheek, steadied her face. "We had some good times together, in the middle of the battles, some fine times. And that's the reason you're going to go with me to see your father."

"My father?"

"Tonight. Now."

"I don't want to do that."

"I know you don't. But it has to be done."

She looked at him, the limp hair falling across her cheek. "Some fine times," she said. "They're still possible, you know."

He shook his head sadly. "I have a taxi waiting. Are you coming with me?"

She paused a moment, then nodded with a distant smile. "Sure. Why not?" she said. "For old times' sake." She stood up unsteadily, not beautiful now, flesh-glistening with steam. "My clothes are in the dressing room. Five minutes. I'll be ready in five minutes."

"I'll meet you in the game room," he said.

The couple was still arguing politics; a woman with ponderous breasts had joined the other man and woman on the pillows. He found the game room, pinball machines for God's sake, nobody playing them, and electronic games, little blips of light moving across the screens, no one in this room except himself. Appropriate, he thought, sex and pinball, both temporary diversions here. A hostess approached, offered him a drink. "There's a couple in the other room who want to know if you'd like to join them."

Politics or sex? he thought, but he shook his

head no, took a drink from the tray and turned his
attention to a pinball machine, watching one of
the chrome balls follow an erratic path between
the bumper breasts of a painted lady, and only
now did he notice that the pinball machine, had a
pornographic motif. Politics and sex, he thought,
and Washington was the perfect center for both,
where it was easy to get screwed, figuratively as
well as literally. He checked his watch. Three
minutes. He would have to tell the taxi to wait.

But as he turned, he saw two men come into the
game room, conservatively dressed, heavily
muscled, cultivated sternness. One of them
approached him with impeccable politeness.

"Mr. Raphael would like to see you," the man
said.

"What's the trouble?"

"No trouble," the other man said. "We never
have trouble here. Now, Mr. Raphael is waiting."

Yes, the cool Raphael, not angry, not upset, but
rather distressed, smoothly chiding. "I'm sorry
you didn't find our regulations comfortable, Mr.
Cameron. I suggest that you leave quietly. The
charge on your credit card will be canceled. We
don't want difficulty any more than you do."

"What in the hell are you talking about? I'm not
leaving without my wife."

"She asked me to convey her regrets."

"The hell she did."

"She informed me personally that you roughed
her up, threatened to kill her. I think it's best if we
both just let the matter drop here. Do you agree?"

Cameron's belligerence collapsed. She had done
it to him again, another one of those terrible and
instantaneous shifts, cutting the ground out from

under him. The men were waiting for him to do something now, to make a move, and Raphael was standing behind his desk, one hand pressed against the polished surface near the drawer. What did he have hidden in there? A pistol? A blackjack? Mace? The other two men had the attitude of professional football linemen: motionless, conditioned to respond only if he moved first.

"I won't make any trouble," he said finally. "I'm going to need transportation."

"Your taxi's still outside," Raphael said. "I took the liberty of asking him to wait."

Cameron nodded and without a word turned and walked out into the snow.

Chapter Four

He spent the next morning preparing for the transfer. He went in to see Saunders first thing and found him preoccupied and fuming over a new directive which had just come in, a result of the congressional reorganization studies which were resulting in a snarl of immense proportions.

"A new order," Saunders said. "We're directed to send all Defense Department summaries through a central liaison now. They're starting from scratch. And we'll not only have to send them budget summaries but a guide to the summaries to let them know what the summaries mean."

"You've got it rough," Cameron said, slouching down in an overstuffed chair. "And I'm going to leave it with you, friend, at least for the time being."

"You've decided to take the transfer then."

"Right. I've counted my accumulated vacation, sick leave, the whole works and I have about three weeks coming. I'll shift my load to some unlucky soul in the next couple of days and leave by the end of the week."

"I'll miss you," Saunders said with a sigh. "I'll contact Adamson this morning and see if there are going to be any complications. In any case, the random audit will stop. What would you say to a commence date in Los Angeles as of first January?''

"Fine," Cameron said. "Hell, I may decide to take a Christmas vacation in South America."

He went back to his office, checked through the in-basket until he found a DIA receipt for the returned print-outs. He could check that off; they could deal with their fictional Russian town in the comfortable knowledge that he would do nothing to compromise it. But they would be scrambling around over there today, debugging their computer, plugging any future leaks.

He called Harv, told him of his decision to transfer, the termination of the audit. "I'm thinking about selling the house in Georgetown," he said. "What do you think it will bring?"

"About a hundred seventy," Harv said without hesitation. "After mortgage, selling expenses, you should clear ninety, maybe ninety-two. But unless you're going to buy in California, I'd hold on to it until next year, keep your taxes somewhat reasonable."

"I'm burning my bridges," Cameron said. "I'll get back to you later."

He inserted a fresh piece of paper in the typewriter, taking the time to light a cigarette, considering what he wanted to say to the Senator.

Dear Senator Beckwith,
 We should have talked about Annie a long time ago so you could have known what was going on from the very beginning. What appeared to be a civilized, even cold divorce was not that at all. Toward the end of our marriage, when Annie's

affairs were not only numerous but flagrant, Annie refused to end our relationship, and it was only when I hired a private detective who collected evidence which I intended to use in court that she finally agreed. Her final consent, I believe, was only made to spare you embarrassment.

I understand your stubborn belief in your daughter; under other circumstances it might be admirable, but it is proving to be very costly to me. I believe you are a fair man. You have a reputation for fairness in the Senate. I think you should have a look at the file which was collected documenting her indiscretions before you continue your vendetta toward me.

I am not trying to appease you. If you continue your sub rosa persecution of me, you will have a fight on your hands. Please do not interpret this statement as a challenge; it is no more than an indication that I don't intend to allow Annie's misadventures to cost me any more than I have already paid.

Sincerely yours,

William Cameron

He addressed an envelope, retyped the letter and then rang for a messenger to hand-deliver the letter to the Senator. They would hold this against him of course, his use of a department messenger for private business, but he did not care.

At mid-morning, Connie came in as usual but he found her slightly subdued. There had been a spark of electricity in her before, perhaps a sexual charge, but now that spark had either been suppressed or had disappeared.

"Good morning," she said. "How are you today?"

"Things are looking up," he said. "I'm transferring out."

"If there's an extra slot in California, let me know. I'm tired of the snow."

No meaning there, office banter. "You have a problem?" he said, getting down to business, glancing at the papers she put on his desk.

"A usual goof-up," she said. "The computer tapes from the West Coast. Do you have them?"

"At home."

"Was there a GAFX-734 among them? From Purdy in Las Vegas? He's doing an IRS survey there."

The conversation tape. GAFX-734. "Yes," he said. "I have it."

"I got another GAFX-734 account tape in the mail this morning so I put it on the computer and got a full print-out, everything Purdy's supposed to supply in a monthly report. So I called Purdy and asked him what was on the first GAFX-734 tape, to see if he was amending his report."

"And what did Purdy say?"

"Besides inviting me to do unspeakable things, he said he only sent one tape, that outside of the bedroom, one of anything is enough."

Cameron picked up the telephone, asked his secretary to get him Purdy in Las Vegas, and shortly Purdy was on the line, cheerful as usual. "I see you have snow up to your navel back there, Willie," he said. "We're supposed to hit seventy degrees today."

"I'm not calling for a weather report," Cameron said. "We got two GAFX-734 numbers out of you

this week. Conie has the numbers and I have a tape
that doesn't make any sense at all."

"Little mix-up here," Purdy said. "Your father
left a tape with me and asked me to send it along if
anything happened to him. I forgot all about it and
then I ran across it and asked my secretary to send
it to you and she put it in one of the regular mailing cartons and got the numbers mixed up."

"The tape was my father's?" Cameron said. "Did
you listen to it?"

"Nope," Purdy said. "I scarcely have time to live
up to my reputation with all the secretaries and
the tourists who've heard of my prowess. I don't
have time for other people's business."

"Thanks, Purdy."

"Come when you can."

He put down the telephone. "Sometimes Purdy
tries my patience."

"Why?" she said.

"He's a devoted family man, completely faithful
to his wife, but his hobby is talking about sex.
About a year ago, he heard we had a new female
operator so he sent her a tape which was supposed to be routine. When she fed it into the
computer, she was faced with an unmistakable
animated display which showed a couple hump-
ing. And written across the bottom was the
legend. 'This is all I want for Christmas, Harriet.'
She was a good sport about it and the program
was run around here until somebody lost it."

She smiled. "Then the first GAFX-734 was a
practical joke?"

"No," he said. "Just a mix-up in numbers." He
leaned back in his chair. "I'm sorry about last
night. It didn't turn out like I planned it at all."

She shrugged slightly, sat down on the edge of the desk. "It was just one of those things," she said. "Did things work out for you?"

"No," he said. "If Annie's involved, things rarely work out."

"Maybe they will. I hope so."

"I hope so, too," he said. "Maybe we can have a drink together before I depart for sunnier climes."

"Sure," she said. "Any time."

2

He went home early, pleased to find that the snow had stopped and the streets were reasonably clear, traffic restored to its usual congestion. When he reached his house and saw that the snow had drifted against the stoop, he realized that he had somehow already begun the mental transition to California and the things he had considered so important yesterday were no longer so. His father's house would pass into other hands and they might paint the original woodwork which his father had restored with great effort. The massive oak door, already beginning to achieve the weathered look his father had wanted, would either be painted or replaced or covered with a modernistic storm door to cut down on the heating bills.
ing bills.

Traditions were worrisome, a burden, and he would be pleased to trade this city of monuments for a culture in which there were no traditions except a free-making rootlessness, where the weather was constant and not an adversary. He vowed to himself to find a different life-style there, to be less serious about his work.

He sorted through the house, listing those things he would sell and those he would have shipped, and the longer the list became the more certain he was that he wanted to keep none of the furniture. It was too bad, in many ways, that he was the last of the line, and his father had been an only child as well, so there were no near relatives to whom he could ship this accumulation of antiques and memorabilia. He would take his library, no more than a hundred books, and leave his father's collection behind.

He worked his way to the arrangement of pictures his father had put on the wall, photographs of his father with famous personages, and a number of them included Nixon and other members of the President's staff. He would take these out of the frames and file them away with the thought that some archive might eventually want to have them. For there was a picture of the President leaving the White House, scurrying along, with the Colonel only a step or two behind him, and it appeared as if Nixon had turned his head to speak to him, a smile on his face. There was tremendous political energy in that photograph which had been one of his father's favorites, for it made them appear to be close friends, and appearances were everything.

Another showed his father at Key Biscayne when the President had gone down to his house there and his staff had stayed in the villas at the hotel. The Colonel was smiling into the lens of the camera in this one, and there was a woman next to him who was probably Rose Mary Woods, the President's secretary. And lettered in ink across the bottom was a date, October 2, 1973.

Suddenly, Cameron went cold, and he began to suspect that the tape his father had sent him was not so unimportant after all. He approached the stack of tapes reluctantly, realizing that he was about to become a part of another of his father's projective dramas. Yet he had to check. He had to make sure. He put the tape in the player, set the footage counter at zero, and then pressed the "fast forward" button, watching the footage counter spin.

Eleven hundred and twenty-two feet.

Approximately eighteen minutes and fifteen seconds. There was no mistaking what it was. He had no idea how his father came by it, but it would be sufficient to stir up the old business once again, the whole thing.

It was the Nixon tape, the missing eighteen and a half minutes which had contributed to the downfall of a president.

And here he stood in his sitting room as the importance of the tape struck him, the enormous implications, for in the millions of words written about Watergate, this was the one missing element. It had been generally agreed that the missing eighteen and a half minutes had been the first part of a conversation between Nixon and Haldeman early in the afternoon of June 20, 1972, the day after the break-in at Democratic headquarters, and that the tape had been erased by Nixon himself, or a member of his staff, because it proved his knowledge of the crime. Supposedly, the erasure had been made during the time the staff was in Key Biscayne in October, 1973, after the tapes had been subpoenaed.

But the conversation had not concerned Watergate at all.

He poured himself a half glass of bourbon and sat down in front of the refectory table, thinking. He had been in Washington long enough to be impressed with a sense of history and he knew he should pass this tape immediately to some branch of the government prepared to investigate the meaning of the conversation and determine its importance. He reached out to pick up the transcript he had made; in that moment the telephone rang and he crossed the room to pick it up, disconcerted, unable to concentrate until he heard Annie's voice, slightly hysterical.

"Willie, please," she said. "For God's sake, don't hang up."

"I'm tired, Annie," he said. "I give up. You win."

"Don't hang up, please."

"You've put me in an impossible bind, so I'm vacating the field, getting out. There will be no more soft reminiscences, no pity, no anger. Nothing."

"I'm sorry about last night. I don't want to be by myself. Please come over here or if you won't do that, let me come over there, just for a while. I apologize for what happened. But I just couldn't face it—"

He put the receiver back on the cradle, not coldly, not dispassionately, because she still had the power to get to him. The last two months of their marriage had been that way, the dissolution prolonged because of her series of appeals, all life and death, that same desperation in her voice, a constant ebb and flow.

But her call, the dramatized hysterics, helped put things into proportion and the cassette which rested in the machine no longer seemed either ominous or dramatic. It was simply a conversation between two men, one known, the other unknown, concerning a project which was being set into motion. He finished his drink, lined up the pencils alongside the transcript, and decided to listen again, to see if he could identify the other man.

He pressed the *play* button, straining to hear the voices. The first was definitely Nixon's and he should have recognized it the first time around but had not. The other man was definitely not Haldeman, too nasal for that, inflections flat. He checked the transcript, ran the tape forward until he picked up the first lead.

> NIXON: I think I had a summary paper. Well, but was this included in the NSC Summary? I . . .
>
> X: No, I don't believe so, sir. This hasn't gone through the Joint Chiefs or the NSC. Clyde was supposed to bring the position papers directly to you, if you'll remember
>
> NIXON: Clyde's daughter, yes, how is
>
> X: I have no recent report but she
>
> NIXON: A real tragedy

Cameron shut off the machine and made a note. A man with the first name "Clyde" who had access to the President and a daughter who had suffered a tragedy should be fairly easy to identify.

He turned on the tape again and let it run, listening to the singsong pattern of the words, Rosencrantz and Guildenstern, and he caught the significance of something he had missed before.

> NIXON: The position paper says you plan to use
>   a hundred and ten men of which you
>   would lose
> X: Not lose, not necessarily, no
> NIXON: But your projection calls for a casualty
>   rate of fifty percent, and

He played it again, listening for the use of the
key word to see if he could be mistaking the intent
here, but he had not. Nixon had said, "You *plan* to
use a hundred and ten men." Plan, not estimate, as
if whatever BRIMSTONE was, there was the
possibility of a 50 percent survival rate. It could
be a military plan, but the transcript showed it
could not be connected with Vietnam. He
searched the tape until he found the part of the
conversation he was looking for.

> NIXON: That's the story of my ... after
>   Vietnam ...

He stopped the tape. *After* Vietnam. He
searched again.

> NIXON: This name, BRIMSTONE, uh, ominous
>   sounding. It's
> X: That's our in-house designation only...

He turned it off again, jotting down notes, knowing he had made a decision without a conscious
resolution, for this was *the* tape all right, a final
pitch by a military man seeking presidential confirmation of a project, something sufficiently

important that the President would break into the
pressured consideration of Watergate to make the
decision. He needed a way to identify X and the
clues were there.

NIXON: This name, BRIMSTONE, uh, ominous
          sounding. It's
X: That's our in-house designation
          only . . . three hundred and fifty-six,
          but then California
NIXON: California has changed.

Cameron could assume that X had been born or
spent a portion of his life in a small town in
Nebraska and at one time moved to California.

He listened to the portion of the tape in which
the word BRIMSTONE was used to make certain he
had not misheard the word "Gemstone," which
had been the code name for another Nixon project,
but the sound was especially clear in this portion
of the tape. BRIMSTONE. No mistake.

He turned to his computer terminal again and
made another search, spelling BRIMSTONE in
various ways in case it had been entered in the
files in some other manner, but he drew a blank.
He let the tape play itself out and when the voices
ended, there was no sound at all. The rest of the
tape had been unused. He turned off the player.
He wondered how his father had come into possession of the tape and about his motives for directing that it be sent to Cameron. Revenge? Perhaps.
An inheritance? Possible. The tape was worth a
small fortune, as a curiosity, if nothing else, but
the implications of that conversation were both
enormous and frightening for they represented a

kind of thinking which had prevailed in the government for a while.

And in this conversation between the President and an unknown visitor, a project had been set in motion which would have required another meeting a year later to countermand. By that time, Nixon was so entangled in charges and counter-charges that he had probably forgotten the project. The possibility of multiple murder. He could understand now why somebody had searched the house the night before last, why every one of the books had been removed from the shelves and replaced, for someone knew that the tape was being sent to him and assumed it was already in his possession and somewhere in the house.

Would they search again? It was possible. He took another mailing carton from his desk, typed a fresh mailing label and addressed it to himself at the GAO, then he slipped the cassette inside with his transcript folded around it.

The telephone rang. Annie, again, but there was something different about her voice this time, the hysteria replaced by a strange lassitude which was not like her at all. "Kings X, Willie," she said. "A couple of minutes of your time, that's all. Not too much, right?"

"What's the point, Annie?" he said without rancor.

"I don't want you to hate me. That was never the point of anything."

"Have you been drinking? What are you on?" He checked himself. These questions were from the past and had nothing to do with now. Annie was always on something; there was always a combination of chemicals and alcohol drifting through her system. "I don't hate you, Annie."

She laughed slightly, humorlessly. "Do you know how difficult it is to make amends, darling?" she said. As she continued to talk, he was able to extract some meaning from her monologue, but he could not be sure of anything with Annie, whether something had actually happened at all or whether she only believed it had happened, or whether it was one of her games.

It seemed she had gone to see her father at the house in Alexandria, and she had tried to explain those years which had led up to the divorce. She had offered her father some insight into how she thought, the way she acted, and she had tried to get Cameron off the hook at the same time. Anyway, he had broken down and wept and when he had finished crying he had begun to rage.

"So he didn't believe any of it," she said. "He thought I was making it up to protect you."

The craziness again, the circle of feelings. "It never ends, does it?" he said, without anger. "I'm grateful for what you tried to do, Annie, but you couldn't bring it off. You try to make amends and you end up exacerbating the situation."

"What does that mean?" she said.

"It means that I know you tried and I appreciate it and at the same time I'm worse off than I was before."

"No, not that. The word 'exacerbate.' That was one of the things that was wrong with our marriage, dear. Much of the time I couldn't understand what you were talking about."

"Oh, come on, Annie. Don't play the dumb-wife role with me." He paused, shrugged. "All right," he said. "You tried to clear things up and it didn't work. I'll take care of it."

"You can't take care of it," she said. "What I mean is, I want to make it possible. I'm really sorry about this and I'm going away and I won't see you anymore." Off on another tangent, drifting into a remembrance of a trip they had taken to California, sheer revisionism, her description of an idyllic time which in reality had been a nightmare, with an English naval attaché following all the way from Washington, calling their hotel at all hours of the day and night because he had mistaken Annie's sexual gymnastics for love and commitment. Annie had forgotten the Englishman. He did not remind her. "You don't have anything to say?" Annie said finally.

"No," he said.

"I really tried to make my father understand."

"I believe you."

"I want to make it right before I go. I want you to come over here. I want to prove that you'll have no more trouble from me. I'll leave the door unlocked. I just want to prove to you that you're the only man I've ever really loved. I never meant to hurt you."

The line went dead. He heard the dial tone and he put the telephone back on the cradle. Always the hook, he thought, always something to keep him on the line. Perhaps once a man was involved with a woman like Annie, there was always a part of him that would respond to her. He remembered the stricken face of the young Englishman over the table at the bar of the Beverly Wilshire when Cameron explained Annie's propensities to him; the young man's face had turned gray and he had retreated without a word. But Cameron knew that if Annie called that young man today, he would begin all over again.

On impulse, he went through the bottom drawer of his desk until he found the envelope containing the report of the private detective which he had not used at the divorce and which he would not use now. Let the old man believe what he wanted. Once Cameron was in California, hopefully the vendetta would end. He opened the envelope at the fireplace, dumped the typewritten sheets and the photographs onto the burning logs and stirred the ashes with the poker.

Cameron put postage on the cassette mailer and put it in the pocket of his overcoat. As he went onto the street, he made doubly sure the door was locked behind him. It had grown dark; the afternoon was gone and he set himself a brisk pace in the long block to the mailbox. He dropped the package in, relieved to have it out of his hands, at least temporarily. He could see a clearing away of problems that had beset him and for which, in many ways, he had to claim responsibility.

There was some truth in Annie's accusation. He had always had the tendency to feel more at home with machines than with people. Even now, on the verge of leaving Washington, he could think of no real friends he would leave behind who were not connected with the section and even more closely identified with computer operations.

He decided to walk to Annie's place; it was no more than a couple of miles from the Georgetown house. The air was brisk. There was an afterglow in the western sky. He could not be sure that her door would be unlocked or that she would be

there, but he did believe she had talked to her
father. Whether she had really had a change of
heart as a result was problematical; she was
mercurial, subject to wild emotional swings, and
tonight, it was possible she was in one of her
tearful valleys.

He passed a bar, one of the watering holes of
Georgetown, a clot of people under a striped
canvas canopy, sleek women in fur coats, army
officers huddled together, laughing, waiting for
their car to be brought around. He felt the same
prickling sensation he had experienced in the
hotel, as if he was being watched, trailed, and one
of the officers glanced at him briefly as he passed,
and for a moment he was certain it was the same
man he had seen at the hotel desk.

He increased his pace, deliberately, watching
his footing on the patchy ice on the sidewalk.
When he reached the corner, he paused in the
shelter of a doorway to light a cigarette, looking
back toward the bar as the party climbed into a
staff car. It pulled of into a side street. His heart
was pounding. Nerves. He remembered an auditor
named Lawson who had uncovered a discrepancy
at some minor agency and developed an absolute
paranoia over an imaginary retaliation which
never materialized.

Erratic power, that was the problem, erratic
power and rampant rumors. Yet, standing here,
chilled to the bone, he did not discount the
element of truth which prompted the wild stories
in Washington. For quite without wanting to be,
he was now at the center of one of the dramas, in
possession of the tape and knowing what it contained.

He began to walk again, calming with the exertion. There was no possible way they could be following him. BRIMSTONE. Probably nothing. One of the thousands of plans hatched during the Nixon administration, during any administration, developed sufficiently that the planning had been funded and had occasioned a chat between the President and the man responsible for the plan.

X was certainly military, but not a field commander. More likely, he was a bureaucratic officer from the Pentagon. His langauge revealed that: phrases such as "FY," "in-house designation." Four dozen possible deaths, a small operation. And then the chilling thought occurred to him. The time frame, yes, and X had mentioned eighteen months at the outside. Dating from June 20, 1972, that meant that this miniature slaughter, this limited killing in the name of the country's defense, could have happened in December of 1974. If so, the men behind it would be most anxious to retrieve the tape.

Cover-up again, suppression of facts, and he pulled his coat collar more closely around his neck. The wind was picking up powdered snow from the drifts. He would not stay in this vulnerable position. Tomorrow, he would retrieve the tape from his mail at GAO and deliver it to the Justice Department and let them do with it what they would.

Annie's apartment house loomed in front of him, one of the giant complexes along the river, and he went into the lobby and took the elevator up to the sixth floor, tired, wanting a drink. The door to the apartment was not locked and he let himself in, welcoming the light, the polka on the stereo, a

German band. He heard the shower running.

For all her wackiness, Annie knew how to live, to create an atmosphere, a pure-white apartment, shining, modern. He shed his coat and poured himself a drink from the decanter on the sideboard and then sat down on the white sofa overlooking the terrace and a view of the bridge with Arlington beyond. The whiskey warmed him; he felt drowsy.

The polka ended; a German march began. The shower continued to drum. The alarm came over him gradually. He put the drink down on a glass-topped table and pulled himself to his feet, anticipating that at any moment the shower would be turned off and Annie would come out of the bedroom, her body wrapped in a large towel. He went to the bedroom door. Her black gown was draped across the white fur on the bed.

"Annie?" he called out. No answer, the shower continuing, the German drums pounding in the other room and he ran across the bedroom and pushed open the bathroom door. The bathroom was all mirrors, walls, ceiling, and they were steamed over, as if there were no hard limits to the room and there she was, slumped in the shower, the stream of water falling directly on the sunken head, the hair like moss, long strands. And the blood was splattered on the mirrored walls of the shower where the spray could not reach. A part of her head was collapsed and with a yell, mindless, he struggled to grab her out of that shower, away from the blood, and the body was slippery, limp, as if even in death she was refusing to cooperate with him. He was blinded by the water from the shower and he put his hands beneath her arms.

Cursing, yelling, he carried her into the bedroom and laid her down on the white fur spread. He was weeping now, angry, and he knew she was dead, her half-lidded eyes glazed, mouth half open, and yet he refused to believe it. He grabbed up the telephone and dialed the operator, forcing coherence out of himself. He told her to call an ambulance, gave her the address and then replaced the telephone with a bang.

He was sick to his stomach and he could not bear to go into the bathroom again, so he went into the kitchen and retched into the sink. Then he splashed cold water on his face and dried with a dish towel, his throat sour. She had given him plenty of warning and he simply had not heard.

He went back into the living room, the German band still playing on the stereo someplace, and he looked for the controls to turn it off, but it was so carefully concealed, hidden in one of the white lacquered cabinets or in one of the tables that he could not find it. Finally, he just stood in back of the white modernistic sofa in a kind of soporific daze, and when he lifted his hand he saw he had left a bloody print on the fabric, a stylized hand, and only then did he become aware that he was soaked with water and her blood.

Incongruous, yes, no organized thought, and she was lying naked and dead on the bed and the police were coming. He could not bear for them to see her that way. He filled a tumbler with bourbon, drank half of it before he gagged and could drink no more. His ears were listening for sirens on the street but he could hear nothing beyond the pounding of the German band.

His skin had no feeling and finally he gathered

the courage to go into the bedroom again. There
she lay, more like an adolescent girl than a
woman, her head rolled to one side so that the
wound did not show. He remembered her lying on
the beach, golden that summer, and he
remembered her coming awake from sleep in New
York, in San Francisco, Paris, and there had
always been a quick delight in her eyes when she
found herself awake. No more.

He wept again, locked in his own grief. When it
had subsided, he opened a bureau, found nothing
but lingerie, went through the closet, unable to
find a coverlet. In the end, he took her sable coat
off a rack and spread it over her body on the bed.
It was then he saw the stereo in the corner of the
bedroom, modernistic chrome and Plexiglas, all
working parts revealed. He turned it off, the
silence overwhelming. He went back into the
living room, his coordination off, the whisky
taking effect.

He answered the door when he heard the chime,
opening it to two policemen, a black man and a
white man, uniformed. He was relieved to put the
matter in their hands. They were trained to deal
with death. He sat down heavily and watched
them, as if from a great distance, as they moved in
and out of the bedroom and the bathroom and one
of them used the telephone while the other came
in to question him. He answered as best he could.

In a few minutes, another crew arrived,
forensic, a photographer, the flash of bulbs, and a
heavy black man with large pores, a rumpled business suit, an impassive face. The black man sat
down next to him, voice impersonal, nonbelliger-
ent, breath smelling of Italian food. Had he been

routed out of a restaurant to take this call?

Facts. What were the facts? Numbers were facts, integers. He gave the black detective movements, times, physical positions, changes, but who would check it out with the Pentagon and it could be suppressed immediately as classified information or it could be classified as a part of the body of the Nixon tapes currently under liti-in a weary voice told one of his patrolmen to drive Cameron home. It was only when Cameron entered the door of his Georgetown house that he realized he had left his topcoat behind.

Chapter Five

General Roffner was being examined at Walter Reed Hospital when Major Shaw arrived and the General knew it was something important but he was in no position to receive the message because he was standing behind a fluoroscope, stripped to his drawers. A young and bearded doctor with hair over his ears was studying the contours of the General's gut and the course of a foul-tasting liquid through the General's system.

"These pains," the doctor said. "How would you characterize them, General?"

"What do you mean characterize? My stomach hurts like hell."

"Intermittently? At intervals? Are they localized or general?"

"I have a goddamned ulcer," the General said. "Now, whatever kind of pain an ulcer causes, then that's the kind of pain I have."

The young doctor straightened up. "You can get dressed now, General. Then if you'll stop by my office . . . "

"And what will you tell me there that you can't tell me here?"

"We'll discuss it there."

He watched the doctor move past Major Shaw

and out into the corridor. Shaw was a good man because he had a sharp mind and an unquenchable ambition. As the General began to put on his clothes, Shaw's one fault, his intolerable caution, demonstrated itself as he looked around the examining room as if searching the place before he felt free to speak.

"What do you have?" the General said, buttoning his shirt.

"Two items," Shaw said. His ideas were always itemized numerically. "We found out how Cameron got the tape from Las Vegas. His father left it with a friend who works for the GAO. On the Colonel's death, it was to be sent to Cameron. His father represented it as a private message, insisted that it was important."

"What's the name of the GAO man in Las Vegas?"

"James Purdy."

"Purdy?"

"Yes, sir."

"Did this Purdy listen to the tape?"

"Negative."

"How can you be sure?" The General examined himself in the mirror, knotted his tie.

"One of the DIA boys offered Purdy a thousand dollars if he could swear the Colonel's voice was not on the tape. Purdy said he hadn't listened to it. At the time he had considered it a private matter, wasn't interested."

"All right," the General said.

"Item two. We have been alerted that there was a BRIMSTONE inquiry made of the DIA computer."

The General's interest quickened. He had installed a questioning loop in the computer a long time ago so that if anybody sought information on BRIMSTONE, the computer would give warning. He had not been sure over the years that it would work at all. Now that it had, he was delighted. "Which computer terminal made the inquiry?"

"One of the GAO remotes. We can't pin it any closer than that. But I think it's *prima facie* proof that Cameron now has possession of the tape."

"No," the General said, looking at Major Shaw's reflection in the mirror. "It is proof only that *some*body in the GAO has the tape."

"I suppose that's true, sir."

"It is true." He put on his trousers and sat down to put on his shoes. "How is Cameron taking the death of his ex-wife?"

"I don't know that."

"Don't you think you should know that, for God's sake?" the General said. "That's bound to make a difference."

"I'll talk to Wicker."

"Yes," the General said, and he realized that his irritation was only serving to make the ulcer worse. He fell back on an old trick which had served him well during the war, looking at what was happening now as something abstract, removed from reality. He could regard it objectively. He did not like Wicker. Wicker was not only a Nixon loyalist but also fanatic about it as well. Even now, years after the fact, Wicker insisted on defining his former leader as a proud and competent man who had been betrayed by his inferiors. The General did not like that kind of blindness but it made Wicker reliable as long as he could interpret his present assignment as a way of correcting the wrongs of the past. "You talk to

Wicker right away," the General said. "There's no reason we should change our approach."

"Yes, sir," the Major said.

The General went in for the chat with the sober young doctor who was no more than half his age, and the doctor put X-rays on a shadow box and with a pointer conducted a tour of the General's duodenum and his stomach which Roffner tolerated with no great interest, for from the tone of the doctor's voice he learned what he had entered the hospital to find out. His ulcer was neither worse nor better than it had been for the past year. It was a borderline ulcer; it could perforate or it could stay as it was. The doctor recommended eventual surgery, emphasized nostrums, diets, pills for the relief of pain as if that were the issue here. But it was not. The General did not mind the pain and had a great tolerance for it as if it only existed to remind him that he was mortal. The messenger was not important, only the message. Not serious.

He had his driver take him back to the Pentagon, the only truly functional building in Washington, the nemesis of visitors who believed that all the concentric rings looked alike and therefore could never find anything without getting lost first. To the General, this vast building was a mataphor for the military complex itself. Outsiders had a tendency to believe that all men in uniform looked alike and thought alike, that there was a single system operative here when in fact there were many systems. In that similarity lay concealment.

He went directly to his office in the E Ring, spacious, clean, uncluttered, passing first through an outer room characterized by secretaries and machines and stacks of paper, a room which was always an organized bedlam and to which he always brought his visitors from Congress. For Research and Development implied papers and plans and diagrams, and he was willing to show dignitaries what they wanted to see.

But the real part of R and D in which he was interested was not here, of course, but in his mind and above all in a patience which would persist through the temporary ebb and flow of various presidents and public whims, all of which had to be ignored. For the strength of the military, the progress of weaponry, had to survive despite outside interference.

The real future lay behind the uncluttered desk in his office, in his ability to synthesize and to remember. The only real security lay in containment, in the strict observance of a rule which was too often stretched to the point of uselessness, the "need-to-know" axiom. He observed it here. None of his subordinates had any more than a partial knowledge at this point.

He asked his secretary to call Stevens at Ramos-Woolridge in California and chatted with him for fifteen minutes. Stevens, a pudgy, brilliant young man, no older than twenty-five, immediately plunged off into an exuberant and scientific discussion of optics and lenses and lasers. The General had the feeling that Stevens did not give a damn about profit and loss and cost overruns and was totally caught up in his work.

"How soon are you going to have a working prototype?" the General said.

"Hell," Stevens said. "I can give it to you now

but I'd like to have a couple of weeks to play with it."

"A couple of weeks is fine." Patience was the key. The General did not want anybody to be able to listen to an assortment of his calls and single out those which were important by the General's attitude toward them. He had no doubt that his telephone conversations were being monitored by various agencies in turn. There was no such thing as absolute secrecy in Washington any more than there was such a thing as absolute trust. But isolated facts were meaningless and only the connection of those facts into a pattern could give them any significance.

He went down the list, making the calls he considered important, from the middle managers at IBM down to the entrepeneur-subcontractors, collecting informal status reports. Shortly before noon, Major Shaw reappeared. "I have a status report on Cameron," he said. "He's being questioned by the Metro police."

The General nodded. "Do you think Wicker's the man to handle this?"

"I talked to him," the Major said, slightly perturbed by the question. "He's ready to move in."

"I didn't ask you that," the General said evenly. "Is Wicker the right man for this job?"

"The DIA thinks so," the Major said. "I agree with them."

"Then tell him to move," the General said. "But before you do anything else, have my lunch brought in. Milk and saltines. And make sure the saltines are fresh."

"Yes, sir," the Major said. "Fresh."

2

Cameron spent less than an hour at the police station. The case was an obvious suicide and he had signed a statement concerning the discovery of the body, retrieved his topcoat, and that was that.

Outside the station house, the cold sunlight was blinding. He stopped at a kiosk on the corner, bought a morning paper. Annie's picture was on the front page, one taken before their marriage, at a horse show, and even in this bad print her eyes sparkled. Dead now, and her family would make the arrangements and he felt in some odd way as if he had never known her at all. The story in the *Post* was purposely vague, the reporting of her death and the discovery of her body by her former husband, William Cameron. Carefully, he folded the paper and dropped it in a trash bin near the taxi stand.

The people in the section were properly solicitous and Connie stopped by to tell him how sorry she was. Saunders called him in and offered him coffee and condolences and news of his new assignment in California. "I talked with Williamson this morning," he said. "Do you know Jerry?"

"I met him once."

"A nice guy. You'll enjoy working with him." Saunders was slightly subdued today. "He'd like to have you out there next week. They're swamped in California."

Cameron sat down in the leather chair, cradled the coffee cup in both hands, welcoming the warmth. He was cold; something was not right within him. "I want to level with you, Harley. I don't know that I'm going to stay with the government."

"I see," Saunders said. He sat down behind his desk, patted the tips of his fingers together. "We have always been candid with each other. Do you have something going with Purdy on the side?"

"Purdy? What do you mean?"

Saunders leafed through a pile of photocopies, came up with one. "We logged in a GAFX-734 from Purdy, addressed to you personally, and you checked it out. And then another GAFX-734 came in. I got a query from the DIA on this, Willie. What shall I tell them?"

And now Cameron knew who had searched his house. "I'm not on the take," he said.

Saunders shook his head. "I know you're not. I don't know why this government has to be run from so many adversary positions. We do our jobs and we accumulate enemies who feel we're interfering with their right to do their jobs and try to blow us out of the water." He lighted a cigarette. "They will also want to know how you can afford to quit. You have another job?"

"My father left me some money. Not a lot, but sufficient."

"And what about this duplicate GAFX-734 business?"

Cameron leaned back in the chair, sipping at the coffee, staring at the ceiling. "It has nothing to do with GAO," he said. "Nothing to do with my work here. My father just sent me something posthumously, through Purdy."

"Then why is the DIA raising hell about it?"

Cameron thought it through, decided not to tell

Saunders the whole business, for Saunders was a man with a strict code of ethics which superseded either curiosity or personal loyalty. "My father sent me a tape recording, the conversation of two government officials. Now, I don't know how in the hell he got ahold of it, but I described in vague terms a military experiment, an operation, I don't know which. It may have taken place sometime during 1974. Up to a hundred people may have been killed."

"Where?" Saunders said.

"I don't know. Have you ever run across a project under the name BRIMSTONE?"

"No."

"It's possible I could uncover the project," Cameron said. "There are enough leads on the tape to make it an outside possibility. It's incriminating enough that they would search my house for it and put the squeeze on you to get it back."

"I want your guarantee that this material did not come from any material sent to us, either leaked or normal, from DIA."

"It happened just as I said."

"Up to a hundred people." Saunders shook his head, dubious. "Sometimes I think of the military as a necessary disease." He sighed. "I can't tell you what to do about this, Willie. Was your father mixed up in it?"

"I don't know. What are the odds of getting action on this if I take it over to Justice?" But even as he asked the question, he knew the answer. The government in operation was not like the government represented in classic descriptions, not separate departments, checks and balances. Practically, if an official at Justice got the tape, he would check it out with the Pentagon and it could be suppressed immediately as classified information or it could be classified as a part of the body of the Nixon tapes currently under litigation. In any case, it would be locked away. And suddenly Cameron knew why the military needed to get the tape back. *They did not know exactly what was on it.* They could rely only on the memory of the co-participant X, if he was available, and it was not probable he could remember every word that had been said or where the specifics of the conversation might lead a skilled investigator. "No," Cameron said finally. "The Justice Department isn't the answer."

"What about a news release?" Saunders said. "A leak."

"I have a tape with some sounds on it," Cameron said. "There's no positive identification of the speakers, not enough hard information."

"This is your business, of course," Saunders said thoughtfully. "But it's also mine in a way because I'm on a one-man kick to keep the government straight. So I'm going to give you some advice after all. I know what I'm talking about. If you leave the government and pursue this on your own, you'll make yourself fair game and leave yourself wide open to any kind of legal action they want to throw at you. You've seen what happens every time some government official resigns and tries to tell the world what's really been happening in his department. They get a brief flurry of publicity but there's an underlying public attitude of sour grapes." He lighted a cigarette. "Precisely what do you have on this massacre? Who killed whom? Where?"

Cameron shrugged. "I don't know."

"But with enough help, you can find out."

"Unless they've covered all their tracks. All I know is that they had a plan under way and that they called it BRIMSTONE."

"This puts a different light on everything, Willie," Saunders said. "Let me make a suggestion. You've been through a great shock, with Annie's death. So take off a couple of weeks and think about staying here, at least temporarily. I can stall Adamson." He tapped his ashes into a brass fish. "You can work full time at tracking BRIMSTONE. We'll cover it in one of the special budgets."

"I appreciate the offer, Harley."

"Which means you're not going to take it."

"It doesn't mean that at all. I'll let you know. And I'll take the two weeks."

"Consider it seriously. When the time comes, I'd like to hear the tape. But regardless of what you decide to do, don't try this on your own."

Cameron went back to his office and just sat at his desk, staring out the window. Saunders' offer appealed to him and he was sure that given sufficient time and the resources of the GAO he could uncover the identity of X and prove beyond a reasonable doubt that this was a bona fide Nixon tape. But in the process he would resurrect his father and place him in the middle of a controversy. His father had held the tape too long and it was not coincidental that he had seen that it was sent to Cameron only after his death. The accusation could be made that his father had used the tape to maintain his pension in some fashion, to hold it over his superiors to gain advantage.

He looked up as a man came into the office and it took him a moment to place the man. Wicker, yes, the security man. "What the hell do you want?" he said.

"I came to see you," Wicker said. "A few loose ends. I expected to find you at the police station. Your ex-wife was a lovely woman. I never really knew her and that's a purely objective point of view, but from other points of view, perhaps there were those who wouldn't have found her quite so lovely." He leaned over, opened his briefcase with some pain. "I'm too old to be playing tennis, but I suppose I'll continue to do it until I fall apart." He found what he was looking for, put on his reading glasses but did not volunteer the page to Cameron. "I make notes to myself on important telephone conversations," he said. "It isn't often that I get a call from a public official of the Senator's stature. He said you had something, a private detective's report. He asked me to investigate with discretion."

"I know what he's talking about," Cameron said. It occurred to him that Wicker could be useful. "I want you to do something for me. Call him and tell him that I've destroyed the file."

Wicker appeared to be pleased. "Sure," he said. "Why don't I do that right now? May I use your telephone?"

"Certainly." He stood at the window while Wicker made his call, having to go through a mobile operator. Evidently, the Senator was in his car. From Wicker's tone of voice, it was evident he was having no trouble convincing the Senator. He put his hand over the mouthpiece. "He wants to have a talk with you. He's on his way to a place in the mountains, his country retreat, he calls it. He would like to meet with you there. I can get a helicopter."

"How long will it take?"

"Not long."

"All right."

Wicker said something into the telephone, then dialed another number and Cameron heard him ordering a helicopter, giving a DIA authorization number, carrying off the whole thing with an offhandedness which implied that this was a usual course of action for him. Suddenly, Cameron remembered, vaguely but certainly, that Wicker had been one of Nixon's men, a part of the White House security force, the palace guards, destined for greater things before the resignation of his leader. And now he was part of a bureau security system, using an excuse to requisition a helicopter to fly to a Senator's retreat. An exercise in personal power.

Cameron put on his overcoat and followed Wicker to the elevator and the helipad on top of the annex building. Freezing cold with the wind sock billowing from a northwest wind, the day was bitter. Wicker stood peering at the sky and rubbing his gloved hands together against the cold. He pursued a conversation which seemed to have no point, talking about various Senators he had known, not in complimentary terms, for he had discovered the grimy world of political expediency shortly after transferring to the White House from the Los Angeles Police Department where he had first met Nixon.

"I've met a lot of people since I've been here. Senators, foreign dignitaries, you name it. I even knew your father," he said, his breath pluming in the cold air. "I can't say I knew him well but I don't think anybody ever knew the Colonel very well. It was not that he was a standoffish sort of man, but he was very efficient. That meant he was busy all the time. Did he ever talk to you about his days in the White House?"

"No," Cameron said. "We weren't very close in his last years."

"Well, there you are," Wicker said absently, interrupted by the noise of the helicopter approaching from the south, a great ugly machine raising powdered snow from the pad as it descended.

They rose over the city, the helicopter tilting to the northwest. Almost immediately, it ran into a snow squall obliterating Cameron's view of the city. He did not look forward to seeing the Senator again, especially under these circumstances. The shock of Annie's death had passed. The grief was gone and he was left with nothing except a deep regret that she had chosen to kill herself and a kind of guilty yet certain relief that he would not have to deal with her aberrant behavior any longer. He wondered if someplace down in the Senator's unspoken thoughts, the Senator did not also feel some painful sense of relief.

"The damned helicopter," Wicker said with disdain, glancing around at the cramped cabin, the solid seats. "They could have sent one of their VIP models."

"Hell," Cameron said with a tolerant smile. "It beats driving."

"Barely," Wicker said.

Cameron settled into silence, turning his

attention away from Wicker. He did not like the man. But hopefully, within an hour or two, he would have completed his business with the Senator and be back in Washington. He would have no further business with Wicker.

At the end of forty minutes, it seemed to Cameron that the snow had intensified. He glanced out the window, shook his head. "If the Senator's on his way to his retreat, we're going to beat him there. Hell, he may not make it for hours in this weather."

"He was well on his way when I talked to him," Wicker said.

The helicopter was descending; Cameron could feel it in the pit of his stomach. The shapes of low and rolling mountains emerged from the storm and he could see the buildings in the compound, the main lodge, massive, designed after a Swiss chalet with separate outbuildings, a vehicle and maintenance shed to the left. The blizzard had been here a long time; the snow was banked around the buildings, scattered in massive random drifts and piled up at the edge of the thick woods.

The helicopter hovered on the sheltered side of the house, gradually setting down, and Cameron felt the contact with the ground. Wicker pushed the door open, caught his breath in the force of the wind, closed the door again as if resting. "I'll give the Senator a ring and find out where he is."

Bracing himself against the seat, he pushed the door open with great effort and hopped out, then pushed through the snow toward the house. Cameron moved reluctantly, his overcoat around him, and, half blinded, followed Wicker to the entry porch where Wicker stamped the snow off his feet, his round glasses frosted with ice crystals, his face flushed. He rang the bell and the door opened, a Sergeant standing just inside, a smooth man in his mid-thirties.

"Good afternoon, sir," he said to Wicker. Then he greeted Cameron and took his coat.

"Do you have any word from the Senator?" Wicker said.

"No, sir."

"I think we could use a good stiff drink, Sergeant," Wicker said. "Bourbon and branch water for Mr. Cameron, a martini for me, very dry." He looked to Cameron. "I'll see if I can find out what the hell is going on. Where's the telephone, Sergeant?"

"In a cabinet by the bookcase, sir."

Cameron migrated to the fireplace, massive logs burning, and he spread his hands to the warmth while he studied the high beams of the cathedral ceiling. The Sergeant opened a sidebar, began to mix the drinks. "This is a non-official question, Sergeant," Cameron said. "But how does the Senator rate an army staff at his private retreat?"

The Sergeant smiled. "I doubt that even the Senator could afford this place," he said. "The property is owned by Defense, used for conferences and T-training sessions. We have various Senators from the Armed Forces Committee who use it as a retreat from time to time." He extended a crystal tumbler to Cameron. "Try this, sir. See if I'm heavy enough on the bourbon."

Cameron tasted it. "Fine."

The Sergeant poured a martini from the shaker,

carried it across the room to Wicker who was still on the telephone, frowning. He accepted the drink, then covered the mouthpiece while he spoke to the Sergeant. Cameron sat down in front of the fire, tired, looking into the flames, thinking with wry amusement how outraged Saunders would be at all this, an opulent chalet staffed for the comfort of a select few, the operating budget undoubtedly buried under a "Training Facility." It was small wonder that the national budget continued to grow each year, this vast interlock of bureaus and agencies, each with its perquisites all neatly tucked away, not subject to review.

Wicker came to join him at the fire, obviously agitated but trying to cover it. "We have to wait awhile," he said. "The Senator's goddamned mobile phone is out."

"Then you'd better notify your pilot," Cameron said. He was aware of the chopping sound of the helicopter over the howl of the wind.

"That's taken care of," Wicker said with what appeared to be a sigh. "You don't think much of me, do you, Cameron?"

"I don't see how my opinion of you makes any difference one way or another," Cameron said. He checked his watch. It was now three-thirty and they were at least forty-five minutes' flying time from Washington. "I think we'll call this off."

"Soon," Wicker said, a quizzical glint in his eyes. "Finish your drink. And I'd like a real answer to my question. You're in a position to inspect the inspectors, so to speak. I'd like to know how you classify me."

"You're not important enough for me to classify," Cameron said. "You're one of a tribe of displaced people, Wicker. You got delusions of grandeur at the White House because you were close to the center of power. And now you're transformed into another minor bureaucrat who takes himself too seriously."

"Not myself, my job," Wicker said, correcting. "It's important that you understand. I take what I do quite seriously. And once I begin something, I'm not easily dissuaded." He shifted slightly. The firelight reflected on his glasses, obscuring his eyes.

Cameron heard the helicopter revving up and he walked over to the window just in time to see the Sergeant running in a half crouch, the wind at his back, almost obscured by the blowing snow. His first thought was that the Sergeant had been sent to relay word of the Senator's delay to the pilot, but this was not the case. The door opened and the Sergeant boarded. The rotors reached maximum velocity and the helicopter lifted tentatively as if to achieve a balance in the wind. Then it rose rapidly and moved off toward the southeast.

"What in the hell are they doing?" Cameron said. "Where are they going?"

"Back to Washington," Wicker said. "I suggest you sit down. We have a lot of business to conduct."

"Who in the hell do you think you are?" Cameron said. "What in the fuck are you trying to pull off?" He went to the telephone, picked it up. A male voice came on the line.

"Your egress code, please."

"This is William Cameron," he said. "I want you to connect me with the GAO."

"Your egress code, please."

He put the receiver back on its cradle. Wicker had not moved from the chair. He had the fingers of his hands laced together across his chest. "It's going to be necessary for you to respect my position here, Cameron," he said. "Otherwise, you might tend not to believe me and that would be disastrous for you."

"What in the hell is going on here?" Cameron said. And quite suddenly, he knew. All that remained was confirmation. "You weren't in touch with the Senator today at all," he said.

Wicker smiled. "Briefly," he said. "But the Senator has never been any more than a peripheral part of your difficulties. He dislikes you intensely, now more than ever, and he would love to see your ass shipped to the North Pole but he's much too busy to spend his time persecuting you. We told him we were investigating you so we've been in touch with him from time to time. Your beliefs about him have proven to be a convenience for us. It gave me a means to get you here, for instance."

"For what reason?"

"All in good time," Wicker said. "First, the ground rules. There will be no games, only positions. You can't be expected to cooperate fully until you're truly aware of your position. If I were you, I'd sit down and finish my drink. You've seen the weather outside."

Cameron sat down, picked up his glass. "There's no way you can bring this off, Wicker."

"I think I can," Wicker said. "First, you should know that the police let you go and have not pushed this case because we requested it."

"Nonsense. The police never made any move to

detain me. My ex-wife committed suicide. The suicide was never in question."

"That's your position," Wicker said. "You as innocent. It's attractive from your point of view and it's supportable. But let's examine a second position, you as murderer."

"Impossible."

"Not as impossible as you might think. What weapon did she use to shoot herself?" He shrugged. "That's a rhetorical question. It was your pistol, of course, not yours but your father's. The police found it in the bottom of the shower. They don't have a trace yet, but I do. I saw it at your house. It's my business to be observant."

"She could have taken it from my house," Cameron said. "She spent that night with me."

"You don't need to be defensive," Wicker said. "You don't have to convince me of anything. Just listen to the whole thing and see if I can't establish a very good position for you as a killer."

His voice droned on and Cameron found himself straining to hear every word above the moaning of the wind and the rattling of a shutter, fighting the belief that this could happen, that he could have been so neatly pulled into this position. "I have a fine base on which to build," Wicker was saying. "Eighty some odd thousand dollars transferred from a blind account."

"Which came from my father."

"Which came from a blind account," Wicker repeated with a half smile. "You have been taking bribes and your ex-wife found out about it, wanted money from you. You threatened her life at Sinbad's Retreat. We have the manager to testify to that. So now we have motive and premeditation.

Your killing her would make perfect sense." Wicker's smile was full now. He lifted the glass, inclined it slightly in Cameron's direction, and then drank. "Believe me, Cameron, we can make it go either way."

"Hell, you're crazy," Cameron said. "And I'm going to call your bluff, you son of a bitch." Wicker was not representing GAO security here. He was being backed by military intelligence, probably the DIA. Cameron relaxed slightly, lifted his own drink. "You didn't set all this up just to get me to confess to something I didn't do."

"Before I'm through, you'll be willing to confess to anything. You'll be anxious to cooperate in any way I ask," Wicker said.

Cameron stared at him in disbelief.

Slowly, Wicker drew a small automatic pistol from his pocket and almost playfully pointed it in Cameron's direction. Quite suddenly, the pistol fired and the ashtray shattered on the end table six inches from Cameron's hand, slivers of glass flying across the carpet. "That's to let you know you can't count on anything," Wicker said. "You can't count on my being logical or rational or humane or reasonable. You are a smoker, I know that, about a pack and a half a day. So I want you to take the pack of cigarettes out of your pocket and throw them on the floor in front of you."

Cameron removed the pack, did as he was told.

"That's very good," Wicker said. "You didn't make the mistake of assuming that I wouldn't risk everything on something as insignificant as this." He removed a folded sheet of paper from his pocket and then stood up and placed it on the end table, next to the shattered ashtray, taking great care that the pistol remained leveled at Cameron's head. "The trade is simple. You sign this paper and you can have your cigarettes back."

Cameron picked up the paper, smoothed it out with his fingers. Insanity, yes, that was what Wicker was trying to project and he was doing a good job of it. Cameron felt slightly sick to his stomach with the knowledge that in this game Wicker could end up killing him and would get away with it. His superiors would back him for they would have to be aware of what he was doing here and assume the risk of failure. He glanced at the paper.

I killed John F. Kennedy.

He looked up at Wicker. "What's the point?" he said.

"The trade is the point," Wicker said. "You can sign that statement and get your cigarettes back."

Cameron took out his pen, signed the statement, put it on the end table. Wicker laughed as he picked it up, then kicked the cigarettes back to him. "Very good," he said.

"We can shortcut this," Cameron said. "What does the DIA want out of me?"

"The DIA?" Wicker said from the fireplace. "Did I mention the DIA?"

"This is an army establishment."

"The DIA is a very good guess," Wicker said. "As good as any. You recognize that I have a very large power behind me. I am an extension of that power. That's all that's important. If you would like another drink, I'm willing to trade for another signature."

This time Cameron signed a typed statement admitting he had sold secrets to the Russians, and later, to join Wicker at a meal of cold cuts in the dining room, he wrote his name again, this time testifying that he had committed adultery many times. He ate sparingly, his appetite diminished by the sight of Wicker's chrome-plated pistol sitting next to Wicker's water glass. He looked out through the dining room windows. The snow was blowing horizontally now, the drifts piling up against a bank of fir trees. He could assume from the direction of the wind that he was looking south now.

Wicker tapped his fork against a crystal glass. Cameron jumped reflexively. "It's much too far," Wicker said, as if reading his mind. "Twenty-two miles to our nearest neighbor. Now, if you are in excellent physical shape, we might negotiate for cross-country skis or snowshoes and give you a try at it."

Cameron was tired, a creeping kind of fatigue. "What will it take to get me out of here?"

"My permission," Wicker said. "I can lift the telephone and have a helicopter here in less than an hour. But let's discuss that over brandy by the fire."

In the living room, Wicker directed him to sit down and poured the brandy, leaving the glasses on the sideboard. He removed another piece of paper from his pocket, a brief typed statement, and handed it to Cameron. And there it was, the reason for everything, finally surfacing.

My father duplicated part of a Nixon tape.

And Wicker had left himself vulnerable with this conditioning game of his, an advantage which Cameron seized immediately. He took out his pen and signed the paper with no more attention than

he had given to any of the other statements. He
held it out to Wicker straight-faced, with no
change in expression. He had caught Wicker off
balance this time. The son of a bitch had expected
a different reaction. But Wicker handed him the
brandy and then stood by the fire, a thoughtful
expression on his face as if he were deciding what
to do next.

"You're a very clever man, Cameron," he said
quietly.

"In what way?"

"Where is it?" Wicker said.

"Where is what?"

"We're still in a trading situation," Wicker said
evenly. "For very high stakes, of course. I
wouldn't be here at all if I didn't want something
from you and you'd have no reason to respond
unless there was something of equal importance
in it for you." He sipped from his brandy glass. "I
knew your father," he said. "I didn't like him. He
was an ambitious man before he was a loyal man.
Nixon was a vastly underestimated president. The
media enjoyed satirizing the way he ran the White
House, but it was run fairly. I doubt that Nixon
knows to this day who erased that eighteen and a
half minutes, I doubt that he even remembers
what was on it."

"Who did erase it?"

"Your father, I believe. After he made a copy."

Cameron lighted a cigarette. "What was on the
tape?"

"You just may push me too far," Wicker said.
"You know damn well what's on that tape. I told
you this was a trading situation. The eighty
thousand dollars didn't come from your father. He

was a profligate spender and he used every cent he could get his hands on. We put the money there."

"For what?"

"Anything we like. We can decide that it was bribe money, and we have the documentation to prove that. Conversely, we can prove it came from your father, if that's what we decide to do. We can even increase it if you wish. We can convict you of murder, make you a free and wealthy man, kill you, let you live. So you see, we're in a position of absolute power over you. And I'll make a progressive bargain with you. If you tell me what was on the tape, as much as you can remember— and believe me, I'll know if you try to fake it— then I'll let you live. When you tell me where to find the tape and I have possession of it, then the murder charge will be dropped against you and the eighty thousand dollars will be yours, plus a cash bonus of twenty thousand more."

"Suppose I do have the tape," Cameron said. The brandy was heady; it was loosening him too much but suddenly he didn't care. "No more pretenses," he said, waving his hand. "I've heard the fucking tape and I know in general what the military did and approximately when they did it. The tape has nothing to do with me. I didn't ask for the knowledge, but I have it and it creates a problem. How do I know that I'll come out of this alive?"

"You have to take my word for it."

He could hear the wind, the crackle of the logs in the fireplace, and he realized in that moment that despite Wicker's threats, the implications of this game, they could not afford to kill him until they had the tape or knew exactly how much it revealed. "No, I don't think so," he said. "And I've never responded very well to intimidation, Wicker. But I'll make you an offer. You lift all this pressure and you take me back to Washington and have the DIA give me a complete briefing on BRIMSTONE. Now, I don't require a hell of a lot of convincing, just enough to believe that this project helped the country in any way. You do that and you not only get the tape but my complete cooperation."

Wicker looked at him quizzically. "A one-man justification committee, that's what you intend to be?"

"Certainly. You're one man and you obviously approved what happened. Why shouldn't I have the same privilege? I'm a good, loyal American."

"Not everybody approved it," Wicker said, as if beginning an explanation which he cut off. "Stand up, Cameron. I think it's time for another trade."

"It would be very foolish of you to kill me at this point."

"That's true." Wicker smiled. "A twenty-two can be more painful than lethal. I can shoot you in the muscle of your calf. I can always put a bullet through your collarbone. You'd end up in the same trading position and be in a good deal of pain at the same time. But that's up to you."

Cameron hesitated a moment and then stood up stiffly. Wicker gestured him toward a hallway and then followed. "This is a T-camp for high ranking officers, Cameron, but I already told you that, didn't I? The concept of the Trading Room was developed during the Korean War by the North Koreans, with help from the Chinese. They had a whole trading protocol designed to extract confessions and it proved to be quite successful, at least on the surface, because there wasn't a single man who didn't write one." He stopped outside a door where a chair sat in the hallway. "Take off your clothes, please."

"The hell I will," Cameron said.

Wicker's pistol fired, the small-caliber explosion almost deafening in the narrow corridor, the bullet chipping plaster off the wall near Cameron's head. Cameron took off his clothes, down to his shorts.

"Those too," Wicker said. "Totally naked."

Cameron took off his shorts, shivering in the chilly hallway. "I'll get you, Wicker," he said. "Sooner or later."

"The basic trade is for your clothes. You write down everything you remember of the tape and you slide it beneath the door into the hallway. I will check every few minutes or so. When you've written enough to satisfy me, the trade will be made."

He opened the door. The room was large, empty, no furniture, with three large windows facing the north, the glass plastered over with snow. The chill poured from the room. It was not heated. In the far corner of the room Cameron saw a stack of blank paper, a ballpoint pen atop it. "You're a motherfucking son of a bitch," he said to Wicker.

"One officer held out for a long time," Wicker said. "He eventually gave in but the toes on both feet had to be amputated. Get in the room, please."

Cameron went in. He heard the snap of the lock as Wicker closed the door behind him and then the fading click of Wicker's heels against the hardwood floor as he went back down the hallway toward the living room and the warmth of the fireplace.

3

He could see his breath in the still air of the room. He checked the windows first, feeling the convective chill pouring down from the panes of glass. The snow had impacted the windows but he found one slight spot, no larger than the palm of his hand, near one corner of the lower right-hand pane where he could see out, dimly yes, through a film of snow but enough to know that there were bars on the windows. And beyond the bars nothing but drifted snow and trees.

He went back to the door, the floor icy under his feet. There was no knob on the inside of the door, not even a place for a knob, and the door was so closely fitted he could not see the bolt which locked it. Ah, Jesus, cold, engulfed by it, his whole body reacting to it but his feet were affected most severely, paining him and then becoming numb as if they did not belong to him and the bright jabs of pain moved into his ankles and up into his legs.

He began to run around the room, a slow jog, keeping himself moving, the blood pumping, angry, demeaned, the whole goddamned thing ridiculous, and the anger pushed adrenaline through him and he decided to survive this just to have the chance to kill Wicker, to watch him die, and after Wicker, who? Nameless, shapeless, the men who had invented this indignity, who had established this obscenity of a room where a man tortured himself and cursed his own body for its inability to stay warm. He jogged around the room and his feet began to hurt again and he flailed his arms against his body. He was fighting a losing battle, for the cold of the room was constant and there was nothing he could do about that. Still he ran, increasing his pace, until it felt as if his lungs would burst and he could draw no more of the thin cold air through his throat and finally he fell against one of the walls and slid to a sitting position.

Not so cold now. Shock. Numbness, and he wondered how long it would take him to freeze to death in this room, a long time perhaps, because the body temperature would slowly sink and at some point he would simply fall asleep, cease to be aware, and death would perhaps be closest to a deep sleep without dreaming, and he wondered how it had been for Annie, if she had heard the noise of the pistol, if the obliteration of thought had been immediate or if there had been a scurrying of random neural reactions, little pieces of memories, aberrant smells, sounds, the cessation of life in a burst of confusions, and that must have been the case with his father as well, struck by a massive truck, never located, thrown fifty feet. And in that hurtling flight, was he aware, conscious of tumbling lights, the sensation of weightlessness?

Dead in the end, the both of them, and now him, and he would drift into it as they had hurtled into it, but in the end it was all the same.

Three, a trinity, death by the numbers. And what was the conversion formula for Fahrenheit into Celsius, zero C was 32 F, and what was the temperature of snow? If he died here, there would be no one to protest his death. They could leave him in a snowbank and manufacture a dozen reasons why his dead body should have been found there.

He stirred slightly. He moved and his muscles jerked in convulsive spasms. He pulled himself to his feet, bracing against the wall. Colder at the floor than up here. He walked over to the pile of paper and the ballpoint pen, picked up a sheet and began walking, realizing with dull panic that his mind was sluggish, non-functional and that what he put down would have to be carefully reasoned. He did not know the rules to Wicker's game. Perhaps Wicker had been instructed to let him die unless he got a full account.

Finally, he propped the paper against the wall and began to write. Difficult. His fingers had no feeling. He dropped the pen twice, finally secured it in the crotch between thumb and forefinger.

"The pres greeted visitor. Flat voice. Bureaucrat. Probably military. Small talk. Brimstone. Budgeted under FY72. Discussion—alternate terms for casualties. 50% of 110."

Enough, yes, not too much, not all Wicker could want. He added one squiggly line as if the pen had slipped and he could write no more. Almost true. He dropped the pen again and this time when he reached down to pick it up, his fingers would not close around it. No feeling at all, dead, and he blew on one hand but could make no hollow fist to contain the warm breath. A bluish cast to the skin, his but not his. He approached the door, holding the paper between both hands for fear that if he dropped it he could not pick it up again.

He heard a spasmodic hollow rattling sound; his teeth were chattering. He could not control it. He knelt by the door, placed the paper flat on the floor and then pushed it through with the heel of his hand, leaving an edge visible so he could see when it was taken. He sat down again, his eyes fixed on that thin white edge of paper. Every few minutes or so. Wicker had said that, no more than a few minutes. The son of a bitch, one of the bureaucrat myrmidons, the slow grinding of the governmental process, nothing swift, the efficacy of numbers. Fifty percent of one hundred and ten. Not enough. No one would be outraged by 50 percent of a hundred and ten. A 747 crashed and 170 died, or the traffic toll for a holiday weekend was eight hundred seventy-six. In Vietnam a good day had meant only seventy-four dead, numbers, yes. Fifty percent of 110 could be rationalized away, a military accident, not enough, and he had known none of these casualties for he knew few people at all, none well, none beyond the section.

He glanced down, blinked. The paper was gone. But when? How could he gauge? Important. If Wicker had taken the paper five minutes ago, he was declaring intent now and the door would not open at all. But if he had just this moment snatched up the paper, he could be making a telephone call, checking, and perhaps momentarily he would be coming back down the hallway.

Slowly, Cameron stood up, balancing, feet numb, feelingless, muscles trembling in his calves, stupid to trust, thrown off balance by that goddamned trading, a constant quid pro quo, something for something, only now the goddamned quo had been removed, not there at all.

He would not lie down and die. He would not

make it easy for them to explain, even in death. The windows, yes, no longer self-protective, no longer willing to pay anything to forestall the inevitable. He held onto the wall and dragged his feet to the window wall, and then, swinging his hand as a dead weight at the end of his arm, twisting his body to provide momentum, he threw his hand at the glass pane which shattered under the force of the blow and the tension of the snow packed against it and the force of the wind behind that snow.

The glass broke and the wind rushed in, fierce, final, and he was aware of his own blood pumping out of the gash in his hand, and he could feel a twinge of pain in that hand. Exultant. He stood directly in the blast of the wind, yelling until he could no longer hear the sound of his own voice, and then he collapsed on the floor and thought nothing and felt nothing.

He came around slowly, feeling the pain before he felt anything else, all over his body, the circulation forcing its way back. His left hand was throbbing. He was aware of a faltering vision and his eyes half opened to stare into the fireplace. Alive, yes, lying on the carpet still naked, hurting. Groggy but alive, and that was the point. Alive. He moved his toes, his feet, his fingers, his hands, a bandage on the left one. He twisted his head slightly, saw the shape of Wicker putting another log on the fire from the woodbox set into the brick wall. Wicker dusted the residue off his hands.

"Well," Wicker said, smiling down at him. "You're a first, Cameron. Nobody has ever broken a window before. I'll have to include that in my report. An interesting footnote." He sat down in the wing-backed chair, lighted two cigarettes, passed one to Cameron. "What you've done is worth a cigarette. Not much more than that, but it's a beginning after all." He leaned back in the chair. "I want you to take your time, but when you're ready you can dictate the rest of it to me."

Cameron said nothing. He drew the cigarette smoke into his lungs, exhaled.

"The next trade will be for your clothes, of course."

"I've already earned them. That was the deal."

"Not quite. You can give me something more."

"The time frame," Cameron said.

"Beg your pardon?"

"The tape said eighteen months at the outside."

"Eighteen months?"

"Yes."

"That's very good," Wicker said. He stood up, removed Cameron's clothes from a footstool, dropped them on the floor. "You can get dressed now."

Cameron sat up, having balance problems, dizzy. Where was Wicker's pistol? In his pocket? On one of the tables where he could reach it? The lamps were on, the room dark otherwise. The sun had gone down. He found his shorts and with great effort pulled them over his legs. Wicker was sitting again.

"How much discussion was there of the time frame? Was Nixon upset?"

"No," Cameron said. He fumbled with his shirt, still chilled despite the fire, wondering if he would ever be warm again. His fingers were stiff, almost unworkable. "Nixon seemed leery of the whole thing."

"Did he approve or disapprove?"

Did Wicker know the answer in advance? Was he fishing, testing? "He let it slide through on a temporary basis."

"What about safeguards?"

Cameron buttoned his shirt awkwardly. He wondered how much damage he had done to his left hand. "Final approval after a year." He could see both of Wicker's hands now, no pistol. In his pocket, certainly. "I want a drink." He examined the bandaged hand. "How bad is it?"

"No arteries cut," Wicker said. "You may need stitches." He stood up, walked over to the sidebar. "Brandy?"

"Bourbon."

"Ice?" Wicker was making a joke, lips pulled back from his gums in a signaling smile, but there was still an edge to his voice. Not satisfied yet, Cameron realized, something still missing.

"No ice."

Wicker handed him the drink. "What did Nixon's visitor say about himself?"

"Nothing," Cameron said. He sat down and with great difficulty put on his pants and began on his shoes. So this was the key, the information which Wicker did not have, and somewhere Nixon's visitor was sweating it out, not knowing if there was anything on the tape to identify him. He would have to give Wicker something else. "They both knew a man named Clyde."

"Clyde who?"

"There was a reference to a Clyde whose daughter had suffered a tragedy."

"Who mentioned it first?"

"I don't know. Does it matter? They both knew Clyde."

"Ah," Wicker said with some relief. "Hollings-worth. On the staff. His daughter was critically injured in a skiing accident. We all knew Clyde." He stood by the fireplace. "Describe the visitor's voice to me."

"Have you heard any of those goddamned tapes?" Cameron said. "They're so full of inter-ference it's not easy to hear the voices at all, much less characterize the speakers. Nixon sounds like Donald Duck."

"Did the visitor have an accent?"

"Not like Kissinger, no. American, flat, that's all I can say." The pistol was in Wicker's left-hand jacket pocket. He could see the slight bulge, the weight pulling against the side of the jacket.

"And you can remember nothing else?"

"Given time, I could probably reconstruct the whole fucking thing," Cameron said. "But we're down to the final trade, the tape itself."

"Where is it?"

"I don't give anything unilaterally," Cameron said. he drank the bourbon in a single draught. It was hot, strong, and it burned his throat. "Once you get the tape, what physical protection do I have?"

"What protection do you want?"

Cameron leaned over to retrieve his jacket from the floor and in that moment, not even knowing he was going to do it, he lurched ahead charging into Wicker who was caught completely by surprise as Cameron's shoulder struck him in the stomach and he was driven back against the rough-brick fireplace, his drink flying out of his hand, his glasses knocked away, and Cameron was yelling, out of control, his uninjured right hand going for Wicker's neck, and the two of them fell over a coffee table which did not splinter but stayed intact, upright. He was on top of Wicker, his hand digging into that distorted blinking face. And then he caught himself, for Wicker was not resistant. He had been stunned by the fall, eyes half glazed, and Cameron fumbled with the coat which was twisted beneath Wicker when he fell. He pulled out the pistol. He backed off, stood up, tired, winded. The bandage had unraveled from his left hand which was bleeding again.

The anger was there, the white-hot murderous anger for the man who was beginning to stir on the floor, struggling to sit up, his hand groping for his glasses, putting them on the bridge of his lean nose. There was bewilderment on his face but there was not the slightest trace of fear.

"I broke my own rules," he said, as much to himself as to Cameron. He rubbed his hand over the back of his thinning scalp. "So there you are." He looked at the pistol in Cameron's hand. "I understand how you feel but you're being foolish," he said. "We have the power to enforce our trades. There's no way you can save yourself."

"You son of a bitch," Cameron said. "I could put a bullet through your forehead and you sit there on your ass and pretend you still have the power." Wicker stirred, started to get up. "Stay where you are," Cameron said. "You don't know how close I am to killing you."

"Yes," Wicker said. "I do know that." He did not try to move again. His hands were flat on the floor.

"So now we trade," Cameron said.

"For what?"

"You answer questions. Take your glasses off. Throw them over here."

Wicker did as he was told. The glasses landed near Cameron's foot. "Who are you with?" Cameron said.

"Defense Intelligence."

"What is BRIMSTONE?"

"A project that went sour." Wicker drew a deep breath. "It was carried out, I think, but it didn't accomplish anything."

"Where? When?" The pain had begun to set in again, intensify. The muscles in his legs were cramping. He needed to rest, to sleep. "Details."

"I don't have any details."

Cameron shifted his foot, feeling the glasses snap beneath the sole of his shoe. He put his heel on one of the lenses, ground it to shattered fragments.

"I haven't been told anything about BRIMSTONE," Wicker said. "My assignment was to get the tape."

"Why does the DIA want it?"

"The man who visited Nixon that day is afraid he might be identified, linked to the project. Now, may I have a cigarette? A trade works two ways."

"Who visited Nixon that day?"

"Top brass, I think. One of the Joint Chiefs, maybe. I don't know. The cigarette?"

"Go ahead." And he leveled the pistol at Wicker's head. Wicker moved slowly, deliberately, cautiously, extracting his cigarettes, his lighter. He clicked a flame, inhaled the smoke.

"There's no need for this," Wicker said, exhaling the smoke. "I apologize for putting you through it. It's none of your affair, after all. And once you return the tape, we make the full transfer of funds and you're out of it. Home free."

"Not nearly," Cameron said. "I think you motherfuckers killed my father. It's possible you killed Annie as well."

"That's possible in your father's case," Wicker said. "I don't think they did because there wouldn't have been any point to it, as far as I can see. I know your ex-wife killed herself. They're just taking advantage of the circumstances there."

"One final question. Are there any support vehicles on the place?"

"I don't know," Wicker said. "But I can call for the helicopter."

"Stand up," Cameron said.

Wicker's eyes were startled. He stood up slowly.

"Down the hallway," Cameron said.

"You're making a mistake," Wicker said, but he moved toward the hallway, Cameron trailing at a sufficient distance to protect himself. They reached the door.

"Strip," Cameron said.

Wicker began to take off his clothes. His body was brown, muscled. He had been spending time on a beach or under a sunlamp. There was a scar on his right shoulder, a jagged streak, long since healed. And the fear had crept into him now, not into the face or the eyes where he had perfect control, but in the shriveled scrotum. "What the hell do you want, Cameron?" he said. "We can help each other."

Cameron opened the door to the room, the wind cold from the broken window, the snow beginning to pile in a splayed drift in a corner of the room and along one wall. Wicker held back. "All right," he said. "There's a jeep in the shed, keys on the wall. There's your trade."

"Inside," Cameron said. Wicker stepped through the door and Cameron closed it behind him, flipping the bolt.

He went back into the living room, so tired he was dragging, and he poured himself another shot of bourbon from the wet bar. He examined the injury to his left hand, multiple scratches, some of them deep, one major cut that stretched from the base of his thumb around the back of his hand, so deep the meaty flesh was separated and pulled back. He was able to regard it dispassionately, beyond feeling, and he wrapped the gauze back around it awkwardly, tightening a makeshift knot with his teeth. He put on his jacket and his topcoat, trying to remember the position of the shed as he had seen it from the air.

The shed was to the west of the house, he was sure of that. He looked through a west window but in the darkness could see nothing except the blowing snow immediately outside the window. There was bound to be a flashlight somewhere in this mansion but he knew he could spend hours looking for it with a minimal chance of finding it. Instead, he concentrated his efforts on the foyer and discovered a battery of switches which controlled outside floodlights. He turned all of them on and then checked through the west window again.

The exterior shell of the house was now bathed in light which extended no more than a few yards into the darkness of the storm. It would not help

him much. He was tempted to say the hell with it
and have something to eat and rest for a while but
he could not take the chance that they would give
him that much time, that they were not following a
schedule which would send the helicopter back
here at any moment.

He braced himself, opened the door and went
out into the storm. On the lee side of the house,
where one wing of the mansion served as a wind-
break, there were bare patches of icy ground
where he could make headway and keep his
footing within the area illuminated by the outside
lights, but once he reached the west edge of the
house he was confronted by a six-foot snowdrift
and an icy wind which took the breath out of him.
He left the protection of the house and struggled
through and over the snowbank, sinking through
the icy crust halfway to his knees. The cold again,
the bitter ache, naked in that room, and he forced
himself to move, one step at a time, dragging himself, reaching the top of the drift to fall sprawling
down the other side, gasping for breath,
momentarily panicked because he could see no
lights at all.

He regained his footing, stood erect. Over the
edge of the drift he could see the aura of lights
from the house, reflecting on the air full of thick
snow. Reference point and he had his bearings and
he continued to push through the drifts until he
came into the protected lee of the shed, a masonry
wall. He followed it, groped hand over hand until
he reached a door and let himself in. Hands numb,
difficult to grasp his lighter, click a flame. He
found a light switch, flipped it on.

A work shed, yes, the walls pegboarded, hanging

tools, chain saws, maintenance equipment and at the far side an army jeep with a canvas top and zippered sides. Laboriously, he checked it out. He found the keys hanging on the wall near it. The jeep was fully fueled. He turned the engine over and it caught immediately. Four-wheel drive, heavy snow tires, and Jesus, the weakness did not lie in the machine but in himself, for his reserves were depleted and the roads outside this compound, if he could locate them at all, would be treacherous. He would have to be alert every second and he was having difficulty staying awake.

He let the engine run and with effort pulled the overhead garage door open and then drove the jeep through it, turning on the headlights. Driving very slowly, he peered through the windshield, trying to catch a glimpse of the driveway, skirting the deeper snowbanks. It was not going to work. Despite the full blast of the heater, the wind came through the canvas, frigid. He saw the lights of the house, drove toward them and left the engine running while he went inside.

He found blankets in a bedroom and added a fresh unopened bottle of bourbon to his load. As he was about to leave the living room, his eyes fell on the telephone. He put his bundle down and picked it up.

"Your egress code, please," the male voice said.

"Tell your superiors that Wicker is in the ice-box," Cameron said. "They may not give a shit one way or the other. If Wicker is still alive, tell him that Cameron observed the trade." And he put the telephone back on the cradle and went out the door.

Chapter Six

The General received the word during a reception at the Norwegian embassy with a tap on his shoulder and the marvelously proportioned blond woman informing him that there was an urgent telephone call for him and that he should take it in the smaller room off the salon.

His first thought as he sat down in the satin chair and contemplated the European-style telephone was that this was a risky place for an urgent call. Foreign embassies were noted for their tapping systems, but then the Norwegians were considered relatively safe. He picked up the telephone.

"Roffner here."

"Major Winn, General." There had been trouble and Winn was extremely discreet in describing it, saying nothing that a monitor could make significant. There had been a call from the Pennsylvania compound and a helicopter had been dispatched immediately and Wicker was found in a poor condition, taken to a hospital in Philadelphia, and there was no trace of Cameron. Despite adverse weather conditions, a search had been made of the grounds. Evidently, Cameron had taken a maintenance jeep and disappeared into the countryside. The weather was too poor to make any search and the Pennsylvania Highway Patrol reported that most of the highways were impassable. "We can advise them about the jeep," Winn said.

"No. Do absolutely nothing," Roffner said.

"Nothing?"

"That's correct. Is Wicker terminal?"

"No, sir. In shock."

"I see. How long before he will be functional again?"

"I don't know."

"Did he get any information from Cameron?"

"We have a few notes in Cameron's handwriting. I'm sending them to you, hand delivery."

"All right, Winn. Keep in touch."

He replaced the delicate telephone in its gold filigree holder and just sat for a moment, his stomach paining him again. The Norwegians always served heavy foods, full of unknown seasonings, and strange liquors that must have been poured into indestructible Viking stomachs in ages past. But food was an occupational hazard, and when he went to foreign receptions he was required to eat and participate in toasts.

He looked up as the blond woman came in, and what was her name, Sonya, Tanya, something Scandinavian, Ingrid, yes, that was it, and she was a marvelous-looking female, flaxen hair, expansive breasts, wide hips, in her mid-twenties, and exuding that sexual air, almost a palpable scent, which hinted that she was available for bedding by a powerful man. Earlier in the evening, he had been intrigued by her and made plans in his

mind to take her back to his apartment after the
reception. But now his interest had switched back
to a more familiar and important track and the
smile he gave her was more apparent than real.
artifact had given him great pleasure and confirmed in some way his philosophy. The object
"I'm afraid it was. I have to leave."

He went through the formality of thanking the
Norwegian ambassador for the evening, and as he
was leaving, the blonde gave him her card and said
she would very much enjoy seeing him again and
talking about NATO. Once he was in his car, and
the entire evening washed out of his mind, he
picked up his white mobile telephone, called his
office to leave word for Shaw to come to the
General's house at Ft. Myer, then changed his
directions so Shaw would come to the General's
apartment in town.

By the time the driver delivered him to his
apartment, Shaw was already there, and if the
Major was irritated at being rousted out of bed or
away from a sexual liaison or a quiet evening at
home, he did not show it.

"Have you talked with Winn?" Roffner said,
removing his overcoat.

"Yes, sir."

Roffner went into his study, a comparatively
small room, the walls lined with books and photographs. It was his favorite place to think, to plan
his moves with all his references close at hand.
For despite all the global displays of power, the
Russians in Red Square on May Day, the ranks of
troops displayed by every country, military
dominance was primarily cerebral, psychological.
True military strength was not necessarily real

but what people believed to be real. He performed his duties at the Pentagon, at the Aberdeen Proving Grounds, but the bulk of his significant work was done here, in this room.

He sat down in the large leather chair behind the desk his mother had given him on his graduation from West Point, a desk reputed to have been owned and used by Ulysses S. Grant during the Civil War, and there was a dark stain in one of the drawer bottoms supposedly incurred when Grant put a whisky bottle in it without capping it. Roffner did not believe that story any more than he believed the history of the desk, for history was another illusion perpetrated by professional historians—a useful illusion to be sure. This bogus artifact had given him great pleasure and confirmed in some way his philosophy. The object was the reality; illusions could be useful.

The Major came in with a silver tray bearing a glass of warm milk. "I appreciate your thoughtfulness," Roffner said. "But I didn't roust you out to see after my stomach." He drank the milk and then unlocked a drawer and removed a manila folder, sliding it across the top of the desk to the younger man. "Read that," he said. "I want your opinion."

The Major sat down, clicked on a reading lamp, and read through the pages, then looked over at the General who was studying him. "You're accelerating the schedule?" Shaw said.

"That's correct."

"May I ask why?"

"We have to move before Cameron surfaces."

"I don't think Cameron is going to surface," Shaw said. "I think he's going to turn up in one of

142 Robert L. Duncan

the gullies around the compound. That's rough country. The storm's a bad one."

"Nevertheless," Roffner said, "put Phillips on BRIMSTONE. If he gets a warning, a red flag from the computer that somebody's probing around, have him begin to feed." He removed another folder from the drawer, handed it to the Major. "This is Wicker's file on Cameron. Get this to the D.C. police and get them off the fence. Use DIA as the source of the information. If Cameron's dead, it will still give us background and the cover we need. If he's alive, he's going to find himself boxed in."

"Yes, sir," Shaw said.

He sent the Major home and then went over his calculations again, the pieces of the schedule which were designed to fall into place automatically. They were all there, of course, all the parts, and despite the delays from the California subcontractors, everything was going to work. Mentally, he fixed the schedule at two weeks from today, setting the hour at 1000 hours. He would have to be thoroughly prepared for the furor it would create.

He went to bed, found he could not sleep. He went to the kitchen to warm more milk in a pan, stirring it with a wooden spoon.

And he thought of Nixon in his new house in New York City and wondered what he was doing at this instant. The General liked Nixon, admired him, and yet within the next two weeks Nixon was going to be thrown into a controversy again, not once but twice. He would like to call him, talk this over with him, but that was impossible, of course, for Nixon was really out of it and had probably forgotten the whole thing.

The milk was hot. He added a little salt, drank it slowly, found his stomach further settled, his mind more peaceful. He was finally ready for sleep.

2

It was almost morning, four o'clock, and Cameron's eyes were heavy and it was only with the greatest effort that he kept them open, the blanket draped around his shoulders, his hands numb against the steering wheel, the jeep inching ahead on the snow-packed road. Occasionally he saw highway signs, so covered with ice he could not read the numbers, realizing only that he was somewhere in Pennsylvania.

No more than ten miles an hour, the grinding noise of the four-wheel drive was constant. No radio in the jeep, no distractions, and he was tempted to stop the jeep where it was, right in the middle of the road, pulling the blankets up around him, allowing himself the luxury of sleep. But if he did not freeze to death the delay would give them time to catch up with him and he could not allow that.

He drove for another hour; the blizzard did not slacken. The country began to level somewhat, farming country, he supposed, distorted by immense drifts, and finally he saw lights ahead, an intersection with a larger highway, the flashing lights from a couple of police cars and a wrecker pulling apart three cars that had tailgated. And now he could see other cars abandoned alongside the highway, almost unidentifiable as the snow banked around them. Police cars, the implication of a town somewhere nearby and the army jeep would be spotted, remembered. Before he reached the intersection, he pulled the jeep off onto what he thought was the shoulder of the road, edging it into a snowbank. When he killed the engine, his ears continued to ring.

He opened the canvas door. Wrapping the blanket tightly around him, he braced himself against the wind and began to walk toward the intersection, the blur of lights in the snow. He fell twice. His hand began to bleed profusely. Ahead of him he saw a policeman, a tall burly man in foul-weather gear, his black boots shining in the reflection of the headlights. As the policeman approached him, Cameron's mind went blank and he could think of nothing to say. But the policeman was looking at his hand, blood dripping on the snow.

"Jesus," the policeman said. "What happened to you?"

Cameron waved vaguely down the highway, out of breath. "My car went off the road. Hit a tree."

"What kind of car?"

"What?"

"The make."

"A seventy-nine Cadillac. Blue," Cameron said.

"Anybody else in the car?"

"No, I'm alone. Business trip." Everything a blur now, and when he was helped into the patrol car, he blanked out, not sleeping, no, but falling into a stuporous state, his body trembling all over, filled with a great dread as if now that he was safe, he would die. He was taken to a large building lined with stainless steel refrigeration cases, a room filled with refugees from the storm, rows of cots occupied by families. National guardsmen were running a radio control post at one end of the building and quaintly dressed women in black caps were dispensing soup at the other. Ah, Amish, Pennsylvania Dutch, and he had some sense of location now, the cluster of towns with names such as Blue Ball and Intercourse.

He was treated by an Amish doctor, a no-nonsense man with a bluff square beard who stitched up his hand, dressed it, and sent him on to the care of the Amish women who provided him with homemade bread, a bowl of heavy soup and a cup of coffee and directed him to a vacant cot where he sat and ate hungrily. He remembered the bottle of bourbon in the jeep and he wished that he had it now. He knew where he was, one of the spotless Pennsylvania Dutch public market buildings.

"I need your name, sir."

He looked up to see a national guardsman standing over him with a clipboard.

"Roger B. Dalton," Cameron said.

"Your home address? Who would you like us to notify?"

"My wife's in Europe," Cameron said. "My address is 7044 Constitution, Baltimore."

The guardsman dutifully recorded it. "What's your ZIP code?"

"I don't know my ZIP code. What difference does it make? Do you intend to send me tourist literature when I get home? I don't know my goddamned ZIP code." He checked himself. He had not known how close he was to a great unresolved anger. "I'm sorry," he said. "It's been a hell of a night."

"Yes, sir. Mr. Dalton," the guardsman said. "If they want it, they can look it up."

"What?"

"The ZIP code."

"Yes." He lay back on the cot, closed his eyes. Numbers, the whole goddamned world full of numbers and bureaucrats whose duty it was to record those numbers, transfer them, add them, manipulate them. Numbers on the jeep, traceable, and they would find it sooner or later, track it to him. Or they would look for the Cadillac which didn't exist. He had had no experience at this sort of a bitch, and he should have let him die—perhaps he was dead anyway—and the words over the telephone had cost him valuable time. Finally, he fell asleep and when he awakened it was daylight and he felt sour. He had been dreaming about Annie, not as she actually had been but a transformed Annie.

was daylight and he felt sour. He had been dreaming about Annie, not as she actually had been but a transformed Annie.

Nine o'clock. He fumbled for a cigarette, smoked it half-way down. Nine o'clock and they would all be in the office at GAO, Connie at her desk and Saunders in his cubicle, just another day for them but his world had turned upside down. Harv would be at work as well, and Cameron was going to need a lawyer, but not yet. He checked through his wallet. He had a couple hundred dollars in cash and the standard credit cards, but he would not use the cards until it was absolutely necessary for they could check those instantly.

The market building was almost deserted. This meant the snowplows had been at work. He went outside to find that the storm had stopped. The sky was slate gray and the highway was a trenched channel through high embankments of dirty snow. From here, he could see a sign down the highway, The Seven Sweets and Seven Sours Restaurant, and he walked toward it. It was jammed with people but he was not hungry. He found a pay telephone in the waiting room and put in a collect call to Harv who accepted it immediately, his voice upset.

"Where in the hell are you, Willie?" he said. "What's going on?"

"That's impossible to explain," Cameron said. "I want you to send me some money."

"You don't need money," Harv said. "You need to get back here as fast as you can move."

"I've got the crazy men of the DIA on my tail."

"That's not all you have," Harv said. The police had gotten him out of bed in the middle of the night, looking for Cameron, and from dawn there had been calls from half a dozen government agencies. It was only when he saw the morning papers that he knew what was going on. Cameron was wanted not only for the murder of his ex-wife but for an attempted murder at a Defense Department T-house in Pennsylvania.

"Then Wicker is still alive," Cameron said.

"Is that all you have to say?" Harv said. "The roof is falling in on you. I've called around, William. The government boys are playing hardball. You make any attempt to run and from the way they have you described, any local cop could shoot you down and be a hero."

Cameron said nothing. His eyes fell on one of the Pennsylvania Dutch hex signs decorating the

wall above the telephone, colorful flowers and
birds, protection against bad luck, the vagaries of
weather, and pestilence, and he had known this
would happen and yet was not prepared for it.

"Are you there?" Harv said. "Do we still have a
connection?"

"Yes," Cameron said. "I've been set up, Harv. I
have the missing eighteen and a half minutes of
the Nixon tape and they want it back." He
described it briefly. "They pulled something off.
They conducted their own little slaughter
someplace and now they're covering ass."

"You can't be serious," Harv said quietly. "No,
check that. Of course you're serious. All right, you
get back here and bring the tape. If what you're
saying is true, then we'll do a little hard
bargaining."

"No," Cameron said. "I don't intend to give
them a chance to cover."

"I'm not only your accountant and your
lawyer," Harv said, "I'm also your friend. I want
you to come back here, put everything on the
table. I don't believe you killed Annie or any of the
rest of it. But we have to straighten this out."

"I'll be in touch," Cameron said. "I'll want five
thousand dollars. I'll let you know where to send
it."

He severed the connection. He had weakened
during the conversation and the desire to give in
was persuasive. If he returned to Washington and
let them have the tape, he could leave it to Harv to
extricate him from the tangle of government
actions. He called the incoming WATS number at
the GAO, asked to speak to Connie. When she came
on the line, he could think of nothing to say for a

moment. He could hear her voice. "Hello?" she said. "Hello?"

"This is Cameron, Connie," he said. "Have you seen the morning papers?"

"My God," she said. "Nothing else. This whole place has been turned upside down. It's suddenly like Jack the Ripper was here for years and nobody knew it until now."

"I didn't kill Annie," he said. "Do you believe that?"

"Is it important?"

"Very."

"I don't believe you killed anybody."

"I don't want to involve you," he said. "But I don't have anybody else to turn to. I want you to do something for me. It involves a little risk—not much, but some. If you don't want any part of it, you can hang up now and I'll understand."

"Let me know what you want. Then I'll give you an answer."

He tried to think coherently, to overlook nothing. "Find a reliable delivery service in Washington," he said. "And then put together a package for me." He wanted a portable CPU terminal and display screen with a telephone interface, the tape carton he had mailed to himself. Then she was to call Harv and get five thousand dollars. "I've already talked to him," he said.

"Where do you want this sent?" she said. "Where are you?"

"I don't know where I am," he said. "I'm so ragged-ass tired I can't think." He closed his eyes, pinched the bridge of his nose, remembering one trip he had taken with Annie through this country, a trip which was supposed to patch their marriage, a motel east of Lancaster, a Holiday Inn, yes. "All right," he said. "There's a Holiday Inn on the circle east of Lancaster, Pennsylvania. Have the stuff delivered there, in the name of Groton, William Groton."

"Groton?" she said. "All right. I think I can manage that. It may take a little time. Are you all right?"

"No, not all right at all. But I'll survive."

"Good luck," she said. "I'll get the stuff to you as soon as I can."

3

There was nothing like pain to sharpen the senses, Wicker thought, nothing like defeat to sharpen the resolve. He had come close to dying and had discovered that he was not afraid of it, not frightened by the darkness. In the Philadelphia hospital, while he was still partially out of it, he listened to the doctors discussing his condition as if they were talking about a faulty automobile. The conclusion was that he needed rest, but he knew differently, and he checked out of the hospital and went back to D.C. and his wife, Gloria.

He had trained his wife not to fuss over him and she had been married to him long enough to know not to try, but she prepared his favorite dinner— rare steak and potatoes—and then sat across the table from him, listening quietly while he rehashed what had happened to him and how he could have done it differently. There had been nothing wrong, either with his training or the new DIA techniques, the trading concept, for he had practiced that technique to a lesser extent while he was with the Los Angeles Police Department.

He ate slowly, chewing each bite of the steak thoroughly before he swallowed. His timing had been off, that was the problem, and he had under-estimated Cameron's recuperative powers. As he stood by the fireplace, his concentration had been misplaced, mental instead of physical, and he had been standing in the wrong position, his weight on the ball of his right foot, so that Cameron's hurtling into him had managed to catch him off balance and push him into the rough brick of the fireplace.

When he finished dinner, he took Gloria to bed, forcing himself over the pain and into a massive erection, making love to her as an expert sexual athlete, bringing her to a frenzied completion, her legs wrapped around his back, but he did not spend himself, and refused to allow himself the physical release. There was too much work to be done. He rolled out of bed and went out to the garage which he had converted into an exercise room, and he went through a full workout, bring-ing himself to the right psychological and physical pitch. Then he put on a jogging suit and took to the path through the park, his breath steaming out of him. He fell into a regular pace, punishing himself, pushing, for out there someplace was a limit, a finite point at which the pain would be so intense, the lungs so oxygen starved, his leg muscles so spasmed, that his body would collapse. It was his duty to get as close to that exhaustion as he could.

He passed three fat old men on the jogging path, the footing sloppy from the beaten-down snow, the trees above him leafless, barren. From this moment, he would think of nothing else until he had Cameron. For Cameron was his responsibility, his assignment. The larger project could be left to the General, to the planners, the leaders, for he considered himself a perfect follower, a man who did not question. He did not know the full implications of BRIMSTONE; did not want to know.

A dog followed him on his last lap around the park, a large mongrel cross between a German shepherd and a Labrador retriever, and it circled him for a while and then took a stance down the path in front of him to bare its teeth and snarl at him. He did not break his pace, but as he passed the dog, he did a quick step and lashed out with his right foot and felt the solid resistance of ribs. The dog retreated, yelping. His timing was back, reestablished.

At home, he took a shower, put on a robe and then went into the makeshift study and dialed the number he had for the General. He got through to Roffner almost immediately.

"I thought you were in a hospital in Philadelphia," Roffner said. "How are you feeling?"

"I just ran five miles," Wicker said. "Do you have any word on Cameron?"

"He's someplace on foot in Pennsylvania. The Pennsylvania Highway Patrol found the jeep at a junction east of Lancaster."

"Have you alerted the police?"

"No," the General said. "I want to give him a little room. I'm glad to hear you're all right, Wicker. It might be a good idea if you take a rest for a week or two."

"I'm going to get the tape for you, General. We used the wrong technique with Cameron. I want your permission to use my own methods with him."

"Certainly," Roffner said. "I'll expect you to check with me if you manage to locate him. We're observing a time frame here."

"I want one other thing," Wicker said. "He's made me look bad, General. That may not count for anything on your level, but it puts a permanent black mark on my record. I want the chance to correct that."

"How do you want to do it?"

"I want carte blanche with Cameron, when the time comes."

Roffner was silent a moment. "That can be arranged," he said finally.

4

Cameron caught a ride with a milk truck to Lancaster and got off just short of the motel on the east side of town. He had little trouble getting a room; the roads were all open now. He checked in under the name of Groton and took a room on the second floor of the back side of the motel where he had an unobstructed view of the snow-covered fields and the Amish farmhouses, the wood smoke pluming from the chimneys in the still cold air.

He ordered a pot of coffee and a carton of cigarettes sent up and then he went to work, jotting down all of the leads he would track through the computer. At the end of the conversation, X had referred to a small town in Nebraska as being his birthplace, population 2,300, and he had also lived in California. Two strong reference points. Cameron would set his population parameters as plus or minus 200 to allow for the vagaries of memory. He would tap into the Defense Personnel files for that one, limiting his search to bird Colonels and above. He wrote down one further note. X was proficient in the euphemistic language of the Pentagon.

Now, as to BRIMSTONE, he was reasonably sure it did not exist under that designation but it was always possible it had an alphanumeric title and unless Cameron hit it exactly, the computer would not recognize the inquiry. He worked until mid-afternoon and then lay down on the bed to wait for the delivery. He promptly fell asleep and awakened to find the room dark and the telephone ringing. He picked it up, groggy.

"Willie?"

"Connie?" he said, coming alert. "Is that you? What went wrong?"

"Everything. Nothing," she said. "I'm here. I'm calling from the lobby."

"Jesus," he said.

"I'll drive around to the back. I'm going to need your help to unload."

He went down the stairs just as her station wagon pulled around the side of the building. She backed up to the sidewalk and climbed out of the car, bundled up against the cold, and he embraced her briefly, gratefully. "Goddamn," he said. "This was probably a great mistake and you probably shouldn't be here at all, but God, I'm glad to see you. What happened?"

"Long story," she said wearily. "An even longer drive. Let's get the stuff inside."

It was all there, a good small CPU in a briefcase with a telephone interface, a small display screen, and he carried the things up to his room with Connie trailing along behind. He put the computer equipment on a table and she took off her coat, dressed in sweater and slacks, her blond hair tangled. She looked at him closely. "You look shot, Willie," she said.

"I am shot. Let me get us some drinks."

"I'm ahead of you," she said, opening a paper bag, taking out a bottle of bourbon. "I didn't know how these Pennsylvania Dutch feel about drinking and I didn't know how you were fixed for money. Speaking of which . . ." She opened her purse, removed an envelope, tossed it to him before she poured bourbon into two plastic glasses.

He riffled through the money: twenties and fifties. "Did you have any trouble getting it?"

"He's a bear when it comes to parting with money," she said, handing him a glass. "He spent a half hour establishing my identity and then another half hour persuading me to persuade you to come back and give yourself up."

He sipped the bourbon, then went about plugging the computer terminal into a wall socket. "Why did you come?" he said.

She took a folded newspaper out of her purse and handed it to him, and there it was, a picture of his face, caught in mid-sentence on some occasion, looking rumpled and angry and slightly maniacal. He scanned the story, the charges against him, the murder, a final sentence that he had been taken to a T-camp for questioning by a DIA agent whom he had assaulted before making his escape. God, they were skillful and Wicker had not been exaggerating. They had dovetailed all the circumstantial evidence against him and made a case. He put the paper down. "Hell," he said.

"Any messenger service would have spotted you right off," she said. "Besides, I was getting tired of the office. Numbers have never been my thing."

"You didn't quit?"

"No. I made a few feminine complaints and told them I was taking sick leave for a few days."

He sipped the bourbon. "I'm grateful," he said. "And now I want to get this equipment set up."

"Have you had dinner?" she said.

"No. I'm not hungry."

"I am and you will be. I'll bring something in." She picked up her coat, glanced at the twin beds in the room. "By the way, I checked in as Mrs. Groton. No implications there, just sure practicality."

"Sure," he said. But his mind was already on the machine and when the door closed behind her, he did not notice.

There was power in the computer, in the keyboard beneath his fingertips, in the display screen, in the telephone nestled in the interface holder. He dialed the GAO computer on the long distance line and then tapped in his access number which connected his terminal with the massive computer. He searched his memory for the access code to the Defense Department Personnel Computer and then tapped it into the keyboard, two digits followed by eight digits.

Once he was connected with the Personnel Computer, he began to ask it to search for one senior military officer who had listed on his personnel records a birthplace in Nebraska. He stopped. The computer could not find information which was not in its storage. It would not have population statistics.

He connected his terminal with the Bureau of the Census computer, asked it for a listing of all Nebraska towns with a population of 2,300 plus or minus 200 between the years 1920 and 1935. As the screen began to roll with them, he put them into storage and then gave the Personnel Computer the new data and asked it to find his man.

He was not prepared for the response. Line by line, the display screen filled up, began to scroll as new names appeared at the bottom of the screen and old names disappeared from the top. Jesus, 640 names before the rolling came to rest. He asked the computer to eliminate all those who did not list service in California in their records. The list of names was reduced by no more than twelve.

Not specific enough, no, and there were few officers who had not been in California, however briefly. But X had mentioned it to the President and that implied a longer stay. He refined the question, requested only those officers who had been based in California six months or longer. Now the list was reduced to fifty.

He sat back, sipping the bourbon. He was overlooking something so basic he had not seen it at first. Undoubtedly, X was based in Washington during that crucial year of 1972. He asked the computer to eliminate the names of those men who were not in Washington in June of 1972. The list was cut to eighteen. He sat back, studying the names on the screen. Then, on a hunch, he asked the computer to list those officers in this group who had access to the White House.

THAT INFORMATION IS NOT INCLUDED ON
SERVICE FILES.

He had not thought it would be. Very well, he
had eighteen names and an almost certain belief
that X was on that list. He punched the names into
storage, cleared the screen and finished the
bourbon, pouring himself another. On another
hunch, he decided to look for BRIMSTONE again.
He hooked his terminal into the Defense Budget
system and then, using lower case, wrote:

Provide budget category for brimstone.

Immediately the answer came back.

STANDBY.

Confusing. The DIA was obviously ready for
him. He should have known they would eventually
feed a garbage program into Defense computers
under the BRIMSTONE heading.
Proface budget category for brimstone, he wrote
again.
STANDBY. And then, in what seemed like
minutes, another single word.

CAMERON?

Ah, clever of them and he was startled. They
were willing to trade information. They would
confirm the name BRIMSTONE if he would confirm
that he was making the inquiry.

Yes. Identify yourself.

I AM OPERATING UNDER RESPONSE TO BRIM-
STONE. I KNOW YOUR PROBLEM. ~~DO~~ YOU
WISH TO COMMUNICATE?

Yes. Who are you?

SOMEONE WHO IS CONCERNED. I'M ON YOUR
SIDE IN THIS. I CAN'T SUPPLY MUCH INFOR-
MATION BUT I'LL TRY TO HELP AS LONG AS
I'M PROTECTED.

Cameron paused, not knowing whether he was
communicating with a very sophisticated program
or a man in a computer room in Washington who
knew what was going on and was using the computers like a teletype machine.

*Complete the following song title. You picked a
fine time to leave me—*

LUCILLE. I DON'T BLAME YOU FOR
VERIFYING. I'M NOT SETTING YOU UP.

Then what was the brimstone project?

I THINK IT WAS A MILITARY PROJECT.

Where? When?

I'M TRYING TO FIND OUT BUT THERE ARE
FEW SOURCES OF INFORMATION. I WILL
HAVE TO COMMUNICATE WITH YOU AT DIS-
CREET TIMES. CAN YOU CONTACT AT 2200
HOURS THIS NIGHT?

Yes.

ADDRESS LOCATION DOD ACCOUNT FILE LF-1113. BE VERY CAREFUL. I THINK THEY WILL KILL YOU IF THEY CAN. END TRANS-MISSION.

His hands were shaking. He refused to believe it. It was possible, yes, but he would have to test this sender, try him out. He had mentioned File LF-1113 and Cameron remembered it, the Russian city which he could not locate, the elevations which did not match. He had moved the material from LF-1113 into the GAO computer memory and it would still be there unless it had been removed. He addressed the GAO files and called for LF-1113 and the maps began to scroll onto the screen. He wished to hell he had a printer, something to make a hard copy of the data, but he would simply have to make do without one. Once he had located the fictitious Russian town, he held the map on the screen and grabbed a pencil and a sheet of motel stationery, making a rough copy.

The door opened and Connie came in carrying a box of fried chicken. "It's time for a break," she said, and then she saw his face. "You found something, didn't you?"

"I don't know." He left the computer and went to the bathroom and washed his face with cold water to bring him alert. By the time he came back into the room, the chicken was on a chair seat between the twin beds, put out on paper plates with containers of mashed potatoes and cole slaw. While he ate, he told her about the response from the computer technician in Washington.

"Can you trust him?" she said, biting into a piece of chicken.

"I don't know. I have to take that chance. It's hard to know who to trust right now."

"I don't blame you," she said. "I've only been in Washington five years and I've seen enough to convince me that government is sometimes a rotten and wasteful business. But every once in a while I run across people who are working within the system, trying to make it better, against great odds. Saunders is one. Maybe I'm saying I think you ought to take Harv's advice and go back. Put it all out in the open."

Cameron shook his head. "Harv can't do anything to help me. Neither can Saunders. Those people, whoever they are, are out to kill me. I'll give you odds they killed my father."

"If they did, you're not likely to find that out on your own. Even that will have a better chance of coming to light if you cooperate with the authorities, give them what you have. What happened to your hand?"

"I cut it breaking a window."

"You'd better let me have a look at it," she said, moving over to the bed beside him. "At one time, before I knew any better, I was in nurse's training." She unwrapped the gauze, her fingers warm against his wrist. She examined the wound with a practiced eye. "Whoever sewed you up did a good job," she said. "Does it hurt?"

"Not much."

"You'll need to get the stitches taken out in about a week."

If I'm still alive. He stirred, restless. "I've got to go back to work."

She put the bandage back in place. "You go ahead," she said. "I'm going to get some sleep." She went back to the other bed, removed her shoes and stretched out, her expression softer now as she looked at him. "I hope things work out for you, Willie."

"I hope so, too," he said. Back at the computer he made more notes, writing down questions that occurred to him, methods, procedures. He poured himself more bourbon, staring at the display screen with the flickering cursor. He believed that all of the pieces were there, hidden in a thousand different locations and waiting for him to find them.

He began with the National Geodetic Survey and put the map of the bogus Russian city into it and asked the computer to match against any similar configurations within the continental United States.

DATA NOT AVAILABLE NGS/447.

Very well, he had been afraid of that. The National Geodetic Survey had not computerized its maps. He would let that approach rest for now. He spent some time gaining access to the Nuclear Regulatory Agency computer and then carefully phrased his direction.

List all nuclear accidents from 1/1/1973 to 1/1/1976 in which loss of human life exceeded 10.

NONE, the computer answered.

He addressed the Federal Aviation Agency

computer and asked it for all air accidents within the continental United States involving the loss of more than ten lives during the same period. Immediately, four appeared on the screen, all connected with major cities, information which could be immediately checked and verified, nothing certainly which could be used to screen a military operation.

He was growing tired now, slightly dizzy from trying to follow the words on the screen. He sat back, smoked a cigarette, and looked at Connie who was sound asleep, one arm across her face against the light, knees drawn up slightly. Maybe she was right, maybe there were people who could help him. Well, he would give it another twenty-four hours and if he came up with nothing, he would contact Harv and turn the Nixon tape over to the *Washington Post* and use his energies to extricate himself.

He checked his watch. It was ten o'clock, 2200. He addressed LF-1113.

Brimstone, he typed into the machine.

CAMERON?

Yes.

I HAD A NEAR MISS EARLIER, ALMOST CAUGHT. COMMUNICATION MAY HAVE TO BE LIMITED TONIGHT. HAVE YOU STUDIED THE LF-1113 FILE?

The non-existent Russian city.

CORRECT.

Is this the project they are trying to cover up?

I BELIEVE SO. I HAVE NOT YET DETERMINED
SIGNIFICANCE BUT I BELIEVE IT IS
SOMEPLACE IN THE UNITED STATES AND
THAT THE INCIDENT OCCURRED IN AUGUST
OR SEPTEMBER 1974. ACTUAL CASUALTIES
SOMEWHAT HIGHER THAN 70-80. DOES THE
NIXON TAPE CONTAIN ANY FURTHER
HELPFUL SEARCH REFERENCES?

*Perhaps. Can you check a list of names for White
House access, June 1972?*

CAN DO. LIST.

Cameron typed the names into the machine, an
assorted list of Generals and Admirals, two
Colonels. *End list.*

IT WILL TAKE ME 24 HOURS TO CHECK
THESE. ACCESS WAS PRETTY TIGHT.

*I have made a computer search for a match on the
Russian town. No luck.*

IT IS POSSIBLE THEY REVERSED GRID DATA
FOR STORAGE. ONE RUMOR: YOUR FATHER
DISCOVERED SIGNIFICANCE "BRIMSTONE"
AND WAS TERMINATED. POSSIBLE?

Possible. Can you provide more?

THERE HAS BEEN A FLURRY OF INVESTI-
GATIVE ACTIVITY HERE CONCERNING YOUR
FATHER'S CONNECTION WITH THE NIXON
TAPE AND THE POSSIBILITY HE WAS IN SOME

WAY RESPONSIBLE FOR THE MISSING
EIGHTEEN AND A HALF MINUTES.

Any hard evidence?

THEY MUST THINK SO. INVESTIGATION IS
BEING CONDUCTED UNDER TOP SECURITY
CONDITIONS.

Cameron paused a moment, thinking, considering.

*Can you leak the information concerning the
investigation without jeopardizing yourself?*

I DON'T HAVE MUCH. WHAT WOULD IT GAIN?

I want to put them on the defensive.

IF YOU SAY SO. ONE FURTHER RUMOR. IF YOU
SURRENDER THE NIXON TAPE, THEY ARE
PREPARED TO TAKE YOU OFF THE HOOK.

More.

DO YOU WISH ME TO CHECK IT OUT?

Yes.

WILL IT BE POSSIBLE TO COMMUNICATE
TOMORROW?

What time?

2100-2300 TIME FRAME. I WILL BE ON DUTY.

Why are you doing this?

I LOVE MY COUNTRY. OLD FASHIONED. BE
CAREFUL, FRIEND. THEY WILL KILL YOU IF
THEY CAN AND NO ONE WILL EVER KNOW.
END TRANSMISSION.

He turned off the computer, terminated the
telephone line. He poured his last drink for the
night and thought about his father and the accident in Las Vegas, and the computer technician's
rumor was probably correct. Cameron's father
was the kind of man who would have been too
curious about the tape to let it pass, and it was
entirely possible that curiosity had caused his
death. And Cameron decided he would wait until
the access list was checked out and if there was
nothing positive there, he would follow Harv's
advice.

Chapter Seven

On Roffner's way to the press corridor, he was seething, not so much at any individual as at his own shortcomings, his inability to cover all the bases. There had been a leak from somewhere inside his organization, he was certain of that, or the investigation would not have reached the media and resulted in such a rash of speculative stories.

He had no idea that there was such an epidemic of Nixon-mania still loose in the country, that the speculation about the eighteen-and-a-half-minute gap would cause such a furor. Major Shaw met Roffner in the corridor outside the conference room, a worried expression on his face.

"I just came from PR, General," he said. "They still strongly urge that you scrub this press conference and ignore the stories."

"They won't go away," Roffner said, feeling better now that he had something negative to play against. "We let them stand and Cameron can feed his tape right into public acceptance." He took a deep breath, clearing his mind, preparing for the ordeal. "Have you briefed Rawlings?"

"Yes, sir."

Roffner nodded. He pushed through the door,

making a shift into another part of his personality, exuding confidence, sweeping the small room with a calculated glance as if to impart his confidence to the batteries of television cameras along the back and the solid mass of print reporters down front, the popping of flashbulbs. The point was to read their mood instantly once the questioning began, to put them at ease, to defuse them, to set precisely the right tone. He was invigorated by the challenge. He recognized Koblenz of the *Post* in the first row, a sandy-haired young man with a hawklike face. It would be from Koblenz that he would get the most flak, for Koblenz had fielded the leak and issued the first story. He had been refusing Koblenz's calls all day.

Roffner mounted the dais, tapped his finger against the microphone although he already knew it was live, then shifted a glass of water and removed two folded sheets of paper from his inside pocket, creating the impression that he was not a tough and calculating man but rather a spokesman perfectly at ease under these circumstances because he had nothing to hide.

"I'd like to set the ground rules before we begin," he said into the microphone. "I have a short statement to make and then I'll answer any questions you have, with no time limit." He sipped from the glass of water.

"None of my remarks are to be construed as partisan in any way. As many of you know, my relationship with former President Nixon was a warm one and I don't intend to get into any interpretations of Watergate. Frankly, I see that as out of my ballpark. I have been advised that I should make no statement at all, that I should not dignify the allegations made in the media by any sort of rebuttal. But there's a principle involved here. I worked very closely with Colonel Harry Cameron for a long time before he joined the White House staff, and since his reputation is at stake and he is no longer here to defend himself, I intend to do it for him."

He paused, looking out at the newsmen, his view partially obscured by the bright, hot lights, but he could see Koblenz's face which appeared to be flushed, predatory, and this young newsman would become his conversion target and his barometer. He spread the two sheets of his statement on the podium and unfolded his reading glasses and put them on, then he sipped the water again.

"Too, there are some elements of the newspapers account that are true and they tend to lend credibility to the parts that are patently false. I want to make sure that the two are separated, once and for all." And now he began to read about Colonel Cameron's impeccable background as a military officer, a purposely dull stretch of words designed to make the reporters restless and indeed it was working. He saw Koblenz fidgeting with his ballpoint pen, clicking the retractable point in and out. Yes, pacing was everything and he was a master of the press statement, veteran of a hundred grillings such as this one.

"Now, I will give you the facts as far as I have been able to determine them, the Colonel's sole connection with any of the Nixon tapes. Parts of what I am about to say cannot be verified due to Colonel Cameron's untimely and accidental death in Las Vegas, Nevada, on November twelfth of this year. When Colonel Cameron retired from military service on one July 1974, I had a long conversation with him in which the subject of the Nixon tapes was mentioned peripherally. This is what he told me.

"On or about one October 1973, Colonel Cameron accompanied the presidential party to Key Biscayne, Florida, at a time when President Nixon was attempting to comply with the order to transcribe the tapes. The Colonel was called into the villa occupied by Rose Mary Woods, the President's secretary, to help interpret the tape of twenty June 1972."

He paused for effect, to heighten the anticipation. He sipped from the glass of water. "I'm sure you're curious about what he heard on that tape. So was I. I asked him quite candidly if he thought the conversation between Nixon and Haldeman confirmed the public suspicion about Nixon's knowledge of the Watergate break-in. The Colonel laughed at that suggestion and I can remember distinctly and exactly what he said. I won't even delete the expletives. 'Hell, General,' he said. 'That damned tape was so garbled I had difficulty making out a word here and there. I couldn't even recognize the President's voice.'"

Roffner paused, shaking his head slowly. "Now, that's simply all there is to it. I will add one simple statement. There has not been an investigation, there is no investigation, and there will be no investigation concerning Colonel Cameron and any of the Nixon tapes. Now, if you have any questions, I'll be glad to answer them."

At least half the newsmen were on their feet now, raising hands, calling out for recognition, and he took his time and looked straight at Koblenz who stood in a casual slouch. "Mr. Koblenz?"

"If I interpret your remarks correctly, sir, you are saying that this is much ado about nothing. Is that an accurate reading?"

"I realize there's great public interest in the subject, Mr. Koblenz."

"But you don't take it seriously."

"That's correct."

"One further question," Koblenz said with an almost boyish smile. "Do you know William Cameron?"

So that was it. Koblenz had made that link. Roffner looked thoughtful. "If you're talking about Colonel Cameron's son, the one who's been in the papers, I can say that I know of him, but only through those newspaper accounts."

"In checking with the GAO, I find that he was involved in an audit of a Defense account LF-1113, and that that account is joint between your department and Defense Intelligence."

"I will look into that for you, Mr. Koblenz," Roffner said, smiling. "I'm not personally aware of William Cameron's activities with the GAO. Too, as I'm sure you realize, the routine audits by the GAO on behalf of Congress cover every account of every government agency on a continual basis. I may not be able to give you full details of LF-1113 because many of our projects are classified, but I'll have one of my people get back to you on that."

He terminated the press conference and went back to his office and closed the door behind him, buzzing his secretary to tell her to hold all calls and admit only Major Shaw. He turned on his sound system to Bach, a composer he had never enjoyed, a man who must have had a musical computer for a mind, no fire in Bach, only precision. He poured himself a glass of milk and sat down in the black leather chair behind his desk, drinking it slowly. His stomach began to stop burning.

He had misjudged. That was the truth of it. PR had been right this time and the matter should have been ignored or handled with a simple press release of denial. He had given the whole matter too much emphasis. There was a slight tap on the door and Major Shaw came in, his usual quiet self, no, somehow changed, more quizzical than usual.

"Well, Shaw," Roffner said. "What do you think?"

"Are you asking my professional opinion, sir?"

"No, man to man."

"I think you did a hell of a job out there."

"It wasn't good enough," Roffner said meditatively. "Where's our leak, Major? That's the question. What son of a bitch is opening his mouth about the tapes and why? We're going to have to plug that leak and fast or we're going to get swamped."

"I don't know," Shaw said. "Maybe it's because I'm getting older, but I find myself wondering if all this is really necessary."

"All what?"

"The whole BRIMSTONE business. I'm sure when it began it was a viable proposition—hairy, unorthodox, but vital. Now I think things have changed."

"This is not the time to doubt, Major," Roffner

said. "It takes a bold plan and bold men not to capitulate to popular convention. BRIMSTONE has been in the works a long time. It's been discussed by some of the brightest men in the country."

"I'll grant you that," Shaw said. "But that was years ago. Most of those men aren't around anymore. They've retired, died, God knows what. And I'm sure none of them has given it a thought in years, and if you asked the ones who are still around, I'm sure they would think that BRIMSTONE was jettisoned years ago."

Roffner was irritated. Shaw was falling under the influence of the breast-beaters and the nay-sayers, the passive critics in the military who used thoughtfulness as an excuse to do nothing. He picked up the telephone, told his secretary to get Wicker on the line. When she found Wicker for him, he told Wicker to get to his office as soon as he could. He replaced the telephone, leaned back in his chair. "What do you think of Wicker now?" he said.

"He's an anachronism."

"Oh?"

"He would have been at home in a feudal fiefdom where the lord of the manor could send him out to do something bloody every day to demonstrate his loyalty."

"That's accurate," Roffner said evenly. "I'd better clarify something for you, Major. I don't like any of the things you're saying. They reveal an inner weakness."

"They represent what I feel."

"Then for the time being, I'm going to require you to suppress what you feel. The next week is going to be a highly critical time. If your feelings get in the way, you will be of absolutely no use to me. Now, if you think you can carry out orders, instantly, without hesitation, then we'll go on with this. If you can't do that, then I'll arrange a transfer for you to a duty where you can be more comfortable.''

The Major straightened slightly. "I don't want a transfer.''

"That's good. I'd hate to lose you. Right now, I want you to get a full trace effort under way. I want that leak permanently plugged. Now.''

Wicker arrived at almost the same time Shaw departed and the General could not help comparing the two men. For Shaw was too much a combination of the intellectual and the idealist. Left to him, action would take the form of words on paper, discussions, computer studies, arguments, cerebral balancings. But Wicker was a physical man, more concerned with the actual than the abstract. As Wicker sat down, the General could see few traces of the ordeal he had been through. It was ironic in a way, that the Major in his uniform should be a civilian at heart and this civilian an ideal soldier. "What do you have?'' Roffner said.

"How do you know I have anything?'' Wicker said.

"Because I know you. Any other man would sit on his ass and wait for orders, but not you.''

"That's right,'' Wicker said. He had been busy. He had checked the doctors in southern Pennsylvania in the general area where the jeep was found and he had located a physician who had treated a man answering to Cameron's description. The doctor had stitched a severe hand wound. Next,

Wicker had checked with a legal secretary who occasionally provided him information and she found out for him that Cameron had talked with his attorney who was upset because Cameron refused to return to Washington. Wicker concluded, therefore, that Cameron had probably holed up somewhere in southern Pennsylvania.

He then checked at GAO and could locate no one who had been in contact with Cameron. Three people had gone on sick leave. Two were home with viruses. The third, a woman researcher, had checked out a portable computer terminal with which to work at home. The super at her apartment house told Wicker she was not home and that she had asked him to keep an eye on her place. A local service station attendant gave Wicker the information that the woman had had her car serviced in a hurry in preparation for a trip. "I think she went to join him," Wicker said. "I have a description of the station wagon, the tag number. They shouldn't be difficult to find."

"Good," Roffner said. "And what about the tape?"

"I think he has it with him," Wicker said, popping his knuckles. "It's logical. Obviously, he asked her to bring him the computer terminal. He's not coming back to Washington and he sure as hell didn't have the tape on him, so my hunch is that she brought him the tape as well."

Roffner was fascinated by the way Wicker's mind worked, all the precision of a Bach fugue and an equal absence of emotion. "You're very thorough."

"It's my job."

"How long would it take you to find Cameron?"

"Forty-eight hours to get face to face."

"We have to cut that time down," Roffner said. "It's critical now. I want that tape before he exploits it."

"I see," Wicker said blankly. "There's just one thing, General . . ."

"What's that?"

"I told you before I want to use my own methods, nothing psychological. More direct."

"Fine," Roffner said. He looked at him directly. "When you have the tape, I don't want him around to contradict what I have to do with it. Do you understand?"

"Perfectly."

"Kill him," Roffner said. "That's what I want."

2

Cameron finished listening to General Roffner's press conference on the car radio and he reached out and turned it off. "We've struck a nerve," he said. "They wouldn't have held a press conference otherwise."

"Maybe," Connie said.

"What do you mean maybe?"

She leaned back against the car door. She shook her head. "Just disregard that, Willie. I don't know how I got into the position of the devil's advocate." She looked out the window at the winter fields, the bleak rolling hills. "Are we still in Ohio?"

"Yes."

"I have a sister someplace in Ohio. Columbus, I think. We never liked each other. She married an orthodontist and we lost touch."

"Are you sorry?"

"About my sister?"

"That you didn't marry an orthodontist and end up in someplace like Columbus, Ohio."

She laughed slightly. "Oh, hell no," she said. "I'm not much, Willie. I don't mean by that that I don't like myself, because I do. But I never had a calling, no special talents, no great beauty. And I never had the overwhelming desire for security that my sister has. I've always wanted to be at the center of things. I think I understand now what your Annie was all about. She just couldn't make do with the ordinary."

"Don't call her 'my' Annie," he said. "And whatever she was after, she sure as hell didn't get it."

"A universal truth," she said. "We all end up dead." She was silent awhile. "Do you know where we're headed, Willie? Or did you get us up in the middle of the night to put distance between us and them?"

"Las Vegas, I think."

"You're not sure?"

"That's where my father was. He talked to Purdy. I know that much. Maybe he had other friends. Maybe he confided in somebody. But you're not going that far."

"Oh?"

"When we get into Missouri, I want you to take your car and go back to Nebraska. Do you still have people there?"

"My mother."

"You go home and when they eventually catch up with you, you tell them you went home because you got sick or homesick or any damn thing you can think of. They won't push you too hard. They want me."

She lighted a cigarette. "This is all so crazy somehow," she said. "I used to have this fantasy when I first got to Washington. I was going to meet this Senator or Congressman and we were going to get married and drive across the country to honeymoon at the Grand Canyon." She snuffed out the cigarette. "It was only after I had a look at the Congressman that that fantasy died."

He saw the highway patrol car in his mirror and tensed reflexively, waiting to see if the flashing lights would come on. He was aware of the pistol in his pocket and the sure knowledge he would not use it if they stopped him. He felt the adrenaline pumping through him. The patrol car moved into the left lane, passed at eighty miles an hour. He watched it pull away, diminish, and he was caught in a visceral trembling that left him short of breath.

"Jesus," he said.

"They think you're alone, right? They couldn't know about me."

"I don't know what they think," he said. But he was afraid in that moment he was not going to get away, for as incompetent as the forces of government sometimes were, they were massive and eventually thorough. He felt like an alien in his own country and he wondered what would happen if he fled inexplicably north, into Canada, into Quebec perhaps where the authorities, being at odds with both the national government and the United States, might offer him refuge. It would not work, no, for if he could not find people to believe him in the United States, he would not find that credence in a foreign country.

He drove all day, occasionally trading off with Connie while he napped, coming awake to find rain showers continuing to obscure the interstate, or to stop at the big service stations to fill the tank or use the toilet or get something to eat. On previous trips he had found these rest stops reassuring, full of cross-country travelers like himself, tired, their accents diverse—flat, nasal, soft, broken—but all American, all akin to him in some way.

But today he felt apart, separate. They all seemed isolated in themselves, and in one diner he heard a middle-aged man and wife talking about a son they were on their way to visit, in an eastern university, living with a girl, unlawful coitus, and he wondered what would happen if he went to their table and introduced himself and told them that their country was going to hell in a handbasket and that as long as one person was being persecuted by the government, nobody was safe. He was not sure what would happen, whether they would hear him out before they called the police. In any case, they certainly would not believe him.

Dark, and he was driving, the rain still intermittent. The digital clock on the dash read eight o'clock and they would have to stop soon to give him time to set up his nightly computer contact.

"What will you do if you get out of this?" Connie's voice startled him.

"I thought you were asleep."

"I was. What will you do? Have you thought about it?"

"No," he said. "Go to California, maybe. Do the same kind of thing I do now, only not for the government. Research of some sort."

"That's not what I'm talking about," she said. "Not work, for God's sake, not your profession or your livelihood. What kind of life do you see for yourself, what kind of feelings, what kind of attitudes toward the world?"

He shook his head. "I haven't got the slightest idea."

"I find men, for the most part, very limited," she said. "My friend in the State Department was like that. There was a whole exciting world around us and so help me God, he could never get in touch with it. When he got up and dressed in the morning, he never once opened his arms to the world and looked forward to the day. His first act after he got dressed was to stand in front of the mirror and worry about how he looked."

"Gray suit, right?"

"On target," she said. She lighted two cigarettes, handed him one. "You're going to find this perverse, Willie, but I've enjoyed this day with you. I've been frightened, edgy, not sure how long anything is going to last, but the threat is real and there's a sound reason for all this anxiety. It's not trouble for the sake of trouble, if you know what I mean."

"All I know is that I want this resolved." He saw a motel ahead of him, high on a buff; he took the next exit ramp, crossed under the interstate, and drove up a winding road with the sudden realization that he had no idea where he was and that it really did not matter.

He checked in under the name of Squires this time, made arrangements for the use of the computer terminal in his room and wearily unloaded the equipment, dragging it up to his room on the second floor. As he climbed the stairs he noticed a swimming pool in a recreation room, truncated by a glass wall which came to the water level, a wall which could be raised during the summer season to convert the indoor-outdoor pool into a single unit. The recreation room was deserted. Perhaps later he would have a swim, lapping the pool until the tension was out of his body.

From the room, he could see the twin ribbons of the interstate below the bluff, winding off to the west, the lights of the cars a steady stream, even at this time of night. He drew the blinds, set up the computer, and made sure it was working. Connie went for ice and when she came back, she looked refreshed, positively radiant. "This is a lovely place," she said. "I'd like to come here in the summer sometime. The country looks beautiful."

"And I think you're just a little bit crazy," he said, smiling.

"I like to think of it as being just a little bit sane." She poured the bourbon into plastic glasses. "Here's looking at you, kid."

He laughed, caught up in the marvelous insanity of the moment, and he put the glass down and lay back on the bed, still laughing. "I don't even know where in the hell we are," he said. "Someplace in Missouri, I think. And I don't give a damn."

"No," she said. "We could be hit by a truck tomorrow. A meteor could fall on us while we're asleep. And if that happened, all this worry would be wasted." She glanced at the computer terminal. "So get your work over with. I'm going to take a shower."

"Right." He glanced at his watch. It was time to make contact. He retrieved his glass and moved to the computer terminal. He was continually amazed at the technology which had been able to miniaturize the components so the microcomputer could fit into a briefcase. The CRT was nothing more than a small television set. He got a direct line from the telephone operator and placed the telephone into the molded interface which fit it like a glove. He could hear Connie singing in the shower. He liked the sound of her voice. He addressed the DOD file number, LF-1113.

Brimstone. The word appeared on the screen as he typed it.

CONFIRMED. IDENTIFY.

Cameron.

YOU'RE LATE. I WAS AFRAID YOU WOULDN'T BE ON LINE TONIGHT.

I'm not late. Time is currently 2148.

YOU'VE CHANGED TIME ZONES THEN. WE'LL HAVE TWELVE MINUTES, SO LET'S GET TO IT. OF THE NAMES ON YOUR LIST, THE LAST FOUR HAD WHITE HOUSE ACCESS, INCLUDING GENERAL ROFFNER. DID YOU SEE HIS PRESS CONFERENCE ON TELEVISION TODAY?

I heard it on the radio.

WE SHOOK THEM UP. THEY ARE REALLY SCURRYING AROUND HERE, LOOKING FOR

THE LEAK. THEY WOULD CERTAINLY TRADE
YOU FOR YOUR TAPE. LIMITED TIME.
THEY'RE BOXING YOU IN. COULD GENERAL
ROFFNER BE THE SECOND MAN ON YOUR
TAPE?

*I'm not sure. The sound quality is poor. What do
you have on Brimstone?*

NOTHING CONCRETE, ANOTHER RUMOR. DO
YOU KNOW PURDY, GAO, LAS VEGAS,
NEVADA?

Affirmative.

LOOK INTO CONNECTION.

Why don't you specify, tell me what it is?

CAN'T DO THAT. I WILL DO NOTHING TO
ALLOW THEM TO BACKTRACK ME.

I understand.

MY ADVICE. IF YOU CAN MAKE A DEAL ON THE
TAPE, TAKE IT. I THINK THEY ARE MAKING
RAPID STRIDES TO COVER EVERYTHING. THE
RUSSIAN CITY HAS BEEN ELIMINATED FROM
THE DIA COMPUTER FILES. DO YOU STILL
HAVE A COPY OF IT?

Affirmative.

IT IS POSSIBLE THAT BRIMSTONE WAS A
NERVE GAS ACCIDENT. I HAVE TRIED TO
CHECK THIS END WITH NO LUCK. IF YOU
HAVE ACCESS ATLANTA DATA BANK,
INFECTIOUS DISEASE CONTROL, QUERY FOR

INCIDENT DURING TIME FRAME. WHERE ARE
YOU HEADED?

I don't know.

EXCUSE THE STUPID QUESTION. MY NAME IS
FRANK REEVES, BY THE WAY. WE'LL HAVE
TO HAVE A DRINK WHEN THIS IS OVER.

Yes. Thank you, Reeves.

REMEMBER THE TIME DIFFERENCE. TAKE
CARE. END TRANSMISSION.

Connie was still in the shower. He took the time
to get the Atlanta access code from the GAO
directory and queried its computer for any listing
of a localized epidemic or unexplained medical
phenomena involving thirty or more people in a
specific place during August or September 1974.

. NO SUCH INCIDENT OCCURRED.

He severed the telephone connection, then on
impulse summoned the map of the Russian town
from the GAO computer memory, putting the map
on the screen, studying the pattern of the streets.
It occurred to him that this was a company town
of some sort, for there was an irregular block of
streets around an area that was large enough to
contain a factory. He sipped the bourbon, looked
around as Connie came into the room, a large
towel wrapped around her. She sat down on the
edge of the bed and started to paint her fingernails. Ah, God, a touch of normalcy and he could
not hold to his anxieties in a situation so non-

critical that this woman felt free to pay attention to her fingernails. She smiled at him. "What's new from your cybernetic correspondent?"

"Rumors," he said. "Rumors and self-protection. He keeps advising me to make a trade." He finished the glass of bourbon, feeling very easy, free floating. "Hell," he said. "Let's give up all this nonsense and spend a week at the Grand Canyon."

"Are you serious?"

"Certainly," he said. "I'm tired of all this and that's the truth. I think the Bright Angel Lodge is open all year."

"Bright Angel. That's such a pretty name for a place."

Foolishness, he realized, on both sides. But logic did not seem important now. "Deal?" he said.

"Why not?" She sat on the bed, painting the last of her fingernails, blowing on them. "Do you like this color? This is my one artistic achievement, mixing fingernail polish."

"It's too red," he said.

"You don't have any taste," she said pleasantly. "Are they going to cooperate with you?"

"I don't know," he said. "You want another drink?"

"No."

He stood up and sat down on the bed across from her. "It's a strange goddamned world, you know that?" he said. "I should feel relieved because I've taken positive steps."

"But you don't?"

"No," he said. "There's something else going on here, something besides a cover-up. They've gone to elaborate lengths, much too elaborate."

"Remember Watergate," she said. "That was pretty elaborate."

"Not in the same way. They assumed a kind of invulnerability from the beginning, as if all they had to do was issue certain public statements and it would all go away. They were stupid then. These people are not stupid in the least." He finished the drink, put the glass on the table, then picked up one of her hands, examining the polish in the light of the lamp. The red appeared to have a silver tinge in the light and her fingers were warm, soft, real, while his uneasy thoughts about a complicated conspiracy were vague, unreal. "What do you call this color?"

"Pink Passion. Isn't that nice? Old-fashioned, somehow."

He saw the look in her eyes—amused, happy, a little wondering—and he leaned down and kissed her and knew in that moment they were going to make love. The towel came away from her body and his hand smoothed over her breasts, the nipples becoming erect, and he traced a path across her stomach with his fingertips to the thicket of hair between her legs. He began to caress her with no seeming urgency, and he could feel her hand on him, freeing him, and then with a great sigh she opened her legs to him and they came together, rocking back and forth, kissing at the same time.

"Oh, darling William," she said into his ear, and he realized she was laughing.

He did not slow down, maintaining the same insistent rhythm. "What's so funny?" he said.

"Me," she said, breathless. "I'm making love

and protecting my wet fingernail polish at the same time."

He put his mouth on hers, more insistent now, absolutely joyous, and suddenly she was with him and he felt himself spending at the very moment she contracted around him. And then she began to laugh again, exhibiting her spread fingers with the polish intact. "My marvelous Willie," she said. "That was glorious. We'll have to try it again sometime when my fingernails are dry and we haven't been driving all day."

He lay back on the bed, more peaceful than he had been in days. He lighted two cigarettes and handed her one. "We should have been together a long time ago," he said. "All this wasted time."

"It wouldn't have worked then," she said, putting her head back on the pillow, blowing smoke into the air. "I'm not going to my mother in Nebraska."

He patted her bare stomach, "I know."

"I'm committed, William, a hundred percent. I think I was totally committed from the minute you called me and asked me to have those things sent to you. I thought about a delivery service, I even called one, but I knew from the beginning I was going to bring them to you myself."

Not logical but real, and he could feel it. "We have to make plans," he said.

"Concerning what?"

"It's not likely that I'm going to emerge unscathed from all this," he said.

She smiled. "I don't have anything to lose, dear," she said. "The only person who would be concerned one way or the other is my mother and I have the feeling she'd approve. She's always had a small desire to be secretly scandalous, I think, and she'd love the notoriety."

"I hope it's as simple as scandalous," he said. He did not believe it for a moment and it was impossible that things would ever be simple again. Lying there on the bed, he turned his mind to details again, for he could afford to make no small mistakes now which, like minor holes in a dam, could enlarge to engulf him. The Nixon tape was one of those weaknesses and as long as he carried it, they both were vulnerable. He sat up, leaned down, and kissed her lightly.

"I have to learn your signals," she said. "That kiss means you're ready to leave my bed, correct?"

"Correct," he said. "There's something I have to do." He sought out the cardboard mailer, found it in the attache case she had brought him. He inked out the former address, then addressed it to William Cameron, c/o General Delivery, Las Vegas, Nevada. He put on his topcoat. "I'll be back in a little while," he said. "Can I bring you something to eat?"

"Fried clams," she said.

"I'll give it a try."

He went down the corridor, through the recreation room to the front desk where he found a young desk clerk watching the color television set in the lobby and he talked the clerk into weighing the small package on a pair of postal scales and selling him enough stamps to send it first class. "Where's the local post office?" Cameron said. "Do they have an outside deposit box?"

"Yes, sir," the clerk said. "It's about four blocks

from here. But it'll go just as fast if we include it in our morning pickup."

"I need the walk," he said. He went outside and almost immediately regretted his decision. A strong wind had picked up from the north, cold, and he bundled his coat about him as he walked down the drive to the street which was all but deserted at this time of night, a couple of pickup trucks parked along the curb, no pedestrians. He crossed the street and went down the sidewalk, past the darkened windows of a few stores until he reached the post office. Then he put the tape in the outside deposit box with a great feeling of relief.

He started back toward the motel. There was a heavy mist in the air beginning to turn icy. He would not be surprised if it snowed before morning. He thought how ironic it would be if the tape now resting in that metal box never reached Las Vegas, if somewhere in the labyrinth of mailing machines and transporting aircraft and trucks it was smashed, obliterated, the burden of it removed from him.

He passed by a store window and suddenly he heard something across the street, a muted, almost whispering sound and the glass smashed in the window as if it had been struck a blow. He jumped reflexively, startled. There was a large round hole in the glass, cracks radiating out of it like a sunburst. He did not move until he heard the sound again, and a second hole was punched into the window immediately to his right side and he realized what he had heard were gunshots, a pistol with a silencer.

He scrambled away, almost losing his footing on the slick sidewalk, running, darting into the dark safety of an alley. He leaned against a brick wall, out of breath. They had caught up with him, who, Wicker maybe, impossible, and the old anger was there again as if it had been just beneath the surface all the time.

He remembered the pistol in his pocket, took it out, the grip icy cold against his hand, waiting. But he heard nothing except the pounding of his own heart and the rasping of his own breath. He could see nothing, but somebody was out there, in the shadows of a used car lot across the street, and he half expected an alarm to start ringing from the violated window or the local police to come rolling up. But nothing happened.

This was a small town, not a city, and that window could remain undiscovered for a long time. He caught his breath, calmed himself, watching the used car lot, aware of a small building at the back of it, one small exterior floodlight shining on the metallic surfaces of perhaps a dozen cars and trucks, a light haloed in the mist.

Wicker, it had to be Wicker, hiding, concealing himself in the back of a pickup truck perhaps, crouched low behind a sports car. Cameron felt the night chill down into his bones, the iciness of a resolute anger.

Wicker and his games. The two holes in the window, meant to terrify. Visible proof that Cameron had been bracketed, that Wicker could have killed him, an introduction to another phase of Wicker's harassing tactics. Cameron moved away from the protection of the brick wall, putting the pistol beneath his jacket, his eyes watching the lot, waiting for the slightest hint of movement, but there was none. He continued to advance across the street, only dimly aware of a pickup truck that had to brake to keep from running him down, the voice of a man yelling at him as the pickup swerved around him and moved on.

Cameron's eyes had not left the used car lot for an instant. He was giving Wicker no chance to retreat, to slip away unnoticed. He removed the pistol from the shelter of his coat, clicked off the safety, walked to the front of a Corvette where he could look down the open space between two rows of cars, all the way to the office with the light. Still no movement.

"Wicker," he said in a conversational voice, knowing that Wicker was listening. "I'm going to kill you or you're going to have to kill me. Here and now."

There was no answer. The mist had turned into rain. It was really coming down now; he could see the slant of it against the worklight on the building, soaking through his topcoat. Dark, much too dark and he simply could not see well enough to know that Wicker had not moved away, was not now gone. He began to inch down the row of cars, moving very slowly.

"You're an incompetent son of a bitch, Wicker," he said, his eyes straining against the rain. "They picked the wrong man when they put you on the job."

And then, quite suddenly, there was another *whomp* from somewhere toward the small building, the silenced pistol firing, and a hole punched through the windshield of a Chevrolet, not three feet from Cameron's head, a neat hole in the center of whitewashed lettering. LOW MILEAGE, ONE

OWNER. And Cameron began to run toward the spot where he thought Wicker was. He splashed through a puddle, the water flooding his shoes, and the headlights of a truck at the end of the row flashed on, blinding him, but he fired the pistol in the general direction of the lights and one of them exploded and went dark. He fired again and the second blinked out. He ran behind the truck, around the side of the building, then stopped short, listening again, waiting for his eyes to adjust. There was an alley behind the building, unlighted, unpaved. Wicker was gone.

He lowered the pistol, half sick to his stomach. Then he heard the car stopping on the street in front of the lot and saw the flashlights, people attracted by the gunfire. He could stay here no longer. He ran into the darkness of the alley, stumbled against a box and hurt his shins, moved on. He came to a lighted cross street, put the gun away, collected himself. He walked back to the main thoroughfare, crossed the street and then stood for a moment, watching the activity at the used car lot. Two more cars had joined the first, one of them the police.

He was into it now and he would have to keep moving. There was another row of motels down the slope on this side of the street and he walked briskly, watching for any sign of a trailing car. There was none. Within minutes he came to the first motel, built like a Swiss chalet. He caught a glimpse of himself in the mirroring glass surface of the door, drenched, topcoat rumpled, his hair plastered down. The fear and the anger in him were visible, the wildness in his eyes.

It would not do. Everything depended on a calm

appearance. A businessman, yes, no more than that. Normal pressures. He could hear the music from the motel's club room, disco, the universal taste. He ran a comb through his hair and went into the lobby.

There was a placard on the counter, WELCOME P.S.M.E., and an older man behind the counter was talking on the telephone, answering a complaint, smooth at it, calming a guest who was protesting the noise from the bar. Cameron heard the words "mining engineers" and guessed that the P.S. stood for "Professional Society" and that the men in the bar were professional mining engineers here for a convention.

The man finished his conversation, ran a hand over his sweating scalp, and then turned to Cameron. "Yes, sir. May I help you?"

"Yes," Cameron said. "I need an airline schedule."

"We have an airport but we don't have any airlines," the clerk said.

"Are there any local planes for charter?"

"No, sir."

Cameron opened his wallet, took out two one-hundred-dollar bills and laid them on the counter. "I want you to find me a car, with a driver, available now, to drive me to Springfield. Then I want you to call the Springfield airport for me and charter a jet, for tonight."

"It may be a little late for a charter tonight," the man said. But he was looking at the money.

"It has to be tonight," Cameron said. "You pay for the car out of this and keep the rest."

"Yes, sir. I'll try."

He left the clerk to make his calls. The cigarettes

in his shirt pocket were soaked through. He threw them away, got another pack from the lobby machine, then went to the row of public telephones, and called his own motel, gave the operator his room number. Connie answered on the first ring. "Where are my clams?"

"We've run out of time," he said. "Wicker's here."

"But how? What is—"

"He's here, believe me," he said, cutting her off. "I don't know whether he's alone, whether he has you located, but you have to get out of there. Don't go near the station wagon. He's bound to have an eye on that. Pack up the computer terminal and I'll have somebody come for you. Use the back stairs and stay away from the lobby."

"I don't understand. How did he find us? What are you going to do?"

"I've had enough," he said. "I'm going to settle it."

"What do you mean you're going to settle it?" Her voice was forceful. "Don't do anything until we talk it over. Promise me that."

He looked down at the circular label on the telephone dial. "Have the man bring you to the Chalet Motor Lodge. You wait exactly fifteen minutes. If I don't show up by then, you go to Springfield and catch a plane for Washington."

"No," she said. "We're going to talk about this."

"There isn't time to talk." He put the telephone back on the hook. The man at the desk signaled him.

"I have the car for you," he said. "I found one jet charter service in Springfield. They say flying conditions are not very good, but if this is an emergency—"

"It is."

"I'll need your name, sir."

"Johnson. H.B."

"They want a destination, Mr. Johnson."

"Albuquerque, New Mexico."

"Yes, sir."

Cameron paced the floor until a new car wheeled up to the office. He told the driver, a man in his thirties, what he wanted done. Once the car was gone, he went out into the rain again and walked back to his own motel, half expecting Wicker to make an appearance at any moment. By the time he reached the motel, his anger had converted into a grim determination. He glanced at his watch, his shirt sleeve wet. At this moment, Connie would be putting the computer equipment in the car at the rear of the motel. Fifteen minutes. Not enough time.

Wicker was not in the lobby. There was a cluster of men in business suits arguing with the desk clerk over reservations which had not been held for late arrival. As Cameron entered the bar, he spotted Wicker almost immediately, the son of a bitch occupying a corner booth, the candlelight reflecting on the twin circle lenses of his glasses, sharp jaw canted upward, lips drawn back in a humorless grin, bantering with the waitress who was serving his drink. No juice in Wicker. Dry sinew. Cameron's flesh prickled and his hand closed around the pistol in his pocket.

He crossed the room, knowing that Wicker had seen him and was pretending not to notice, purposely keeping both hands in sight as if to signal the fact that he was unarmed. His right hand cradled a cocktail glass. The fingers of his left hand raised a pretzel. He grimaced slightly as Cameron sat down, but he did not take his eyes off the pretzel.

"We gave them quite a show," Wicker said pleasantly. "Probably the first gun fight they've had in a century." His teeth clamped through the brittle pretzel. "Did I get your attention, Mr. Cameron?"

"Oh, you have my attention all right," Cameron said. "I have a pistol in my pocket, Wicker, and I'm just seconds away from putting a hole in your stomach."

"Of course you are," Wicker said evenly, picking another pretzel from the bowl. "That's the chance I'm going to have to take." The jaw teeth worked against the pretzel. "I could have killed you out there. And now you can kill me. I do hope you can hold off until we have a chance to talk."

The smile was on his face again and Cameron became aware that the waitress was at the table, smiling down at him with her wide, moist smile. Cameron wondered if she could read the feelings in him, if she knew how close he was to killing the man who sat across the booth from him. And what would she do if he pulled the trigger suddenly, here and now, Wicker jerking back in the booth from the sudden, rupturing shock?

"It's wet out there," the waitress said.

"Yes."

"A drink will make you feel warmer. What can I bring you?"

"Bourbon and water."

She departed. "I like conventions," Wicker said, sipping his drink, looking around at the booths filled with men. "My wife doesn't much. But there you are."

"How did you find me?" Cameron said.

"It wasn't very difficult. You've been monitored all the way across country. I work for a big organization, lots of contacts, and I managed to requisition a government jet. All in all, it hasn't been that difficult."

"You've pushed it too far this time," Cameron said. "You should have killed me on the street, when you had the chance."

"I'm a tidy man," Wicker said. "Orderly." The automatic grin flashed on his face as the waitress served Cameron's drink. Wicker put some bills on the tray, his eyes following the waitress' retreat. "You trail a lot of loose ends, Mr. Cameron. If I had taken advantage of the situation out there, I could not be sure the tape would be contained. And that's my job, first of all, to keep it from surfacing."

Cameron tasted the drink, his hand still on the pistol in his pocket. And he saw himself forcing Wicker out into the night, into some quiet place where he would raise the pistol and put a hole through that tanned forehead. He could do it without a twinge of conscience. No remorse. Loose ends. True on both sides. He could not be sure that Wicker was alone, that Connie had not already been taken.

The bourbon was strong. No watering-down here. It warmed Cameron, counteracted the wet chill of the topcoat and suit. He studied Wicker who continued to eat pretzels with an almost compulsive orderliness. Wicker could not know he had mailed the tape, otherwise he would not be sitting here now.

"I'm still willing to trade with you," Wicker said. "I'd say that we're just about even, all in all. Perhaps you're a bit ahead because I suffered more in the cold room than you did." His face wrinkled with a speculative expression. "But then, on the other hand, I think I put the fear of God into you tonight."

How much time had passed? Ten minutes? Cameron could not afford to check his watch, to let Wicker know that time was an issue here. If Connie had been picked up, she would be waiting for him now. He finished his drink, put the glass down.

"How did you get here from the local airport?" he said.

"A taxi."

"I want your wallet," Cameron said. "Put it on the table."

There was a spark in Wicker's eyes. He was on familiar ground again. "What's the point?" he said. Then he shrugged and placed the wallet on the table.

Cameron opened it, stripped out the cash, folded the money, placed it in his pocket. He removed the identification cards from the glassine windows, pocketed those as well, then pushed the empty wallet back across the table. "You do have a pistol?"

"Yes."

"Give it to me. I would be very careful if I were you."

"No need for reminders," Wicker said. His hand moved toward his jacket, very slowly. "I am taking my pistol out of the shoulder holster now," he said, with the same deliberate tone of voice an air controller might use to talk a plane down. "I don't want to provoke an incident here. That would be very foolish of me." He glanced around to make sure he was unobserved. His hand held the pistol by the barrel as he handed it to Cameron.

Cameron put the pistol in his pocket. "How many men do you have in town?"

"One," Wicker said. "My pilot. Out at the airport. He doesn't know why I'm here, what I'm doing."

"I don't believe you. You wouldn't come alone."

"Why not?" Wicker said expansively. "Call the airport and check it out. His name is Edwards." Another pretzel stick snapped as he bit into it. "It's a point of pride for me to be able to persuade you by myself. And I know that you're already thinking about it, the advantages."

Cameron looked around. There were three pay telephones on the wall of the alcove leading to the rest rooms. "You stay here," he said. "I'll check it out."

From the telephone, he kept his eyes on Wicker who raised his glass in Cameron's direction before he drank. Cameron dialed information, asked for the number of the Chalet, then dialed it. He recognized the desk clerk's voice.

"This is H.B. Johnson," he said. "You rented a car for me."

"Yes, sir," the desk clerk said. "It's here now. I can see it through my window."

"I want you to do something for me. Go out to the car and tell my secretary I'll be delayed another fifteen minutes and ask her to wait for me. Ask her if she needs anything. I'll hold on."

In a long minute, the clerk was back on the line. "She says she'll wait," he said., "She said she doesn't need a thing. Everything's fine."

"Very good," Cameron said. He put the telephone down and went back to the table. His drink had been replaced by a fresh one. He did not touch it. "There's something I want," he said to Wicker.

"Oh? What's that?"

"The name of the man who killed my father."

"Difficult," Wicker said. "In any event, he wouldn't have known why. He was simply ordered to do it."

"That makes no difference."

"And what would you do if you had it?"

"That's my business."

"You might be able to backtrack BRIMSTONE from that name."

"I can backtrack BRIMSTONE now, given enough time," Cameron said, bluffing. "I know who was talking to Nixon on that eighteen and a half minutes of tape. I know his name and I know his rank."

Wicker pursed his lips slightly and in that moment gave himself away, displayed belief that it was possible. Cameron stood up, chilling slightly; the damp shirt still clung to the small of his back. The wound in his hand had begun to throb again.

"So," Wicker said. "If you get the name of the man who killed your father, then you surrender the tape. Is that what you propose?"

"That's it."

"How do I get in touch with you? I'll have to

clear this with Washington. I'll have to get the information. Where are you going?"

"We'll be in touch."

Wicker made no move to stand up. There was the slightest trace of annoyance on his face. "I'm sure we will."

Once Cameron was in the lobby, he remembered the station wagon. He could not leave it here at the motel; Wicker would know instantly he had used another means of escape. He stopped at the desk, took the keys from his pocket and handed them to the clerk. "I want my station wagon serviced right away. Do you have someone who can take it to an all-night station?"

"Yes, sir," the clerk said.

"I'll need it done in the next hour."

"I'll have somebody take it down there now."

Cameron nodded, went outside into the rain, determined to wait long enough to see the station wagon moved away and to make certain Wicker did not leave the bar in time to make the connection. He stood under an elongated eave at the motel entrance, the light reflecting against the slant of rain, and in a few moments a boy came out of the office, wearing a blue windbreaker and a red baseball cap, his long yellow hair already damp and stringy. The boy made a dash down the driveway, an exuberant sprint. Ah, to have the energy of a sixteen-year-old again.

But then, Cameron had never been sixteen, not in the way sixteen was supposed to be for a boy. Always serious, sober, as if to mirror his father's intense preoccupation with advancement. Well, better late than never, and once this business was

over and done with, he was going to lead a far less
serious life.

He shivered slightly, hopefully. It was possible
he could surface the unknown man in the conversation with Nixon, air the whole business of the
tape, put his father's murderer in the hands of the
authorities, and walk free of it. He shook a
cigarette from the slightly dampened pack, lighted
it, an edge of worry intruding into his mind, ill
defined but there nonetheless. There was something about his encounter with Wicker that struck
him as nonsensical. Wicker could have killed him
out there on the street, dropped him with a single
shot, but did not. Why? Too many loose ends
would be left dangling, he supposed.

And in the bar, Wicker had shown no particular
stress. It was almost as if Wicker could agree to
anything after making a show of proper resistance, knowing that the whole problem would
be resolved in his favor without any activity on his
part, everything dealt with at the same moment.
No loose ends.

A terrible possibility occurred to Cameron. He
flipped the cigarette into the rain and started to
run down the driveway, waving his arms frantically as he spotted the grill of the station wagon as
the boy drove it around the back of the motel, a
hundred yards away. As the station wagon cleared
the turn, it exploded, as if a great orange fireball
grew inside it with a heat that incinerated the boy
in the baseball cap and then, in an instant, blew
out the doors, hurling one aloft and through the
glass wall into the swimming pool.

The concussion caught Cameron and tumbled
him backward into the bushes and when he looked

up the momentum of the fiery car carried it into the brick side of the motel and there was another explosion, the gas tank. The heat seared his face. Through the inferno he could see the skeletal remains of the chassis.

The boy could not have survived the blast. Dead, instantly. Confusion. Men streaming out of the motel, yelling, approached the station wagon only to be driven back by the intense heat. Yelling, yes, but he could not hear them distinctly. Ears closed by the blast. Numbed, on his feet, anger surviving the numbing effects of the shock. The pistol was in the hand dangling limply at his side. Half dazed, he moved into the open, eyes searching the shadows for Wicker.

Wicker had meant for Cameron and Connie to be consumed by that holocaust. The tape, papers, everything going up. No loose ends. He would kill Wicker instantly if he found him, witnesses or not. He watched the shadows, the faces of the men backlighted by the fire, the spray of a garden hose leaping from the group nearest the fire. No Wicker. Wicker would be gone, the explosion signal enough.

Cameron sucked the cold air into his lungs, only now aware that the rain was still coming down, the fire too intense to be affected by it. Anger, rage, and another feeling, there despite his disapproval. A shameful sense of relief. Someone else had died, not him, and now the pressure would be off for a while. He slid the pistol back into his pocket. He turned his coat collar up against the rain and began to walk down the street to the waiting car.

Chapter Eight

Roffner was in a foul mood, antsy, irritable, but this was a time when he could not show it. It was late at night and he sat in his office, studying a press release on a report which his office was about to make public. It concerned discovery of a new Soviet airborne radar which would allow Russian pilots to defend against low-flying bombers and fighter planes trying to penetrate Soviet airspace. The story also contained an estimate that it would take the Russians $50 billion and eleven years to come up with a defense against a possible attack by American cruise missiles.

It was the latter part of the story which disturbed him. There was a tendency in the Pentagon for officers to attach too much significance to material deleted from the press releases, and he did not want that to happen here. At the same time, he wanted nothing issued from his office which would increase discussion about cruise missiles.

In the end he called the Captain who had written the press release on the telephone, congratulated him on a fine piece of writing, discussed the Soviet airborne radar, and then asked the Captain to hold up on the release until new intelligence reports could be declassified so the Captain could plug additional information into his story. The Captain was mollified. The press release was killed, in effect, and once the call was finished, Roffner did not give the Captain another thought.

At the moment he had other concerns. He was receiving partial reports from Missouri. The late news dispatches included an account of a station wagon dynamited in a small town in Missouri, and FBI agents were swarming over the area. The station wagon had been identified as belonging to a woman named Connie Stryker, a federal employee working out of the GAO, and the implication was that her car had been demolished by mistake as a part of a mining dispute. A sixteen-year-old boy named Carl Merriam had been driving the car at the time of the explosion.

No further details. None. The General was sickened by the stupidity of the incident, the senseless violence, knowing it was Wicker's work. And Wicker would be calling in soon and Roffner had to decide what he was going to tell him.

Roffner was standing at the window, looking at the lights across the river, when Major Shaw came into the office, looking strangely bemused, rubbing his hands together. "It's getting colder by the moment," he said.

"Help yourself to the coffee," Roffner said.

Shaw nodded, poured himself a cup from the automatic coffee maker. "Would you like some?"

"No."

He sat down in a leather chair near the stand of divisional flags hanging behind his desk, regarded the Major. "What did you find out?"

"Not a great deal," the Major said. He blew on the coffee. "The FBI doesn't know why a woman employee from the GAO was in Missouri."

"And Cameron?"

"They know she was registered with a man in a motel room but they don't know it was Cameron."

"I have an appointment with Senator Livermore later," Roffner said.

"Tonight?"

"He never sleeps. He wouldn't go into any detail about why he wants the meeting. Have you heard anything from the Hill?"

"No, but I can call Colonel Rawlings, if you like."

"No. I'll find out soon enough."

The red light flashed on the telephone on his desk and he knew instantly that would be Wicker. He stood up slowly, then picked up the telephone and sat down behind his desk.

"General," the voice came, Wicker certainly, the connection not a good one. It sounded as if Wicker were underwater.

"What went wrong?" Roffner said.

"The wrong baggage was delivered," Wicker said.

The irritation returned full force, exacerbated by Wicker's continual indirection on the telephone. It seemed that since the Nixon business Wicker was in mortal fear of being taped and had to state everything in an ambiguous way as if he were preparing a defense against being confronted with his own statements every time he said a word.

"This is a secure line, Wicker," Roffner said.

"It's my impression, sir, that you can't

guarantee that."

"If it's not, I would have been shot down years ago," Roffner said. "I need some direct answers from you. What in the hell is going on out there? What did you do?"

"It seemed expedient," Wicker said. No defensiveness now.

"Blowing up a car?" Roffner said. "You call that expedient?"

"I was convinced he would have the tape with him. It seemed the best method for getting rid of him and the tape at the same time."

"But it didn't."

"No."

"Where is he? Where is the Stryker woman?"

"I don't know yet. But I will."

"What makes you think I'm going to leave you on the assignment? Have you seen the news? The FBI is all over the case. Can they tie you in with it?"

"Of course not," Wicker said.

"Why should I leave you there?"

"I had a conversation with him," Wicker said quietly. "He knows who you are. At least he says he does."

Roffner was suddenly cold. "Did he mention my name?"

"No. He just said he knew your name and your rank."

"My rank? He used the word 'rank'?"

"Yes, sir."

"Did he say 'military rank' or was he using the word generically?"

"'Rank,'" Wicker said. "Just 'rank.'"

"But not my name. I think we can discount that."

"Possibly," Wicker said. "Now, if you want to take me off this, General, then that's your right. But I detected a change in him. He's tired. That's the truth of it. He's at the end of his rope. All he wants now is the name of the man who killed his father. He's willing to let the rest of it go by the board."

Insanity, yes, wishful assumptions. "My God," he said. "You don't know that. You tried to incinerate him. It doesn't make a goddamned bit of difference what he felt before, what he believed, what he would settle for. You changed all that. Hold on." He put the receiver down on the desk and stood up, stretching, walking over to the window, knowing that the Major was standing with his coffee cup cradled in his hands, watching him. Roffner had to think, to sort out, and he did not mind leaving Wicker holding the telephone.

"What's he up to?" the Major said respectfully.

"Cameron claims to know who I am," Roffner said.

"I doubt that." The Major sipped his coffee. "If he did, he certainly wouldn't keep it secret."

"He might," Roffner said thoughtfully. He returned to the telephone. "I'm tempted to relieve you," he said to Wicker.

Wicker was unfazed. "Who would you replace me with?" He paused, sucking the air between his teeth. It made a slight whistling noise over the telephone. "I have an idea, if you're interested in hearing it."

"Go ahead."

"Give me the name of some army Sergeant who

was stationed in Las Vegas when Cameron's father was killed, somebody who's been transferred out of the country."

Roffner could see the point immediately. "Why not a cover name?"

"Won't do. He's got that goddamned computer terminal. He'll check personnel files with it. The man has to be authentic."

Roffner leaned back in his chair. "I'll get you the information," he said. "But you're not on your own anymore, Wicker. That was a stupid business you pulled up there. You've attracted far more attention than you can imagine. So I'll leave you on this temporarily. But you make no move without calling and checking with me first. Do you understand?"

"Yes, sir."

During the drive across the river, Roffner gave the Major a list of items he wanted taken care of, then leaned back against the seat of the staff car, his large hands folded across his stomach. He did not look forward to this meeting with Senator Livermore. Livermore was from South Carolina and during his twenty-five years in the Senate he had earned the appellation of "the Silver Fox" because he was supposed to be astute and forthright and fiercely devoted to representing the people of his state. As a ranking member of the Armed Forces Committee, he frequently made speeches full of technical references to Russian military strength, the cry of the super hawk, but Roffner knew as a matter of fact that all of his expertise existed only in the phenomenal work of a legislative aide who wrote speeches for him. Then Livermore delivered them with vituperative

zeal and understood very little of what he was
saying.

Livermore was primarily interested in living
well, in turning everything to his advantage, in
preserving a sense of southern charm and a mis-
tress he had brought up from Charleston to serve
as his secretary, and little else.

As the car drew to a stop in front of the building,
there was a slight mist in the night air. Roffner
told the Major to make the calls and come back for
him in half an hour, then he braced himself, and
went into the Club. He found Senator Livermore
sitting in an overstuffed leather chair near a bay
window. The Senator was a corpulent man with a
puffy pink complexion which told Roffner that he
had been here for some time and the glass of
bourbon he held in his hand was not the first of
the night. He smiled up at the General, made no
effort to rise, but waved a large hand at the chair
across the oval cocktail table from him.

"Grand to see you, General," he said. "Excuse
me for not getting up but I've got arthritis in my
knees and that makes graciousness damned near
impossible."

"Haven't seen you in a long time, Senator,"
Roffner said, sitting down.

"Too damn long," Livermore said, his hand in
the air, a vague gesture which summoned a black
waiter, a young man with close-cropped hair.
"Sam," he said to the waiter, with a conspiratorial
air. "You suppose that we could find something to
warm up the General on a cold, nasty night like
this?"

"Yes, sir. I think so."

"You suppose that the General here would be

offended if we found him a glass of that rare old bourbon we keep here for special occasions?"

"I'll have a Scotch and water," Roffner said.

"Well, Sam, we'll have to make a convert out of this Yankee another day," Livermore said. The black waiter moved off, a foolish smile on his face, and Roffner thought that the world had changed and the blacks had been liberated but in this one private enclave Senators like Livermore would have their black waiters a hundred years from now.

Livermore leaned back in his chair gingerly, as if his whole body was sensitive to the pressure. "Well, General, is our country still safe from the Russians tonight?"

"Absolutely," Roffner said. The waiter brought him the drink in a crystal glass on a silver tray. "What do you have on your mind, Senator?"

"I like that," Livermore said. "You come right to the point." His manicured fingers toyed with what appeared to be pearl buttons on his vest and Roffner realized that Livermore was not going to come to any point immediately. He had the air of a country lawyer with a final devastating piece of evidence in his pocket and a want for something which he would have before he was through. "I've always been a plainspoken man myself. That gets me into trouble with my colleagues occasionally; but the people back home seem to appreciate it. Is your drink strong enough, General?"

"Yes," Roffner said.

"I appreciate this chance to just meet with you one on one, so to speak, a little confidential chat." The Senator's eyes followed a woman across the room. Blond. White-skinned. His fires had not been banked. In his late sixties and still a hungry man. He sipped his bourbon gently, then turned his ice-blue eyes back to Roffner. "I'm sure you won't mind a little bit of constructive criticism, General, but I think that press conference of yours was a mistake. I'm sure you military men need to display your aggressiveness from time to time, but you put your team on the defensive, if you know what I mean."

"No, I don't know what you mean, Senator."

"What I mean is that when you go on the defensive, there are always certain types who mistake that for weakness and try to capitalize on it." He sipped the bourbon again and the habitual smile remained on his face, but there was no warmth in it. "I want to talk about a facility which is under your jurisdiction. It has been sticking in my craw for a long time, General, I have to admit that. Because there are still parts of my state where folks don't have a pot to piss in. Now these are not pobuckra, General, not dumb whites or niggers but people who are capable of working if jobs were available."

"What facility are you talking about, Senator?"

"That prison facility you have in Nevada that's repairing military vehicles. What do you call it, General? I've always hated these goddamned places that go by initials."

Roffner felt a shock, as if electricity had suddenly been run through the chair in which he was sitting. But his control was sufficient that it did not register on his face. There was no tremor in the hand that raised the glass, but his mind was racing ahead, trying to determine if this was a coincidence. How much could this dandified old man know? He drank from the glass, using the time to collect himself. "It's a Military Ordnance Rehabilitation Center," he said calmly. "It's called MOREHAB."

"Yes, that's the one," Livermore said, leaning back in his chair. "In my opinion, MOREHAB is just about the worst idea that some dense-headed analyst ever came up with. It gives a bunch of nigger felons about twice the annual wage that a poor white can make in my state."

"All the participants are not black," Roffner said.

"Ninety-two point six percent," Livermore said precisely. "That's pretty goddamned close to being pure black. I've always been curious to know what keeps those men from driving the tanks right through the walls." He attracted the attention of the waiter, ordered another round of drinks. "But then, I imagine that you keep a close eye on what goes on out there. After all, that's your department."

"Not exclusively," Roffner said. "It's a joint project with the Federal Bureau of Prisons."

"Which somebody in your department instigated. Correct me if I'm wrong."

Roffner's stomach twinged with a painful spasm. "Ordnance was having trouble with equipment repair and the Bureau of Prisons was having trouble attracting industry. So we set up an experimental facility in Nevada to train men with long-term sentences in the repair of heavy equipment, tanks, half-tracks, personnel carriers. It's all perfectly safe."

Livermore shrugged slightly as if that were beside the point. His fingers plucked at the lapel of his coat, then slid inside to take an envelope out of his inside pocket. He did not hand it to Roffner immediately but instead tapped it on the table absently. "I received this letter yesterday afternoon, addressed to me, personally. I have to admit that I get a lot of letters—complaining, whining, begging, asking—but this one was a little different, and my nose tells me that there's something to it." Only now did he slide it across the table.

The envelope and the sheet inside were embossed with Defense Department insignia. The note was typewritten with no signature.

Dear Senator:

The MOREHAB facility in Nevada is an unsafe facility. A scandal of enormous proportions will be uncovered there very shortly, with a possible loss of lives on a wide scale. I am advising you, sir, instead of following the usual course through the Bureau of Prisons, because I have no wish to harm the military. I would suggest that you contact the GAO for an immediate surveillance of that facility with a view to a special investigation.

Roffner's eyes stayed on the paper, even after he had read the message. A betrayal, certainly, somebody in his organization who wished to stop the project without being caught at it. But he would deal with that later. Livermore was his concern at the moment. He folded the paper, put it back in the envelope.

"It sounds serious but vague," he said, handing it back to the Senator. "My first guess is that this is some middle-grade bureaucrat trying to make trouble for a superior. Hardly anything to get very upset about."

"And that's the way you see it?" Livermore said quizically.

"I'm on top of the situation there," Roffner said.

"Ah, the scandals," Livermore said, turning away as if trying to catch a glimpse of the woman across the room again. "This is a city of scandals, General. Human nature. We feed on them. I don't wish to make things hard for you, sir. Not at all. But then it's a matter of conscience, after all. To disregard a letter like this would be derelict on my part."

Roffner looked up at the glittering intricacy of an immense crystal chandelier and wondered how many pieces constituted the whole. A thousand? Ten thousand? He would have to reverse his field now. He could see what the Senator wanted and he would give it to him. Livermore was a gobbler, sucking up projects for his state like a vacuum cleaner.

"All right," Roffner said quietly. "We do have problems in Nevada."

Livermore's eyes glinted. "Ah," he said.

"I would ask you to keep what I'm about to say in confidence."

"You're saying the letter is true then?"

"No. Untrue."

"What's the problem then?"

"The note is nonsense, of course. No major scandals ready to pop. No possibility of a riot. Nothing like that. We're having problems in a different direction. MOREHAB's a fine concept but poorly executed, grossly inefficient. An average overhaul of a tank diesel runs somewhere in the

neighborhood of twenty-six thousand dollars. I
have had some preliminary reports made that
suggest abandoning the Nevada prison and setting
up another large-scale repair center somewhere
else, not connected with rehabilitation."

He had put out the bait and he could see the
quickening interest on Livermore's face. "I see
that could be embarrassing to the military."

"Yes," Roffner said. He concentrated on his
drink, giving the Senator room.

"I appreciate your telling me this," Livermore
said. "It does tend to put my mind at ease because
it offers us both a practical solution to a pair of
problems. I want to make this clear though,
General, that there is no coercion of any kind. I
have simply approached you with a problem and
you have been candid with me and since we are
both on the same team, we are both looking for
solutions which would be beneficial to the
country. Do you agree with me in that, General?"

"Certainly."

"Since I am on Armed Forces, it is perfectly
logical for me to institute a site search, subject to
your requirements, of course. And I will be the
first one to defend the frank admission of what we
will consider a mistake, not a failure, a rather
noble mistake to be sure."

"I don't consider the project a mistake," Roffner
said. He could not give in too easily, even though
any agreements made here were going to prove
senseless in the end. "We were hit by inflation,
soaring costs."

"Yes, yes," Livermore agreed suddenly, sooth-
ingly. "I can agree with that. And you're not going
to get the best work out of prison labor. History

has shown us that. None of the prison experiments have ever worked, but then, we have to continue to try to find a solution." He continued to talk and Roffner could see that he had already formulated the whole plan in his mind, and that from this conversation would grow an ordnance depot and repair center near Charleston, soaking up South Carolina's unemployment problem. But to Roffner, there was only one important thing at this point. Time.

He waited until Livermore was through, then nodded thoughtfully, agreeing. "I appreciate your calling me, Senator," he said. "I'll have Colonel Shultz put some figures together for you in the next two weeks. There's no point in involving the GAO in this. They would simply discover what we already know. Were you the only man on Armed Forces to get a copy of this letter?"

"As far as I know," Livermore said. "I've made informal queries of the others. No, I think we can assume I am the only one."

"Do you mind if I borrow the letter? I'd like to see if my boys can track it down."

Livermore thought it over. "As long as you don't take any actions against the man who sent this."

"I'm sure he or she is a conscientious citizen," Roffner said firmly. "If they have further information we don't have, I think we should know about it."

Livermore handed him the letter. "Call me sometime for lunch, General. I'd like to talk about Russian missiles, the SS20's, the SS16's."

Roffner shook the Senator's warm hand, put the folded letter in his pocket, then made his way across the deeply carpeted room, his stomach cramping severely with the effects of the tension and the whisky. Major Shaw was waiting in the foyer and fell in beside him, recognizing his mood, saying nothing. The doorman opened the heavy glass door for them and Roffner saw the staff car waiting at the curb but he took a moment to get his breath in the fresh air.

Once he was in the car, Roffner punched a can of Maalox and drank it down, then leaned back against the seat and waited for his stomach to ease. Old, goddamnit, stiff in the joints, with a nervous stomach that responded instantly to trouble. None of this would have bothered him ten years ago. Major Shaw had not yet started the car and Roffner handed him the letter. Shaw read it through.

"What do you think?" Roffner said.

"Somebody in DOD suspects something," Shaw said. "They don't know what the hell is going on, but they suspect something and they're trying to get a big investigation started."

"The use of DOD stationery isn't coincidental," Roffner said, his stomach roiling.

"It could be used just to lend importance to the note, to make it seem like inside information."

"It could be almost anything," Roffner said with a sudden burst of irritation. "It could be that somebody wants to put a stop to BRIMSTONE without putting his own ass in a sling." Ah, the intricacy of military politics and it could be any one of a half dozen Colonels or a dozen civilians in high-ranking positions. "I don't want the word getting around," he said. "Nobody gets any feedback on this. But I want a check made of typewriters in the Pentagon. I want to know whose office this letter came from."

"We can eliminate," Shaw said. "I'm not sure we can pinpoint."

"Then elimination will have to do for the moment," Roffner said, calming himself deliberately.

"How did you handle this with the Senator?"

A direct question. Good. Shaw was coming along. "A trade," Roffner said. "He knows something is going on—he has a highly developed nose —but he really doesn't want to find out what. I've suggested a new ordnance-repair depot in South Carolina." He drew a deep breath. "But I've gotten us time and that's all we need. Drop him a memo tomorrow and let him know we're developing a time frame for the information he wants. He enjoys phrases like 'time frame.' "

He lapsed into silence, a little surprised at the depth of his own bitterness toward men such as Livermore. Roffner had been in the Pentagon for more than a decade and he thought he was used to congressional interference, but he rankled at the idea that a man such as Livermore could rise through sheer longevity to a position of power and have an influence on a whole military structure and tradition he knew nothing about.

He turned his attention to the business at hand, the clipboard and the crop of messages Shaw had taken down during the thirty minutes Roffner had spent with the Senator. Roffner pored through them. Dirsten reported that the equipment had been shipped to Nevada. Colonel Garver had called, wanted an immediate callback.

He put a checkmark on the Garver item. The Colonel would need reassurance. There were a dozen other items. He would take care of them later. He handed the clipboard back to Shaw. "Did you make contact with Brigid?" he said.

"Her name's Ingrid, sir."

"Brigid, Ingrid, the names are all alike. Did you reach her?"

"Yes, sir. She said she would be delighted if you stopped by her apartment for a drink."

"I want more than a drink."

"She's aware of that."

"I don't want any misunderstandings. What's her background?"

Shaw brightened perceptibly. He enjoyed gossip. "The word's gone around, sir, that she fancies herself as a secret agent."

The General chuckled. "A spy?"

"Yes, sir," Shaw said with a smile. "She does secretarial work for the Norwegian embassy but she gets a monthly check from the Swedish government. A hundred and twelve dollars a month, if my sources are correct."

"Jesus Christ," the General said. "The Swedes regard the Norwegians as dumb cousins. They made jokes about them. What the Norwegians could have that the Swedes want is beyond me. But it's the same the world over. Everybody's watching everybody else, just in case."

"It might be better, sir, if you let me find somebody else."

"I like her. Besides, a few days from now it won't make any difference. And she might be useful. A few more days."

"A few more days," Shaw echoed. "What do you want me to do about Wicker?"

"Have personnel dredge up the name of a

Sergeant who was stationed at Nellis for the last year and recently transferred overseas," Roffner said. "Give Wicker the name and let him keep Cameron occupied if he can."

Time and negotiation and the eternal trades, he thought, and Wicker would be kept occupied and Cameron, if he really knew that Roffner was the other man on the Nixon tape, would try to press his advantage and gain the name of the man who had killed his father, and in the end it would all come down to nothing, make no difference, because sufficient time would have passed that BRIMSTONE would be over and done with, everything revealed.

His mind turned to the Scandinavian blonde, the time ahead. Sex was the ultimate expression of personal power and he never entered into one of his temporary liaisons strictly as a release from tension. He always gave more than he got and he was aware of the stories that circulated about him Washington, tales of the "General's ladies." It was good for his reputation. A few more days and that too would not matter.

He thought about the statement he would have to make, the wording he would eventually dictate, the way his actions would be interpreted, the rationale which only he could provide. He had no illusions about a place in history and, fifty years from now, he would be a footnote in the military textbooks, nothing more.

"Mintz," he said aloud.

"Beg your pardon?"

"I just remembered the name of the son of a bitch," Roffner said. "Captain Mintz. Did I ever tell you about him?"

"No, sir."

"I was in Germany, the end of the war," Roffner said. "I was at a party, one of those goddamn victory celebrations with the Russians." And he told Shaw what had happened at the party, only the bare bones of it, but he could remember every detail, that young Russian Captain in his coarse uniform that looked as if it had been made out of burlap and the broad Slavic features, a wide gap of a mouth and Napoleonic black hair that curled down over a square plane of forehead, and wild, black, cunning eyes, wary, the eyes of an animal always looking for advantage.

Roffner had been bone-weary at the time, after enduring Patton's grueling pace, the push that left everyone reeling, and in this stinking little ballroom of some German castle which smelled of mold he had ended up by drinking with young Captain Mintz who drank vodka by the tumbler and became so drunk his face turned red, glowed like a coal.

"He spoke good English," Roffner said. "Not perfect but he could have gotten along in Washington without any trouble. Now, he kept talking to me confidentially, all evening, as if there was some kind of bond between us, kept poking me with his elbow, no sense of distance. It turns out that the son of a bitch thought that Roffner was a Russian name, that Roffner must be Russian in sympathies."

"I see."

"I had been drinking pretty consistently, matching him drink for drink," Roffner went on, caught up in it now. "I didn't like him but we were under orders to have no incidents. But then the son of a bitch, thinking I was Russian, began to tell me how within not so many years we would be having dinner together in New York City, and how, since he spoke such good English, he was going to have a position of power, and it took me a little while to realize that he was letting me know that the Russians intended to take over the United States, perhaps not right away, but eventually. He was offering me a job working with him when he finally got stateside."

"What did you do?" Shaw said.

"I hit him," Roffner said. "Right in the middle of his square Russian face. I broke his nose." The memory of that moment was sufficient to make his adrenaline pump. The gushing blood. The stupid expression on the Captain's face. So drunk he was immobilized. The wary black eyes still gleaming.

Shaw smiled.

"It wasn't funny," Roffner said. "It isn't funny now. Because he was telling the truth. And nothing has changed."

The smile faded. "Yes, sir."

"So when the time comes that somebody asks you why I pushed through BRIMSTONE, you tell them about Captain Mintz."

"Yes, sir."

The car stopped. They were at the apartment complex. A light snow had begun to fall again.

"She's in apartment 776D," the Major said. "What time shall I pick you up, sir?"

"In the morning," the General said. "If there are any brushfires between now and then, you handle them. Or let them burn."

"Yes, sir," Shaw said.

Roffner did not get out of the car immediately.
"I mean that about the Russians," he said, trying
to articulate his thoughts exactly. "The Russians
have been turned into a paper tiger in the past few
years. Every time the administration wants to
goose the public into one kind of activity, they
make the Russians out to be bloodthirsty, and
then they turn around and soften the Russian
position to manipulate the public in some other
direction. But the Captain Mintzes are in power
over there at this moment, and by God, I intend to
let them know that there are still a hell of a lot of
strong men over here who won't let them win. Do
you understand what I'm saying, Major?"

"Yes, sir. I do."

Roffner got out of the car.

A car, and he was in it with Connie. A relaxed
time, and they had been talking about the Grand
Canyon and laughing, and then he saw the sheet of
flame which suddenly enveloped the roof lining of
the car immediately over their heads, a fire which
Connie did not see, and he was frozen in position
behind the wheel, unable to speak, to move, and
the flames engulfed her while she continued to
smile, her shoulders burning, her hair. He jerked
awake in a cold panic, mouth dry. It took him a
moment to realize where he was.

The chartered Lear Jet. The powerful hum of
the engines. Connie asleep in the seat across the
aisle, arms folded across her breasts, lips pulled
back slightly from her teeth. He looked out the
window, saw nothing, no reference points in the
darkness. He checked his watch.

They had been aloft thirty minutes now, and roughly calculated, that would put them somewhere over the frozen earth of western Kansas. His hand was hurting, a slow throbbing. He unwrapped the bandage, noted with detachment the inflammation, the puffy redness which marked a minor infection. A small thing now, an injured hand. There were much larger problems. He would have the hand seen to sooner or later.

He rewrapped the bandage, poured himself a cup of coffee from the chrome Thermos on the rack, sipped it. Tired, mind fogged with fatigue. A boy had been blown to bits in a station wagon back there in an explosion meant for him. It seemed distant, as if it had happened a long time ago, or had never happened at all.

From here he could see into the cockpit and the dim shape of the pilot—who reminded him of a modern version of the old comic book character Smiling Jack—a handsome, blond athletic young man who chartered Lear Jets out of the Springfield airport and who was able to quote a price of $2,200 to Albuquerque without so much as a flicker of apology.

Distance condensed, time collapsed, and Cameron was aware of the outflow of money at an alarming rate. The $5,000 was going to be consumed in no time at all. He would have to make arrangements to get more.

He felt like slipping back into sleep but he remembered the dream and forced himself to come awake. He clicked on the pinpoint light above the seat, then took out a pen and a scrap of paper, an old cleaning bill that had been in his pocket for weeks. He began to scribble on the back of it. It had always been easier to think on paper.

The death of his father, the destruction of the kid in the baseball cap, Wicker's deadly games were all to cover something that was history by now. All to shut him up. All to keep him from discovering what had happened and the name of the man in the conversation with Nixon in the Oval Office.

"1. A military operation," he wrote.

Certainly connected with the military. Wicker was a part of the DIA. The tape referred to casualties. Had to be military.

"2. Probably overseas."

No. Not worth the risk they were running to cover up. There were too many foreign involvements, and multiple deaths in Nicaragua or Iran were so commonplace that there would be no more than a brief stir of public indignation.

"3. Possible operations in the United States they covered."

His pen paused. He lighted a cigarette, watched the smoke being whisked away by the ventilation system. He was overlooking something obvious, something right in front of him.

Suddenly, he knew what he had been missing. He reached across the aisle, put his hand on Connie's arm. Her eyes blinked open, momentarily confused.

"I have to talk," Cameron said. "I've been stupid."

She turned in her seat, her eyes still dull. "You'll have to give me a minute. I'm not quite awake." She sat up, took the cup of coffee he offered her. "All right, I'm with it. What's going on?"

"I've been on the wrong track," he said, his voice excited. "They're out for blood and they wouldn't do that just to protect somebody's reputation, some incident from the past. They wouldn't go to all this trouble just to cover something Nixon let slide through. Hell, he's the perfect scapegoat. They wouldn't have to take the horrendous chance of getting caught blowing up a car in Missouri when all they had to do was release details of this massacre, whatever it was, and lay it all at Nixon's feet, another example of his megalomania."

She sipped her coffee. "Perhaps the other man doesn't want to be implicated."

"No. It's so goddamned simple I couldn't see the forest for the trees. Whatever BRIMSTONE represents, whatever kind of massacre it stands for, it hasn't happened yet. That's why they're so frantic to shut me up, to get the tape."

"Possible," she said. "but what does that change?"

"Everything," he said. "Whatever it is, there has to be a whole rack of elaborate plans for it. I've been looking into the past and that's the wrong direction." He smiled humorlessly. "Ah, the son of a bitch," he said. "He's probably feeling pretty smug right now, because even if he didn't kill me, he's certain that I'm going in the wrong direction, looking for a trade of information, the safety of his client in return for the name of the man who killed my father."

He made his way forward to the cockpit. Smiling Jack removed his earphones. "Just listening to a weather report," he said. "Albuquerque's clear but cold as a witch's tit. We should be there in another hour."

"That's what I want to talk to you about," Cameron said. "Are you carrying enough fuel for Los Angeles?"

"Sure," the pilot said. "No problem. I can even let you have the direct-route rate. Thirty-three hundred."

"Will you have to file an amended flight plan?"

"It's not absolutely vital," the pilot said. "You have your choice of three airports—Los Angeles International, Orange County, or Ontario."

"Orange County."

Smiling Jack checked his vast array of instruments and panels that glowed in the semidarkness. "I can give you an estimated arrival time of 0348, Pacific Coast time."

Cameron nodded, went back to the cabin, calming somewhat now. Connie was looking out the window. "It's incredible," she said. "I just saw a river down there, or a lake, the moon glinting on the water. It's difficult to believe we're seven miles up."

He sat down in one of the heavily padded seats. "It makes as much sense as everything else," he said. "The whole thing's crazy."

"Specify."

"Us, the situation, especially us, you and me."

She put her hand on his leg. "Yes," she said with a half smile.

"I feel as if I've known you a long, long time, as if we're old friends as well as lovers. And I don't know a damn thing about you, not really."

"I think I wear well," she said. "That's my long suit. I'm impatient sometimes, downright bitchy, but over the long haul, I'll work out fine. I'm also forthright, outspoken. You'll never have the

slightest doubt what I think, or where I stand."
She sighed slightly. "What do you intend to do?"

"I've changed our destination to Los Angeles,"
he said. "I hope in the general confusion out there,
we can gain a little time. Then we go to Las
Vegas."

"Why Las Vegas?"

"If there are to be any answers, I'll find them
there. My father was killed in Las Vegas. The tape
was sent to me from Las Vegas. But I want you to
think about the risks by the time we reach Los
Angeles. You're going to have to make a choice."

"At least you're not pushing to get rid of me."

"No," he said. "I'm torn about that. I need all
the help I can get at this point."

She pursed her lips, a thoughtful expression in
her eyes. "What would happen if you turned yourself in to the nearest police station once we
reached Los Angeles? Wouldn't you be safer?
Couldn't you accomplish just as much?"

"No. I think I would be dead before I
accomplished anything. And I couldn't stop
BRIMSTONE even if I stayed alive. I don't have any
hard evidence."

"And it's possible you won't get any hard
evidence anyway, isn't it?" she said. "It's possible
that you'll run all the risks and come up empty-
handed, that BRIMSTONE will go right ahead and
happen, whatever it is."

"Yes."

"I appreciate your honesty," she said. "And
now, you should get some sleep. You have hollows
under your eyes. Would a drink help?"

"It might."

She mixed him a bourbon and water. She kissed

him briefly and then curled up on her seat, tucking her feet beneath her before she turned out the light overhead. She was asleep almost instantly. He was grateful that she had accepted without argument what he intended to do. He would see that she remained safe.

He finished the drink only to find that he could not sleep. He clicked on the small light again and picked up the newspaper containing the account of Roffner's press conference, the follow-up stories. It appeared that the military strategy might be effective after all. For there was more comment on the news leaks in Washington than there was on the press conference, and Cameron's father's connection with the Nixon tape was less important than the feeling it aroused about the original Watergate scandal.

He shrugged, looked out the window at a string of lights in the darkness far below, a settlement of some kind, a town, a tiny collection of people in the middle of a black world. For a moment, he projected himself and Connie into that town, cutting off the past, but there would be no safety there and he knew it. There was no escape, no defense except attack. Wicker had been able to pinpoint him in the small Missouri town as if by magic.

He scanned the rest of the paper for more news from Washington. Debate over the neutron bomb, the eternal Russian threat, a quarrel over the declining economy, debate over the diversion of Colorado River water to Los Angeles.

He put the paper aside. When he was certain he was not going to be able to sleep, he went forward to the cockpit and Smiling Jack pointed out the glow of lights on the horizon. Palm Springs. The beginning of the massive luminous display that would become the Los Angeles metroplex.

He stayed in the cockpit long enough to reassure himself that Smiling Jack had received no alarming messages through those oversized earphones and then returned to his seat, watching Palm Springs come and go and the dark bulk of mountains and then the incredible sea of lights, the whole sprawling cluster of cities.

He awakened Connie, helped her fasten her seatbelt, the jet beginning a slow descent and its approach to the Orange County airport.

"Did you get any sleep at all?" she said.

"I'll have time enough for that later," he said. "What credit cards do you have?"

"American Express, Visa, something else, I think."

"What bank is your Visa drawn on?"

"Someplace in Virginia. What difference does it make?"

"If they're tracking electronically, I want you to make this as complicated for them as possible. I want you to rent a car and make reservations at a hotel in El Paso and arrange to drop the car there as well. I want them to think we're bound for Mexico the hard way."

"I'm beginning to catch on," she said with a smile.

"I also want you to call the *Washington Post.*"

"Oh?" she said, startled.

"Tell them you're calling for me. Give them your name and have the operator connect you with somebody at the City Desk."

"And tell them what?"

"Tell them I know about a secret military project called BRIMSTONE. Tell them I also know the name of the man who conferred with Nixon in those eighteen and a half missing minutes." He paused, thinking it through. "You can tell them that I'm out to avenge the death of my father and I've decided to use publicity to do it. Tell them everything that's happened to us."

"Do you think they'll print that?" she said.

"If you're convincing enough."

"I'll give it a try."

When the jet landed and taxied to a private terminal, Smiling Jack lowered the hatch steps, bounding down them as if flying the jet for the past few hours had consumed none of his energy. "It's been a pleasure serving you, Mr. Johnson," he said. "If you're going to be here a day or two, I can give you a special standby rate and fantastic savings on the return trip."

Cameron counted out the money and handed it to him. "No, thanks," he said. "We have some calls to make in L.A. and then we drive to El Paso."

"Thank you," Smiling Jack said. He wrote out a receipt with a flourish. "There you are, sir."

"Fine. If you'll just unload the baggage . . . "

"Yes, sir. Right away."

A balmy night with temperature in the sixties and he was momentarily disconcerted. He stood with one hand against the fuselage of the jet, envying the boundless energy of the pilot who was in his late twenties. He wanted nothing more than to check into a motel and sleep, but there was no time for that. He went through the formality of tipping the baggage man who loaded the computer equipment into the rented car and then slid behind the wheel.

"I made the call. Are you sure you don't want me to drive?" Connie said.

"Positive. This is my home territory. I know the freeways."

He eased away from the airport, followed the boulevard until he found the Newport Freeway which fed like a massive concrete river into the Riverside Freeway and the clear Interstate which connected Los Angeles to Las Vegas like an umbilical cord.

"Well?" he said finally.

"I was superb," she said, laughing slightly. "It's absurd, really, the whole thing. I was pretending to be frightened, scared out of my wits, and then I realized I really *was* frightened, *am* scared. But the night man at the *Post* was trying so hard to manipulate me that the whole thing turned funny."

"What did you say and what did he say?"

"I told him about BRIMSTONE and your father and the information you have. And he told me to hold on while he wrote the material down." She paused, lighted a cigarette. "And suddenly, I realized I was playing a role, that I didn't know how to *sound* frightened, and I remembered an actress in a southern picture, and I suddenly realized that I was deep into a southern accent. But he didn't even notice, he was so anxious to get more information, and I told him about the attempt on our lives in Missouri."

She inhaled the smoke, studied his face. "I didn't go too far, did I?"

"No," he said. "You gave them something they can check out. You didn't mention Wicker?"

"No. Do you think I should have?"

"You did exactly right. How did you leave it?"

She laughed again. "He wanted to know where he could reach you and I said you would be in touch. Anyway, he said he was going to have to check things out and that he was very interested."

"Which means they'll print it," Cameron said.

"About the car. I told the rental agency we were going to El Paso and would take a week to get there."

"Good."

They lapsed into silence. She sat against the door, her feet tucked beneath her, and quite suddenly he remembered Annie, the quixotic way she had of leaping from subject to subject, no interest in the past. She could not understand why anybody would want to spend a moment of the present dealing with something which no longer existed. Poor Annie. Dead, unbreathing. Despite the evidence of his senses, the memory of her dead in the shower, the whole thing seemed untrue, as if it had never happened, as if he had invented it.

"Did you love her very much?" Connie said.

He was startled. "How did you know I was thinking about her?"

"You looked very far away, very sad."

"Annie was an experience, like a roller coaster," he said. "But I'll always be grateful to her, in a way. I've spent most of my life with machines and what relationships I've had weren't very significant. But Annie woke me up, if that makes any sense."

"It makes sense," she said.

They stopped for coffee in Barstow and he was feeling more alert now. The sky was beginning to lighten in the east, the sun coming up over the sparse landscape of the high desert, the barren mountains.

By the time they reached Las Vegas, it was nine o'clock and he could feel his wariness returning, for he was no longer isolated. His father had died here, on one of these streets, and it was very possible he would die here as well. On the Strip with its high-rise hotels in the thin bright light of the morning, the casinos looked drab and the sprinkler systems were working to keep the lawns alive. He saw a group of women on the street, heading for the MGM Grand, all of them wearing formals and ornate badges. They had probably been up all night for the first time in years.

"What do we do now?" Connie said. "Where do you want to stay?"

"Not at any place with a casino," he said. "If we tried to check in with a sophisticated computer terminal, the word would be all over town within minutes."

He drove through the center of town and found a quiet motel on the road to Boulder City and checked in. He unpacked the computer equipment himself. The rooms were pleasant, early American, with chintz curtains and maple furniture. And once they were inside, Connie gave him a light kiss and proceeded to inspect the bedroom and the sitting room, smiling, cheerful. "Not elegant but sufficient," she said. "Now, let me have the car keys and I'll get us some breakfast while you sack in for a while."

He gave her the keys. "I have some work to do first." He checked his watch. "It's shortly after noon on the East Coast."

Once she had gone, he took a shower, examined his lean face in the mirror, stubbled with beard. The blond hair, shaggy, needing a haircut, his blue eyes bloodshot, cheeks haggard, a certain appearance of madness there. He had not been unaffected. He put a new bandage on his hand and found that his left arm was trembling, the muscle jerking slightly. The wound had begun to hurt him again. The pain reminded him of Wicker and the shattered glass of the window in the icy room and the exploding car last night. He would have to get himself together.

When he had dressed, he walked to the office, inquired about the location of a drugstore and walked down the street to buy toilet articles. Bright sun. Normal traffic. A few people on the street. Safe for the time being.

By the time he got back to the room, Connie was already there with breakfast laid out on the coffee table and a single rose in a vase. The moment she saw him, her smile faded. "What happened?" she said.

"Nothing," he said. "We're secure for the time being." He ate his breakfast in silence and then poured himself a hot cup of coffee from the Thermos before he sat down by the telephone. Purdy was the next step, a necessary risk. He could not be sure of Purdy's position. He would have to take precautions. He dialed Purdy's number and a secretary answered.

"This is Saunders," Cameron said. "Let me speak to Purdy, please."

Purdy's voice came on the line. "How goes the nation's capital?" he said.

"This isn't Saunders. It's Bill Cameron."

"Cameron?" Purdy said, startled. "My God."

"I want to see you. But I need to know where you stand on what's happened."

"We've been getting a lot of scuttlebutt," Purdy said. "But I haven't taken any of it seriously."

"Does the term BRIMSTONE mean anything to you, Purdy?"

"Not much. Only what your father told me. I can't talk over the phone. Are you in town? Can we meet?"

"What are you driving?"

"A little topless MG," Purdy said. "Fire-engine red."

"Then meet me in the parking lot behind the Circus Circus in half an hour. Park away from the other cars and be by yourself."

"I'm a friend, Willie."

"I'll see you in half an hour."

He severed the connection and then interfaced the computer terminal with the telephone and had the operator dial the access telephone number. He punched the proper code into the keyboard. It was early, far too early, but it would do no harm to try. Reeves was the next link.

Brimstone, he wrote.

He waited what seemed like minutes.

CAMERON?

Affirmative.

YOU'RE VERY EARLY BUT WE HAVE BEEN MONITORING, JUST IN CASE, HOPING YOU WOULD MAKE EARLY CONTACT. RUMOR HERE SAYS YOU HAVE THE NAME OF THE MAN ON THE NIXON TAPE. PLEASE VERIFY.

Ah, there it was, the suspicion, bright and glowing in his mind, the use of the first person plural, "we," the different tone of the phrasing. Somebody else was communicating with him through the computer, not Reeves. He wanted to be wrong, mistaken, but he had to know for sure.

You picked a fine time to leave me, he wrote, praying that the next word to the song would appear on the screen. But instead there was a pause, a long silence. Then:

REPEAT. PLEASE. WORDING GARBLED.

Please standby.

Something turned very cold within him and he knew that he had to verify. He looked to Connie who was refilling his coffee cup. "I want you to go to the lobby," he said quietly. "Call Saunders at the GAO and have him check the current status of a Frank Reeves in the computer section, Department of Defense. Tell him it's very important."

"Do you think something has happened to Reeves?"

"I have to know for sure."

She nodded wordlessly. He waited a few moments, taking the time to smoke a cigarette. He would have to resume contact.

You picked a fine time to leave me during the last transmission. Abrupt. I was afraid they had you spotted.

WE HAD A CLOSE CALL.

Are you still secure?

YES. PLEASE CONFIRM THE RUMOR THAT YOU HAVE THE NAME OF THE MAN ON THE NIXON TAPE. WE ARE CURIOUS.

Affirmative.

WE CAN PROVIDE FURTHER INFORMATION ON THE NAME. DOUBLECHECK.

Standby, please.

Connie had just come into the room. From the ashen look on her face, he knew what she was going to say. "Damn it," she said. "He was only twenty-six years old."

"Was," he echoed quietly.

"Saunders checked. If it was the same Frank Reeves, he died of a heart attack last night."

"Ah," he said, an exhalation of breath as if a hand had pressed against his midsection and squeezed the air out of him. "The sons of bitches," he said, his anger too strong to be anything but quiet, the realization sudden within him that the computer was still on line, the faceless men waiting on the other end. They had caught their fish this time certainly enough, and he could see in his mind's eye the intricate telephone tracing equipment at work, circuits closing, digital lights flashing. They would know where he was by now. But never mind. He no longer wished to avoid, but to draw them here.

Reeves dead, never seen, known only from a pattern of words on the screen, and yet Cameron felt his death as deeply as the rest. It would cost them dearly.

You're a goddamned liar. Frank Reeves is dead.
End Transmission.

Cameron left the terminal on line. Connie had a stricken look on her face. She fumbled with a lighter, could get no flame from it. He struck a match, lighted her cigarette. "It's going to be all right," he said.

"The hell it is." She drew smoke from the cigarette, then crushed it out. "You're putting yourself right in the line of fire."

"I can take care of myself."

"No," she said, shaking slightly. "You can't take care of yourself. There are a hell of a lot of them and only one of you. They're going to roll over you like a bump in the road and you're going to let them do it."

"No," he said.

"I won't let it happen," she said, her voice intense. "You pick a Senator out of a hat, anybody you trust. You call him and tell him the whole thing. If you don't trust Senators, then make it a priest, a labor leader, the head of the FBI, the Attorney General."

"I'll handle it myself."

"That's the bottom line, isn't it? Handling it yourself, I mean." She stood up, trembling with anger. "If you won't do it, then I will. I'm going to the police."

He reached out to touch her arm and she whirled and slapped him across the face and quite suddenly he was grappling with her as she tried to kick him, the anger giving way to tears, and without knowing how it happened, he was making love to her, no preliminaries, no tenderness here, and she moaned beneath him and bit him on the lip as if in the coupling she was entering into a mortal struggle with him. And his rhythm became savage as she matched him thrust for thrust and finally, all thought obliterated, he put his hands under her pale buttocks and lifted the lower half of her body up off the divan, extending himself fully within her. She went beyond control now, straining against him and then, released, fell back, away from him, all tears and passion spent. He lay beside her, knowing that the anger was gone.

"You are a son of a bitch," she said, out of breath.

"Yes."

"And I can't stop you, can I?"

"No."

She put her hand on his leg. "Make me one promise."

"All right."

"Don't let them kill you. If it comes to the point where you don't have a chance, where you have to admit that black is white or the sun rises in the west, then you admit it. There are no words left worth dying for, no tapes."

"Agreed."

He went to the bathroom, shaved, examined his face in the mirror. Not so desperate now. Normal. He would have to make the best use of his time. None to waste. He knotted his tie as he came back into the sitting room. Connie was sitting on the couch, putting on her jeans.

"We can expect Wicker to be fairly close," he said. "An hour or two at the outside. I think Wicker will play this one safe. No surprise moves because he doesn't have to make them. He won't want to chance any commotion. I need you to help. Do you feel up to it?"

"What do you want me to do?"

He put his hands on her shoulders. "You go to the front desk, ask them to call you a taxi. Tell them you are going to the Dunes because you hear that the slots there are lucky. When you get into the taxi, go to the Riviera instead. Have a drink, play the slots. Meet me under the front portico in an hour."

She nodded, accepting. "All right. I'll meet you in an hour."

Busy work, certainly, something to keep her occupied, but if she understood what he was doing, she did not question it. He watched her leave and then smoked a cigarette while he thought about what he was going to do. The confrontation would come soon and he was ready for it.

He went to meet Purdy.

Chapter Nine

"We have you scheduled for 1030, second December," Colonel Barr was saying over the telephone and Roffner was having a hard time concentrating, knowing that Pearson was waiting for him in the outer office. Pearson was a physicist, a tall, thin, bony man with a crane-like neck, a nervous disposition, and he considered all military men his intellectual inferiors. And beyond Pearson, there were the rumors buzzing through the corridors of the Pentagon, engendered by the story in the *Post*, and he would have to deal with them sooner or later. Yet here he sat, his voice perfectly calm as he dealt with the accelerated schedule in Nevada.

"Would you repeat that schedule, please?" Roffner said.

"That's 1030 hours, second December," Barr said. "I realize this is rushing a bit, General, but we have to accommodate a great many groups during Operation Red Flag. We're running a heavy national guard training exercise just before Christmas. Too, our long-range forecasts call for a true-blue norther to come blowing in by the sixth and we can't guarantee photographic tracking. Now, if you prefer, we can offer you an alternate time slot after one January."

"No, Colonel. We can accommodate to the advanced time."

"You might want to catch a few shows in Las Vegas while you're out here. You want me to set something up?"

"I'll take care of that from here."

"Well, then, I'll look forward to seeing you tomorrow."

"Yes, tomorrow."

Roffner put the telephone down, sat in silence a moment, thinking it through, planning. He could not afford to make a false move at this point. Finally, reluctantly, he reached out and pressed his intercom and told his secretary to send Pearson in. He stood up, turned to look out the window, aware that Pearson would be pushing, irritable. The only way to deal with a man such as Pearson was to cool him down, to underplay everything. He heard him come into the room, clear his throat, but he did not turn to look at him.

"Ground zero," Roffner said.

"What?"

"Had you ever considered, Carl, how many missiles in Russia are targeted right on the center courtyard of the Pentagon? I would say just offhand, at least twenty, perhaps more." Now he turned, nodding at Pearson who was still standing just inside the door, looking very physically uncomfortable in an ill-fitting gray suit, scowling out from behind his rimless glasses, his hands full of papers. "Did you know, Carl, that the Pentagon was originally designed as a military hospital to take care of the casualties from the projected invasion of the Japanese islands? But we didn't have to invade, so the space was taken over by the

War Department."

"I don't see the point, Roffner," Pearson said. "What's this about an accelerated schedule?"

"There's a profound point to the history of this building," Roffner said. "If it had not been for the success of the atom bombs, this building would have been filled with the bloody casualties of a campaign we didn't have to fight. And that's precisely what we are doing here. Forestalling."

"We can't go with an accelerated schedule," Pearson said, sitting down at the conference table, beginning to spread out his papers. "You're sticking your neck way out on this one as it is."

"We're all right if your calculations are correct."

"My calculations are perfect," Pearson said. "The thing will work but if you clamp down on our time, we can't make any accurate prediction of the effects. You tactical boys don't know the difference between assumptions and facts. You try to treat what you're doing as an exact science when it's not a science at all. Now, you give us more time for computer projections and we can give you reasonably hard data."

"We don't have any more time," Roffner said, feeling the stirrings of indignation. "And if we had it, I wouldn't give it to you. My God, I've seen the way your boys do business, don't forget that. I've seen your fat-ass team and your scheduling. You've turned our laboratories into country clubs."

"I'll match our scheduling against any similar groups anywhere," Pearson said. "You can't force scientific development the way you force troops."

"The hell you can't," Roffner said. "The atom

bomb was a crash effort."

"Adequately funded."

Roffner shrugged, his stomach signaling him, the slight, sharp edge of pain, the barometer of the gastric juices. His tension level was high. *Was the newspaper account true? Did Cameron really have the information?* He forced the thought out of his mind, poured himself a glass of milk from his Thermos. "Hell, Carl," he said in a mollifying voice. "We'll fight the past some other time. Let's take a look and see what we have to work with."

Carl spread the papers and the charts on the oversized table and Roffner joined him, the better to follow the lines of the intricate contour map. Pearson's lean finger traced a jagged route from north to south, following the general configuration of the hills.

"I'll just give you objections," he said. "I'll give you the glitch points and then you're free to do what you want." His voice still carried that goddamned abrasive edge to it. "You've already proved the TERCOM guidance system on the missile, so it seems to me you're gilding the lily here. You're trying to cram too many tests into one operation. Every time you complicate the flight path, you create more opportunity for error."

Roffner followed that jabbing finger and the pattern of that strident voice, but his mind refused to stay fixed. For Pearson was merely pointing out objections he had voiced a dozen times before. This time, Roffner realized, it was for the record, so if anything went wrong, Pearson could always report he had made his objections known forty-eight hours before the test itself.

Roffner found himself thinking about the Scandinavian woman, his night with her, that fantastically skilled body of hers, the inexhaustible sensuality. He would have her fly to Las Vegas this afternoon. She would be the perfect window dressing.

Pearson had peeled off one paper, was examining another. "But here is the main problem," he said pointedly. "All of these circuits and measuring devices were installed in 1972-73 and the wiring may be inadequate to carry the load. Too, you don't have sufficient population control for an adequate scientific measurement. Out of a thousand people, using that as a base, you should have no more than two hundred of them inside the two-hundred-fifty-meter circle. The rest should be grouped into units of a hundred and placed here, here, and here." The fingernail tapped against the paper with a popping sound. "There should be an age distribution, sex as well."

Roffner shook his head. "You can't have your mathematical ideal," he said. "You'll have plenty of data to work with."

"If it's not balanced, the results won't be statistically valid."

The quantifiers of the world, Roffner thought. In the end the important thing was not the scientific data but the test itself. The Russians would get the message. Nothing else counted. He glanced at his watch. Time was running out and there were a hundred details to cover and most of the technicians were already in Nevada.

"Have you written down these objections?" he said. "Do you have a prior-date memo to cover your ass in case you're proven right?"

"I won't need a memo," the scientist said coldly. "We need more time and adjustments to the testing system and we're not getting it. Your ass is on the line, not mine. This is your baby." He rolled up the charts. "I'll see you in Nevada."

The moment Pearson left, Roffner returned to his desk and took the checklist out of his locked drawer. The preliminary section had been completed and he was reasonably satisfied with the procedures but he did not have check-ins from Walters, Saldi, Chavous, or Glassic. He would have to notify them of the shortened time, get them busy.

He flipped the intercom and told his secretary to get Major Shaw for him right away. Then he leaned back in the chair and studied the story in the *Washington Post*, under Koblenz's byline, and he felt the strain again. Koblenz was masterful at his craft.

His article was a blend of fact and innuendo. He detailed the demolition of the car in Missouri and the fact that it had been registered to a Connie Stryker, employee of the GAO, and he reported a telephone call to the *Washington Post* offering information about the Nixon tape and a secret military project named BRIMSTONE. He rehashed the business of the suicide of Cameron's wife and the death of his father.

Nothing was put together properly. Koblenz did not know the truth and the story was fishing for facts. Roffner had seen the method used before, and there was always the possibility that someone connected with BRIMSTONE would begin to get nervous, have second thoughts, and call Koblenz and begin to feed him information in return for an eventual immunity. The letter to Senator Livermore confirmed that possibility.

His secretary buzzed him and told him Colonel Hughes was on the line. He put the line on the scrambler and then picked up the telephone.

"Yes," he said.

"Hughes here." Hughes had worked with the British for a while. The accent and the attitudes could still be heard in his voice. "We've been in touch with Cameron through the computer, sir, but our cover has been blown. He knows Reeves is dead."

"Where is he?"

"Las Vegas. We ran a trace on the telephone."

"He contacted the *Post*," Roffner said, thinking aloud. "Are you aware of that?"

"Certainly, sir."

"What do you advise, Colonel?"

"I would suggest termination."

"Hold on." Roffner poured another glass of milk from the Thermos, giving himself time to think it through. He drank the milk, then addressed himself to the telephone again. "All right," he said. "Take him out of there."

"I do think that's best. I'll give you a ring when that area is secure."

As he put down the telephone, the door opened and Major Shaw came in. Shaw looked bedraggled, his hair rumpled, his tie askew. There was a vagueness about his eyes Roffner had seen before, a troubled expression which meant that, given the slightest chance, Shaw would drag out his doubts like a stringer of fish. Roffner did not want to deal with those doubts. He told Shaw about the change in schedule. "I want you to get

Glassic off his can," Roffner said. "I want a medical section report."

"The key medical team flew out three days ago," Shaw said. "They've already gone through the alert routine. They're ready to monitor. They'll adapt to the new schedule."

"Very good. Then get me a suite at the Riviera. Call Ingrid and tell her I want her to come to Las Vegas for three days."

The intercom buzzed again. "Mr. Koblenz is calling for you, sir."

"Tell him I'm not available." He flipped off the intercom, sat back in his chair, fingers laced. He observed Shaw making the call to Ingrid, adequate, conveying and receiving information, but not really there. Finally, Shaw turned from the telephone.

"She'll be delighted," he said.

"What have you found out about the letter to Livermore?" Roffner said.

Shaw shook his head vaguely, began the ritual of taking the cellophane top off a pack of cigarettes. "The experts say it's impossible to trace, General. The typing balls are distinctive, not the typewriters themselves, and there are literally thousands of those around." He sat down, a perceptible hesitation in his voice as if it were difficult for him to concentrate. "We could make a very large-scale investigation but that would take weeks."

"Did any other Senators or Congressmen receive similar letters?"

"No, sir."

Now he just sat, still fumbling with the cellophane. There was no sense putting it off, Roffner realized. Shaw would only get worse, more morose. "What's eating you, Major?" he said.

"Reeves."

"Who?"

"Franklin W. Reeves."

"The leak in the computer section, DIA. Is that who you're talking about?"

"Yes."

"I'm pleased you put yourself on top of that situation. DIA concludes he was working alone. Do you agree?"

"He has two children."

"What?"

"Allen and Georgia, the names of his two children," Shaw said. "He was a computer hobbyist when he wasn't working. His wife said he was curious about everything. Very patriotic. Shit, he even had an American flag flying outside his apartment." He fumbled with a cigarette, managed to get it lighted, blew the smoke out of his mouth with a plopping sound. "Alone. No conspiracy. He was just curious about BRIMSTONE when it popped up on the computer. So he communicated with Cameron through the computer. Just curious, that's all."

"So you've had a drink or two," Roffner said.

"He wasn't any threat," Shaw said to the wall. "It wasn't any goddamned heart attack."

Roffner's mouth became a skeptical oval. "No? Are you a medical expert?" There was no barb in his voice. "Did you look at his medical records, come to a conclusion with the pathologists?"

"He played handball, jogged every day." Another belch of smoke. "His wife is twenty-two years old."

"It's a wicked world," Roffner said. "Now, I don't presume to know how this young man died, Major, and I don't propose to find out because it's none of my business. But I'll tell you this. I don't give a damn what his motives were. If his staying alive put what we are doing in jeopardy, then I would have ordered him killed myself."

Shaw smoked in silence, finally nodded. "Necessary, then."

The worst had passed. Shaw was too philosophical, that was his problem, always looking for meanings when there were none, eternally poring over entrails which contained no message.

"I suggest that you headquarter at the Riviera instead of Nellis," Roffner said. "After the test, before we begin data analysis, you're going to need to unwind."

"Yes, sir," Shaw said finally. "I'm going to need to unwind."

2

Cameron found Purdy sitting in his MG in the almost deserted parking lot behind the Circus Circus. He was a short man, characteristically slumped back in the seat, sunglasses covering his eyes, his pinkish face exposed to the warm sunlight. His car radio was tuned to a disco station and his fingers were drumming on the steering wheel in time to the music.

Cameron parked his car next to the MG. As he climbed out he was aware of the stiffness of his legs, the fatigue that had settled over his body. But his mind was quick, aware, and he scouted the parking lot for any possible sign of trouble before he approached Purdy's car. He touched Purdy on the shoulder and Purdy jumped slightly, opening his eyes. "You startled me, Willie," he said. "What the hell's happening?"

"Imminent collapse," Cameron said.

"Imminent collapse is about right," Purdy said flatly. "Then all the stuff in the *Washington Post* is true."

"They printed it then," Cameron said, almost to himself.

Purdy clicked off the radio and climbed out of the car. "You look like hell," he said. "Understandable. But I find that there are no unsolvable problems in the world which can't be ignored. Come on in and I'll buy you a drink."

Incredible, Purdy refused to take anything seriously. His eyes blinked while he cleaned his sunglasses as if he was unused to any unfiltered exposure to the world. He sauntered toward the casino with Cameron, one hand hanging on Cameron's shoulder. Incredible, certainly, because Purdy was now on his working hours and he was wearing a flowered sportshirt and red trousers, as if he was on an eternal vacation.

"I have a simple philosophy," Purdy said. "I let the machines do the work and if they turn up a bad batch of figures, I simply pass on the information and let somebody else worry about it." He ran his hand over his sparse sandy hair and his pinkish scalp. "Do you really have one of the big boys in a crack, Willie? Are they really trying to blow you up? They're all dumb assholes, you have to remember that. If you have the clout, I say use it. Sink them before they scuttle you. You'll come out all right. I meant to call you or write you or something to tell you how sorry I was about your father. But I never got around to it."

"How well did you know him?"

"I got to know him quite well after he came out here," Purdy said. "He used to come over to the house and play backgammon and tell Nixon stories."

They went to the mezzanine overlooking the gambling tables and a convention of women playing keno immediately below them. Cameron felt unreal. For at this moment, Wicker and his men would be moving in on the city, locking him in, and here he sat in Purdy's relaxed fantasy world, watching as out above the floor the trapeze artists were performing, the circus music subdued. Purdy signaled a floor waitress and ordered a mai-tai. Cameron settled for a bourbon and water.

"I sure as hell would hate to be a morning trapeze performer," Purdy said, watching a sequinned girl spinning through the air to be caught by her feet. "Jesus, none of those poor suckers down on the floor give a flying fuck about what's going on overhead."

The waitress, a stunning red-haired girl with a dazzling smile, delivered their drinks, and Purdy put the money on the tray and watched her retreat. "Ah, the land of the perpetual poontang," he said. "The valley of bliss where the ass is always fresh."

"So you've really started fooling around?"

Purdy smiled. "I'm still a looker, not a toucher. Alice knows that." His smile was remote, a facial reflex. "Poor Annie," he said. "A mixed-up broad."

"I'm running out of time," Cameron said, with some effort. "If you have any information that can help me, I want it."

"Then you don't have one of the big boys by the short hair?"

"No."

"It's a good bluff. Why are they on your ass, amigo?"

"They're after the tape you forwarded to me from my father."

"I'm not surprised," Purdy said, sipping at his drink. "Rambling Richard at his rarefied best."

"You heard it?" Cameron said, startled. "You know about it?"

"Absolutely. Your father played it for me a half dozen times." He ran a fingertip around the rim of the mai-tai glass. His eyes were in constant motion behind the colored lenses. "Your old man was a secret celebrity, you know, really volatile potential. Real chutzpah. He erased the original eighteen and a half minutes after he copied it. Did you know that?"

Momentarily struck dumb, Cameron shook his head. A bell was clanging somewhere below. Someone had hit a jackpot. He cleared his throat. "Jesus Christ," he said. "You knew all that and you kept it to yourself?"

"No interest in politics, old sport, that's my trouble," Purdy said. "Watergate bores me. Anything Nixon does bores me. I don't do double crostics. I put in my time as painlessly as possible and then go home and fool around with Alice and the kids. Your father didn't echo any of those sentiments, of course."

"He told you he erased it? He admitted it?"

A thin, knowing smile. "He agonized over it."
Cameron listened to his bland voice, a quiet recital
as if Purdy were discussing the weather, but
Cameron could see his father in Florida where
Nixon had taken his people to sort out the tapes,
getting the combination to the safe in the Key Biscayne villa, sneaking in early on the morning of
October second, copying the eighteen and a half
minutes on a small recorder and then erasing the
original on Rose Mary Woods' machine, backing
up, erasing again and again. Always the thorough
man.

"He was really split," Purdy went on. "If you
know what I mean. He wanted to find out the
secret of the tape and at the same time he didn't
want anybody else to know about it, in case he was
wrong. I told him the pursuit of poontang would
be much more rewarding and just as challenging,
but he never believed me. And then he got hit by a
truck. He had asked me to send the tape to you if
anything happened to him, so I did."

"They murdered him," Cameron said.

"They?"

"You know goddamned well who I'm talking
about. They. Somebody in the government."

Purdy finished his mai-tai, ordered another.
"Maybe," he said. "Probably not. The police
labeled it hit and run and they're pretty thorough.
I'd like to be able to contribute to your sense of
drama. But I wouldn't go along with his and I see
no reason to start now. Sometimes he was
paranoid about that tape, convinced somebody
was trying to cover something up. But hell, he was
out here a year and everybody knew where he was
and he wasn't any closer to a solution when he was

killed than he was at the beginning. No, I think he was a hit-and-run victim of some drunk who was never found and probably never even remembered hitting anybody."

Cameron watched the trapeze artists, the catcher a wiry little man with bulging shoulders, the girl, a broad red smear of an automatic smile on her face as she dropped into the net and checked her fall, bounced back to a standing position and cocked one arm in salute to a crowd which was paying no attention to her. Uninvolved.

"No," Cameron said. "He was closer than he realized or they wouldn't have killed him. What kind of lead was he working?"

Purdy's eyes followed the spangled lady up the pole. "With muscles like that, I'll bet she's a fantastic piece of ass." He shrugged. "Your father was chasing wild geese," he said. "He was following another brimstone, a nickname used for a government Law Enforcement Assistance Administration project, where federal prisoners are being used to repair military equipment. It's on the desert and during the summer it gets hotter than hell out there. So the locals refer to the housing around the institution as 'hellfire' and the prison itself as 'brimstone.'"

"What did he find?"

"He didn't find a damn thing," Purdy said. "That's one of the federal projects on my beat and it's probably the most fucking crazy boondoggle in the country. Other than being totally screwed up from the beginning, nothing's ever happened there to require a cover-up. Shit, read one of my annual congressional inspections on the place sometime, any one of them since 1972. They spend a half million a year to maintain systems to measure radioactivity when above-ground testing ended years ago. There's absolutely no quality control in the buildings, some of them insulated like bunkers, others plain metal frame." He clicked his fingers at the waitress. "Bring me some black coffee, sweetheart," he said. "All that goes up must come down."

Cameron cradled his glass in his hands, distracted by the music, the girl with the bright-red mouth, the swarms of people on the gaming floor below. Another bell went off. Another jackpot.

The nagging thought was there, something important, but his mind was too tired to see it clearly. "Federal convicts repairing military equipment," he said. "Where's the prison?"

"On the highway toward Reno." The coffee was served. Purdy grimaced, drank the cup halfway down. "There's nothing out there that would interest you, believe me."

"Somebody's getting ready for a slaughter," Cameron said. "I don't know how, who, or why, but the blood's going to run. You can't stay out of this, Purdy."

Purdy stared off into space. A spotlight reflected from his colored lenses. Cameron could not see his eyes. "Nobody really gives a shit," he said. "Hell, read the transcript of the Church Committee hearings in 1975 sometime. The special operations division at Ft. Detrick made a simulated test in the subways of New York in the mid-sixties. They set off gas bulbs in two subway lines, reported that if the gas had been toxic, they could have wiped out New York City. And somebody asked the question about the kind of gas that was actually in the bulbs. It could have been a gas with long-range effects, but there wasn't any hue and cry.

"In the end nobody knew for sure who had done it, the army or the CIA. And what about the army LSD experiments in the sixties? People jumping out of windows, going bananas." He finished his coffee, put the cup back on the saucer.

"I care," Cameron said. "And you're going to back me up."

"Sorry, old sport," Purdy said flatly, easily. "I like my life and I don't have any desire to change it, risk it, even adjust it. I'm sorry about your predicament but nothing I could say would pull you out of the soup. I'd just be in there with you. As for the larger cause, the big picture as they say, I'm with the majority. I simply don't give a shit, one way or the other."

"And if BRIMSTONE goes through and you could have stopped it—"

"Don't do that," Purdy said. "Don't try to guilt me, friend. Won't work. I don't play anybody else's game. I do wish you well though, and that's sincere."

"You son of a bitch," Cameron said.

"That's right," Purdy said. He stood up. "I have to get back on my horse. No offense, amigo. And if you need any information I can supply, just give me a call. But your father was climbing the wrong tree so I wouldn't get sidetracked if I were you."

Cameron sat in the booth for a few minutes after Purdy had gone. Purdy was one of the true policy makers in the country, a bureaucrat who allowed decision by default. It became quite clear to Cameron, in this moment, that the decision to handle this himself had been a right one, for there were too many Purdys in the government, too many people who would refuse to move.

Hell, the answer to the riddle was there and quite suddenly he knew it, but he had no hard facts, nothing that would convince anybody of the truth. He needed the computer to confirm it.

He went back to the rented car. The sunshine was dazzling and he could see the high fortress wings of the Riviera Hotel across the boulevard. Connie would be inside, killing time, and he would have to pick her up soon. Traffic was increasing along the Strip.

A police car passed him. He considered taking time to track down the accident report on his father, the exact time, the exact place, the circumstances of his death, but at the moment that accretion of facts was useless. They would have killed his father with the same care they had used in removing Reeves, the same sense of detail they would use to dispose of him, if they had the chance.

He passed the pawnshops and stopped at a sporting goods store with a western motif. He went inside and bought an automatic shotgun and a box of shells. Then he drove back to the Riviera to find Connie waiting for him under the portico. She reached out and touched his cheek with cool fingers as if to reassure herself.

"Nothing has changed, has it?" she said, resigned. "Purdy didn't do you any good, did he?"

"He's a son of a bitch," Cameron said. "He leads a perfectly uninvolved life. He does his job faultlessly. His ratings are perfect, his work uncompromising, honest, and he loves his wife and kids and enjoys good whisky and girl watching. But underneath all that detail, he's the coldest bastard I ever met. Hundreds of people are going to be slaughtered and he doesn't give a damn."

He eased the car into traffic, driving out in the general direction of the airport, needing time to think. She kept her eyes on his face. "You found out something, didn't you?" she said. "You know what's going to happen."

"I think so, yes." he said. "I know what's going to happen, the end result, and I know where it's going to take place, but I don't know when, why, or how."

She breathed a sigh of relief. "Thank God for that. Then it's over, isn't it?"

"No," he said quietly.

"Why the hell not? You call somebody and pass the information on to them and then you're out of it legitimately." Her voice trailed off. Her eyes were on the leather guncase in the back seat. "Is that what it appears to be?" she said incredulously. "My God, what do you think you're doing? Are you going to try to outshoot them, is that it?"

"Don't make it sound so damned flip," he said. "I'm doing what I have to do."

"You're doing what you *want* to do. There's a difference, you know."

"Yes," he said. "I have this coming to me."

"I love you, Willie," she said. "I appreciate the fact that you're so damned tired you're about to drop and that you feel abandoned, sold out. But if that gun in the back seat is your solution, then love or not, I'm dropping out."

He pulled over to the side of the road, stopped the car. Tired, yes, so goddamned tired he was having trouble thinking. He sat in silence a moment. "All right," he said. "A compromise."

"What kind of compromise?"

"You call the Attorney General, the Justice Department, anybody you can think of. You tell them we need immediate help, that a lot of people are about to get killed. If you get any real assistance, then I'll call it off and let them handle it."

"Tell me what's going to happen."

He looked out across the desert. "No," he said. "At this point, it wouldn't do any good. But you find one reliable source that's willing to move instantly, and I'll dump the whole load."

She was quiet a moment. "You really mean that, don't you?"

"Yes," he said. "Right now I'd give anything for a soft bed, sleep. And a normal life."

He drove back into Las Vegas, past the Red Sands to an adjacent motel, then stopped the car across the street. "You check in here," he said. "Take a room on the second floor, overlooking the Red Sands parking lot. Wicker's not going to take me on by himself and I want to know what I'm up against. If you see any government types—men in business suits, short haircuts, conservative—you let me know. And if you line up any help, you let me know that too."

She was reluctant to leave the car. "And if I can't turn up anything, then what?"

"I'll let you know when you call."

"All right," she said. "But it won't come to that." She leaned over, kissed him briefly. "I should have something in a half hour. I'll call you."

He watched her crossing the street, then he

drove to the parking lot of the Red Sands, at the rear of the main building. He sat in the car a long moment, rubbing his eyes, trying to come fully alert. He made a visual sweep of the motel and the second-floor terraces. If Wicker's men were here, they were not yet in evidence. Everything quiet. A couple walked out of the motel and headed for a car, the woman steaming ahead, the man following in a passive and stony silence. Cameron could hear her angry voice as she said something to him. He made no reply.

Finally, Cameron opened the back door of the car and took out the guncase and the paper bag with the box of shells and went into the motel. The corridor was empty. He unlocked the door to his suite and opened it slowly. No sound except the hum of the computer terminal. He disconnected it from the telephone, then locked the door behind him. One thing at a time now, no mistakes, no wasted motion. He poured himself a cup of coffee from the Thermos and drank it down, then he removed the shotgun from the case. Opening the box of shells, he put four of them in the magazine and then checked the bedroom and the bathroom before he went back into the sitting room.

The telephone rang. He picked it up to find a male voice on the line. "Cameron?"

"Yes."

"The name you're looking for is Roffner."

"Who is this?"

"Run it through your computer. I'll call back." The line went dead.

The computer terminal.

He sat down in front of it, poured himself a second cup of coffee. More alive now. The caffeine, he supposed. He could not identify the voice he had heard on the telephone but he was sure it was one of them. He asked the operator to connect him with a Washington number, then he placed the telephone in the holder, interfacing with the computer. He typed the eight digits into the computer keyboard to connect him with the Defense Department Personnel files, and then the code words to connect him with the Pentagon roster.

Roffner, General, but what was his first name? George, yes, and he typed the name into the machine and waited while across the country, millions of electronic pulses searched it out, and then the information began to flow onto the screen —Roffner's current status, financial statistics, his whole history in the army—scrolling on the screen until Cameron was almost dizzied by the words. He watched for one date, one phrase, and there it was, dumped in the middle of a distinguished career.

1955-1967.

Ft. Detrick, Maryland.

He severed the connection. A minor elation, everything falling into place. He took another drag from the cigarette. That goddamned misplaced Russian town. The files had been returned to the DIA but the map still existed in the GAO computer memory. He went on line again and summoned up the map of the Russian town, then left it displayed on the screen to free the telephone line again. Ah, it made sense now and he knew what it was. All that remained was for him to check it out.

He called Purdy's office and Purdy came on the line, friendly, cool, as if nothing had happened to change the relationship.

"I need some information," Cameron said. "Where is this prison you were talking about, the ordnance-shops?"

"Up Highway 95, north of here about sixty miles, just off the road, on the edge of the AEC Nuclear Testing Site."

Cameron studied the map on the computer screen. "Does it back up to a mountain range on the east?"

"Check."

"And it was funded in fiscal year 1972, right?"

"Dead center," Purdy said. "What do you have?"

"How was it funded, an LEAA grant?"

"It's a joint project of the LEAA and the Department of Defense. Are you on to something?"

"Nothing that would interest you. What was the inmate population at the beginning of the experiment?"

"Hell, I'm not sure. Close to a hundred."

"Could it have been a hundred and ten?"

"That's close. It mushroomed in the mid-seventies with all the correctional grants floating around. I'd say they have a stable inmate population of about eleven hundred. Then there's a small town on the west side of the institution, another three or four hundred people."

"That's all I need to know." He severed the connection in the middle of Purdy's curiosity. The telephone rang immediately. It was the voice again.

"Did you check the name?"

"Yes. Who is this?"

"I'm Major Shaw. There is a telephone booth in front of an Exxon station on the main street in

Brimstone. I'll meet you there at nine o'clock tonight."

Again the line went dead. When the telephone rang again, he knew it was Connie, even before he picked it up. She was highly distraught. "It's crazy, darling," she said. "The whole thing is crazy."

"Who did you call?"

"A half dozen people," she said. She had begun with the Justice Department, had been given access to a clerk who was willing to take down information and write a report which would lead to an investigative decision. "I called the local office of the FBI and told them you knew about something terrible that was going to happen. They wanted to know where you were but they didn't even ask me about the information you have. I called two Senators and didn't get to speak to either one. I got professional sympathy from a couple of secretaries who said they would pass information on but nothing more. Did you know this was going to happen?"

"Yes," he said. "Even if they believed you, they couldn't move. I'm sure the DIA put in a claim on the case at the Justice Department. And I was with the GAO long enough to know how slowly the Congressmen move. What do you see out your window?"

"There's a black car in front of the motel, four men, I think. And there's a man in a blue car in the parking lot. He's just sitting there."

"They're here then," he said. "I can expect Wicker any minute."

"Isn't there anything I can do?"

"Just stay put. And remember that I love you."

He pulled back the drapes, looked out into the parking lot. There was a blue sedan sitting in the space next to his car. He could see the shape of a man in the driver's seat. No details, no features but he knew it was one of them. Were there other DIA men in the motel, scattered through the corridors, covering the lobby? It made no difference.

There was a knock at the door. He took his time and cleared the computer display screen, then he picked up the shotgun before he answered it, unfastening the safety chain, unlocking the dead bolt.

"Who is it?" he said. He stepped back, brought the shotgun up to waist level.

"It's Wicker."

"Come in. It's open."

The door opened and Wicker came in and stopped dead in his tracks when he saw the shotgun, a reflex action, no fear that Cameron could see, only dismay. "What are you doing with a shotgun? You know you're not going to kill me. You don't have that instinct in you. Some men do and some men don't. Believe me, you don't."

"Close the door behind you."

Wicker did as he was told. The door clicked shut.

"Empty your pockets on the table," Cameron said. "Turn them inside out. Take off your jacket. Put your pistol on the table as well."

Wicker shrugged and then, in an orderly fashion, removed his jacket, then lifted his pistol from its shoulder holster, and laid it on the table with great respect. "This isn't very rational," he said.

"I'm not rational," Cameron said. "Get on with it."

A wallet and a memo pad came out of the jacket pocket. Wicker emptied the pockets of his trousers. Keys, change, a comb, a small pen-knife, a handkerchief. A pack of cigarettes from his shirt.

Cameron gestured with the shotgun. "Over there. Sit."

"May I take my cigarettes?" Wicker said, picking them up before he sat down. He removed a book of paper matches from the cellophane around the pack, lighted a cigarette. "I don't blame you, Cameron. You've been through a hell of a lot and that's a fact. Everybody in Washington thinks quite highly of you. And in the end you're going to surrender to me and we're going to walk out of here like reasonable men." He inhaled the smoke through thin lips, tapped the ash into a ceramic ashtray, perfectly at ease, almost smug.

And quite suddenly, beyond thought, beyond the plan he had so carefully thought out, Cameron swung the shotgun around, the butt catching Wicker squarely on the side of his lean face, not so much a blow as a solid push, and Wicker fell off the chair and went sprawling, his glasses miraculously remaining in place, the cigarette showering sparks as it rolled across the floor. And Cameron stood above him, the muzzle of the shotgun pointed at his head. The rage was so intense within him he did not want to control it and he had to restrain his finger from tightening on the trigger.

"The boy," Cameron said. "You killed a sixteen-year-old boy last night."

Wicker remained perfectly motionless, eyes

glittering, a rabbit freezing against the onslaught of a hawk. A red flush had begun to rise on his right cheek, where the butt of the shotgun had struck him. He said nothing. His breathing was very shallow.

"What was his name?" Cameron said.

Wicker ran his tongue over his lips, shook his head, said nothing.

"You incinerated him and you don't even know his goddamn name," Cameron said. His hands were trembling. He moved away slightly, the rage beginning to sour. Too much to do; he could not kill him now. "No more killing," he said. "No more killing nameless people." He sat down in a chair, keeping the shotgun trained on Wicker who still did not move. He sat in silence a long time.

"I know how you feel," Wicker said tentatively. "I'm sorry about the boy. I truly am." A sigh escaped him. "It's a shitty business."

"I want information from you."

"All right. Can I get up?"

"No." Cameron inhaled the smoke. "I know about General Roffner," he said. "He was at Ft. Detrick, a part of the army's experiments with drugs and exotic weapons and human guinea pigs in psychiatric hospitals. And I know that sooner or later, those poor bastards in that prison are going to be used as guinea pigs in some kind of nuclear test."

Wicker's eyes were on the cigarette he had dropped when he fell. "Do you mind if I put that out?" he said. "It's going to burn a hole in the carpet."

"Don't move," Cameron said quietly. "I want information."

Wicker rubbed his mouth with his hand, shook his head. "I'll say anything you want me to, of course. If you want to believe that, then I'll confirm it. But I really don't have any information."

"You work for Roffner."

"I know Roffner. He's one of my superiors."

"I intend to keep the BRIMSTONE experiment from happening."

Wicker's fingers touched the inflamed cheek as if to assess the damage. His expression was placid. If he felt any pain, he did not show it. "Assuming you're correct, just assuming, because I don't know what's going on," he said, "then you're fighting a lost cause. The same men are in power because the same mentality is always in power. Even if what you say is true and you could get a handle on it, the best you could do would be to delay, postpone. You certainly couldn't stop anything. And it would be extremely costly to you."

Cameron smiled. "You're perfect, Wicker," he said. "Absolutely perfect. I'm going to blow BRIMSTONE out of the water, totally abort it, not just postpone it." He backed to the telephone, dialed the operator, put the instrument to his ear. The line was dead. "What did you do to the telephone?" he said to Wicker.

"It's a precaution," Wicker said. "I had the telephone cut off." He shifted position slightly. "Have you considered the girl, Mr. Cameron? You should think of her, what further involvement is going to do to her."

Slowly, Cameron returned the receiver to the cradle. He shook his head, picked up the drink he had mixed for himself. The ice had melted. He drank it anyway, straight down, his eyes never leaving Wicker for an instant. At any moment he could squeeze the trigger of the shotgun and mangle the man who lay there on the floor, raised on one elbow.

"Get up," Cameron said. "Get up and sit in the chair."

Wicker's expression was no longer even. There was a quizzical gleam in his eye, an almost perceptible nervousness. He raised himself to his feet, sat down. Cameron gestured with the shotgun. "Raise your left hand straight up in the air."

"Why?" Wicker said. "What's the point?"

"Stick it up there."

The arm moved, raised. Cameron poured himself another drink from the bottle, laughed again. "What have you got left when you can't use your reason, Wicker? You can't predict a goddamned thing. Put that arm down and raise the other one."

The left arm came down. The right hand went up. "You can't win," Wicker said.

"Take off your left shoe, very carefully. Then place it parallel with the stripe in the carpet."

Slowly, Wicker did as he was told, placing the shoe on the stripe in the carpet. "You're wasting time."

"You're fucking it up," Cameron said. "I didn't say to put the shoe *on* the stripe. I said parallel *with* it. So move the goddamned shoe."

Wicker moved the shoe.

"Good," Cameron said. "Excellent. Now, how many men do you have, Wicker? How many in this motel?"

"Enough," Wicker said, face slightly ashen, off balance now. "You can't solve anything like this."

"How many?" Cameron said evenly.

"Seven."

"Where?"

"Two in the lobby, one in the parking lot," Wicker said. "And four more out front. Beyond that, an unmeasurable force."

"Nothing is unmeasurable. Stand up."

Slowly, Wicker rose to his feet. "What do you intend to do?"

"Take you out into the corridor," Cameron said. "I'm not sure of the power of this shotgun, what would happen, for instance, if I shot you in the groin, whether it would rip the genitals right off you or kill you outright. You're the expert at these things. What would happen if I shot you in the right knee? Would it splinter the bone, fragment it? Or is there sufficient force to blow the leg away?"

"Before you do anything, let's talk about it," Wicker said. There was a slight quaver in his voice. "Nothing's gone too far."

"Oh, it has," Cameron said. "Way too far. Now, walk over and open the door into the hallway."

Without one shoe, Wicker's walk had a limp to it. He opened the door.

"Look outside," Cameron said. "Tell me what you see."

"A maid. Pushing a linen cart. About three doors down."

"We'll stake your life on that," Cameron said. Prodding Wicker in the back with the shotgun, he followed him out into the hall. The maid was there, a buxom Mexican woman in her forties. Her eyes widened but she did not panic when she saw the shotgun. "I'm the police," Cameron said. *"Policia.* Do you speak English?"

"Yes, sir," the woman said.

"Go out the door into the parking lot," Cameron said. "There's a man in a business suit, sitting in a blue car. Tell him that an officer in here needs help."

"Yes, sir." She went outside. Wicker stood perfectly erect, balancing on the single shoe.

In less than a minute the door from the parking lot opened and a young man in a dark-blue suit came in. He stopped short when he saw Wicker and the shotgun. Young, Cameron thought, but not inexperienced. Cold, calculating eyes.

"That's right," Cameron said. "You're doing the right thing. Take out your pistol. Drop it on the floor."

The young man hesitated.

"For God's sake, Grotta," Wicker said. "Do as he says."

Slowly, Grotta's hand went beneath his coat. He dropped the pistol to the carpet.

"Now we're going across the parking lot to my car," Cameron said. "Wicker here can tell you, Mr. Grotta. I'm perfectly willing to trade everything for the chance to blow him away. Tell him, Wicker."

"He means it," Wicker said.

Was Grotta persuaded? Had the other men been instructed to stay put at the front of the motel? Were there more men in the parking lot, along the roof? The whisky was warm in his stomach and he was feeling easier. The complications were all wisping away, unreal, but this shotgun solid in his hands was real and Wicker limping along in front of him was real.

The parking lot was empty, no people, and the sun was warm overhead. Grotta walked directly to the car. "You get in the driver's seat," Cameron said to him, tossing him the keys. "Drive out the back way. We'll be going north on 95, out of town."

Was Connie watching now from her window? He could not tell.

He put Wicker in the back seat and then sat opposite him, the barrel of the shotgun across his lap, no chance for Wicker to deflect it. The car started, pulled away, and Wicker looked straight ahead. Cameron watched the boulevard give way to the interstate, the hotels and casinos receding, the town diminishing to residential sections which in turn surrendered to the desert. The four-lane highway narrowed.

Grotta drove in silence, a steady, legal speed. "All right," Cameron said finally. "Pull off the road ahead. After you stop, put the car in neutral. Leave the engine running."

Grotta pulled the car off the road and then sat waiting, his hands in his lap.

"I want you to deliver a message to General Roffner," Cameron said. "Tell him I know about BRIMSTONE. I'll be in touch."

"I don't understand," Grotta said.

"You don't have to understand. Just do it," Cameron said. "Now, get out of the car and walk ahead on the shoulder of the road. A hundred yards."

Grotta opened the door, climbed out, began to walk. There was a wind blowing. It flapped the tail of his suit coat, revealed a red lining. Cameron looked to Wicker. "You'll drive now. Get out of the car, very slowly."

Once Wicker was behind the wheel, Cameron eased in beside him on the passenger side, keeping the shotgun on him. "All right, drive," Cameron said.

"What makes you think I'm going to cooperate with you any further?" Wicker said.

"Because you know something now you didn't know before. I'll kill you if you don't."

"You son of a bitch," Wicker said. "You can't win against us all."

"If you want to be alive to see the victory, start driving."

Slowly, reluctantly, Wicker shifted into gear. The car moved back onto the pavement, picking up speed, creating an eddy of dust as it passed Grotta who stared after it, then slowly turned and began to walk in the direction of Las Vegas.

Chapter Ten

Roffner was never free of paperwork but he did not really mind. It was through the memos, the checklists, the trivia, that he kept firmly in touch with what was going on. Even now, in his suite at the Riviera, the coffee table was covered with neat stacks of papers and he sat on the divan, his reading glasses perched on his nose, going through them, aware that Major Shaw was talking with a man from the hotel about setting up a small telephone switchboard in the suite. Finally, the hotel man departed.

"Did you get the set-up?"

"Yes, sir. Six telephones."

"I want a full staff meeting at midnight. Rawlings, Jensen, Masters, Willoughby, and Chylinski to handle post operation. By noon tomorrow, we're going to be besieged and I mean that literally. Our communications center is going to be swamped. We're going to have Congressmen raising hell and the White House and a dozen local officials who will be scared shitless that the radiation is going to spread."

He picked up the sheaf of papers, sorting through them, knowing the details firsthand but checking them again anyway, for he had never participated in a test in which something did not go awry at the last minute, human or electronic or mechanical. There were always 10,000 diverse elements which were required to come together at precisely the right instant, the total testing of a weapons system and a defense against that system. And then the follow-up, in this case an explanation of this terrible accident, the result of an electronic failure.

The telephone rang. Shaw answered it and then covered the mouthpiece. "It's Colonel Askins at Nellis, sir."

"I'll take it." He picked up the telephone. "What do you have for me, Al?"

"We're projecting an SSW breeze, five knots maximum, General."

"Visibility?"

"Unlimited. High cirrus clouds. That should give us an absolute minimal drift, totally dispersed by 1400 hours, well within our range limits."

"Thank you, Al." He put the telephone down. Almost immediately, it rang again.

"Dearborn's on the line, sir," Shaw said.

"You take the information," Roffner said. He put the papers aside, suddenly restless, walked to the window where he could see the swimming pool. He spotted Ingrid immediately. Even from this distance, she seemed to glow, the honey-colored hair catching the sunlight. There were a few girls like Ingrid in the pool and a handful of muscular young men, but the majority of the bodies moving through the water or laid out like carcasses on deck chairs to catch the sun were older, flabby, dead white, and he had a brief glimpse of his own near future. For he was approaching that age.

"You'd better take this one, sir," Shaw said. Roffner picked up the telephone.

"Yes," he said, and Dearborn was off and running in that pleasant public-relations-man voice of his as he recounted the episode in the motel room and Cameron's escape with Wicker at gunpoint.

"He left Grotta on the highway north of Las Vegas," Dearborn said. "He told Grotta to relay a message to you, that he knew all about BRIMSTONE and would be in touch."

"I see," Roffner said finally.

"We've gone through possible scenarios," Dearborn said. And he went on to talk about all of the moves Cameron could make at this point but Roffner was only half listening, his mind already projecting beyond the test to the change in plans which would now become necessary. Scenarios, fictitional projections, hypotheses. "I think we should assign two teams to the area," Dearborn concluded.

Always a team, Roffner thought. When there was a problem, the solution always seemed to lie in numbers, as if many men could solve what one man could not. He needed time to think. To turn Dearborn loose would result in a flood of men pouring into the field, blocked highways, a ruckus which would involve state police, local authorities, cause questions to be asked. He rubbed his palms together.

"Wicker had six men at the motel and they couldn't bring it off," Roffner said. "All right, you hold off on the teams. If Cameron calls, you handle it. I want to know what he's done with the information he has. I want the tape, and then I want him killed. Do you think you can manage that?"

"Yes, sir," Dearborn said.

Roffner severed the connection and went back to his checklist, only half aware of the telephone men installing the switchboard. He was interrupted by a call from Senator Livermore. Roffner did not hesitate. It was vital to remain instantly responsive to the Armed Services Committee. "What can I do for you, Senator?"

Livermore was indirect as usual, in his slow and southern meandering way. It seemed that Livermore was in Los Angeles with his wife and his grandson and the boy was fascinated by airplanes and Livermore understood there was to be a test of a cruise missile as a part of Operation Red Flag and he thought it would be an excellent idea if they stopped in Las Vegas long enough to see the demonstration on their way back to Washington.

Once Roffner had extracted the intention from Livermore's monologue, he ceased listening and considered the possible ramifications of the Senator's presence. A complication, yes, but he could see possible advantages down the line.

"How old is your grandson?" Roffner said, when he had the opportunity.

"Ten years old. Robby's a bright boy, a very bright boy."

"I'm sure he is. Robby. Is that spelled R-O-B-B-Y?"

"That's correct."

"We'll be delighted, of course," Roffner said. "Maybe we can make a pilot out of him. Will you be driving up, Senator?"

"Unless you happen to have a military helicopter that will be making a run down here to Los Angeles anyway," Livermore said. "Robby loves helicopters and he's never flown in one."

"I'll make one available."

"Only if you have a run scheduled this way."

The little rituals, the ass-covering semantic dances. "I'm sure we do," Roffner said. "Where are you staying in Los Angeles?"

"The Beverly Wilshire."

"Fine. I'll do some checking and get back to you, Senator." He put the telephone down, leaned back on the divan. "Senator Livermore is bringing his wife and grandson to the test tomorrow," he said. "I want you to get a special hard hat for the boy. Have his name put on it. R-O-B-B-Y. Alert the Nellis PIO and have him set things up to show the Senator a good time. Have him flown out to the range a half hour before the test." He paused, scratched his chin thoughtfully. "But Cameron's your top priority. If he calls, you drop everything, take care of it."

"Yes, sir," Shaw said. "I understand."

2

As Wicker drove through the desert, Cameron felt a sense of desolation, of extended barrenness for hundreds of miles to the east. His eyelids were heavy. But at the same time he was aware of the quick brightness of Wicker's eyes. He sat there behind the wheel, fully rested, peak physical condition. Cameron knew what he was thinking, that constant gauging as to whether he could be quick enough to push the muzzle of the shotgun to one side before Cameron's finger could pull the trigger.

"I don't think you could make it," Cameron said. "But I'd welcome the try."

Wicker smiled, a tight pulling back of the lips from the teeth. "I know the feeling," he said. "To have it done with, one way or the other." He sucked the air in between his teeth. "So let's get to it. What do you want from me?"

"Information."

"About what?"

Words were an effort now. The sunlight was bright, the car warm. He rolled down the window slightly, felt the cool and reviving air. "Roffner intends to kill a lot of people at Brimstone in an experiment. You're going to tell me how. You're going to tell me when."

"I don't have any details, Cameron." Wicker kept his eyes straight ahead on the deserted road. "But even if what you say is dead accurate, information won't do you any good. Bloody things go on in this country. That's simply the way it is. Nobody really cares."

"I'm going to stop BRIMSTONE."

"No. I'll tell you what will happen, eventually," Wicker said evenly. "I don't have anything against you personally. I wouldn't enjoy killing you and I certainly don't want you to kill me. So I'll cooperate. But sooner or later, you're going to realize that there's nothing you can do. You'll give it a good try, do everything you can, but you can't really do anything."

Lulling words, eminently reasonable, leading him along a mental track. Probably true. Probably futile. He flipped his cigarette out the window. "The boy you killed last night was sixteen years old."

"I repeat," Wicker said spontaneously. "It was extremely unfortunate."

"A computer technician named Reeves. And my father."

"Reeves?" Wicker said. "I don't know about him. And I wasn't responsible for your father. But the boy, well, I do have to take responsibility there."

A quick repentance, an immediate *mea culpa*. And for one brief instant, Cameron almost gave in to the urge to pull the trigger, splattering Wicker against the side of the car, ending the words, that goddamned manipulative flow. But then he saw the road sign. U.S. GOVERNMENT MILITARY ORDNANCE REHABILITATION CENTER. 1/2 MILE. And at the same moment he saw the craggy peak rising ahead and to the right. He told Wicker to turn off ahead. He was filled with a sense of *déjà vu* as he glimpsed the prison on the slope, the white walls gleaming in the sunlight, and next to the highway the drowsing town, shade trees along the streets.

The exact pattern, the fake Russian town on the computer. This was the place, entered into the DIA computer to allow all the data for the test to be collected covertly, all here. A main street ran from the highway up to the prison itself and beyond, into the Atomic Energy Commission test range. Suddenly everything fell into place, the shielding devices which had been built into the prison in the first place, the military data on the map, the concentric rings marking a damage level away from the prison itself, the projected road blocks, the estimated casualty figures. A nuclear explosion was going to happen here. People instead of sheep and goats.

They drove past a nursing home, a low adobe building back from the main street. Cameron could see a row of elderly people in wheelchairs on the terrace, taking the sun. Wicker slowed the car.

"Where do you want me to go?" he said.

"Straight ahead. A newspaper office. A town hall."

The car crept past an Exxon station where a young attendant sat in a wooden chair, reading a magazine. Cameron saw the telephone booth next to the street, thought of the call from Major Shaw. Another trap certainly with information as bait. The car moved on. A general store, a convenience store, a tavern, but there was no newspaper, no town hall, no post office. The settlement was undoubtedly too small, unincorporated, getting its services from the prison administration.

Cameron saw the sprawl of side streets, small houses, mobile homes. An elderly man wearing a green eyeshade was adjusting a water sprinkler on a struggling lawn.

"What kind of nuclear device are they going to detonate here?" Cameron said.

"A nuclear bomb?" Wicker said, startled, skeptical. "Not likely." His fingers drummed against the plastic circle of the steering wheel. "That wouldn't make any sense at all. They might run some minor experiment at the prison, but they could never get away with anything like a nuclear explosion."

It was nonsense to discuss anything with Wicker

who would simply mirror his own doubts, amplify them. He stirred, shifted the shotgun on his lap. It was growing increasingly heavy. One step at a time and he would have to cover himself for Grotta would have made it back to Las Vegas and Wicker's men could already be on the way. He was too vulnerable, one tired and desperate man armed with a shotgun in his hands and in his pocket the automatic he had taken from Wicker at the training center. They could take him like a bird in a net, make him disappear without a trace and only Connie would be left behind to ask questions.

He had seen enough. He told Wicker to drive back toward the highway, then directed him south. Cameron turned on the car radio, found an FM news station, listened fitfully for a few moments, and then clicked it off. A military convoy was approaching on the highway, three trucks led by a jeep carrying a Captain wearing fatigues and sunglasses, lolling back against the passenger seat.

Soldiers. In his imagination, Cameron could see the jeep make a sudden swerve across the highway to block the car, the trucks screeching to a halt to disgorge troops, and his hand tightened involuntarily on the shotgun. In that moment he knew that if they cornered him, he would kill Wicker first, before he took any other action. But the jeep did not veer from its course down the highway. It continued straight ahead, the trucks following at spaced intervals with another jeep bringing up the rear.

"It could have been them," Wicker said. "I don't blame you for being nervous."

Cameron said nothing. The sun was beginning to go down and the peaks to the west were casting deep shadows across the highway. Another night, and he would have trouble getting through this one. Trouble concentrating. Trouble remembering exactly what it was he had to do. He saw the sign ahead, faded, weatherbeaten. LAS VEGAS RANCH-ETTES. 5 BEAUTIFUL ACRES. $1495 AND UP. TODAY IS THE FIRST DAY OF THE REST OF YOUR—but the last word was sandblasted away, illegible. He could see the crumbling brick columns that marked the entrance to the land development.

"Turn in here," he said. Wicker responded immediately, following a graveled road which led past the concrete foundations of a sales office which had either burned down or been carted away. And beyond it was a grid of bulldozed streets, the metal signs still identifying them. CASINO LANE. EASY STREET. THUNDERBIRD DRIVE. No houses, no people, nothing but desert. Wicker slowed the car, looked to Cameron for instructions.

"Go up to the end of the graveled road, then stop."

When Wicker killed the engine, the silence of the desert was overwhelming. Wicker sighed. "What time is it, Cameron?"

"Six-thirty," Cameron said. "Get out of the car."

Wicker took a deep breath. When he was out of the car he stretched, as if his legs were stiff, then looked up at the sky which was already beginning to darken in the east.

"Tell me what they are going to test in that prison," Cameron said. "When?"

"I don't know."

Cameron kept the shotgun leveled at his stomach. "Take off your other shoe."

Wicker shrugged. He pulled the shoestring on his right shoe, removed it.

"You're going for a run," Cameron said. "Down the graveled road to the street sign and back again." He gestured with the shotgun and for a moment it seemed that Wicker was not going to respond. There was no show of resistance, just a pause as if Wicker were killing time before he turned and began to run. His feet sloughed through the gravel and when he reached the street sign he turned and ran back. He stopped a few feet away, breathing heavily, his face flushed, and at first Cameron thought the gravel had had no effect. But then he saw Wicker's feet, the socks shredded, bloody. Jesus, the man was either impervious to pain or else he fed on it.

"I'm ready to trade," Wicker said, catching his breath. "They're going to test a cruise missile armed with a neutron warhead on the AEC range. It's supposed to be a regular test but something will go wrong and the goddamned thing will go off over the prison."

"Go on."

Wicker shrugged. "That's enough for a cigarette."

Cameron moved the shotgun to one side, pulled the trigger. The blast of pellets screamed off the gravel, kicked up dust. Wicker jumped reflexively but he did not flinch. His face was set. "We're pretty close to the same point, Cameron," he said. "You're willing to die rather than be pushed any farther. So am I."

"One cigarette," Cameron said.

Wicker's face came into sharp relief with the flame of the lighter. He inhaled the smoke with relish, held it in his lungs, then blew it out. "I feel the pain, by the way," he said casually. "I could run another five miles on gravel like this. I can go about sixty hours without any noticeable fall in my energy level." The cigarette coal glowed as he inhaled again. "You're really pretty good at this, you know, for an amateur. Only twice during the day did I have a chance of taking that shotgun away from you. And then the odds were fifty-fifty."

"You've used up your time," Cameron said.

Wicker nodded, took another drag on the cigarette. He held his left hand straight out, palm up. He ground the cigarette out against his palm. A hiss. The smell of scorched flesh. "You've used up yours," he said. "Right about now, that military convoy going north when we passed it will be setting up a roadblock five kilometers the other side of Brimstone. And another will have blocked off traffic a few miles south of here. So you're pretty well sealed in."

The darkness was deepening. Only a glow remained in the west, over a range of mountains. "Then the test is tomorrow," Cameron said.

"First thing in the morning."

"It won't take place."

"There you go," Wicker said softly. "You're fighting the problem. It *will* take place. Now whether that's good or bad is beside the point. And you've had a hell of a good run at it. You'll get credit for that. And I'll get even more credit for bringing you back. You've been a good adversary. You won't lose any face by deciding to deal with me at this point."

Very dark now, everything indistinct, only the
white of Wicker's shirt was plainly visible. In that
moment, everything was suspended, frozen, and
then a rustle of movement from Wicker, a blur, a
whisper of motion and Cameron pulled the
trigger. The shotgun kicked and the blast seemed
to catch Wicker dead center, yet he spun around,
began to run as if he were untouched, kicking at
the gravel for perhaps ten yards before he pitched
forward and went down. Cameron stood stock-
still, listening to the barrage of echoes from off in
the distance. He walked around the car, slowly,
reached in through the open window, clicked on
the lights.

Wicker lay sprawled on his back, arms outflung,
something metallic glinting in his right hand. His
left leg was jerking slightly, convulsively, but he
was dead. Cameron approached him, found it difficult to breathe. Wicker's chest had been per-
forated, torn away. His eyes glinted dully. There
was a pistol in the half-opened fingers of his right
hand, small, chrome. Illogically, Cameron was
tempted to search him, fascinated by the
mechanics of concealment, the man's profession-
alism. Where had he hidden that pistol? Where
had he kept it stashed? No matter. Wicker had
been off by a split second, beaten by his own sense
of superiority.

Cameron took a deep breath, adrenaline
pumping. He had killed a man. A sense of
imminent punishment washed over him, archaic,
the presence of a scowling and displeased God
who would strike him down. He ran back to the
car, shut off the lights, comforted by the fact that

he could no longer see the body. He waited, listening, expecting to hear voices in the darkness, far-off commands as the troops came over the hill, attracted by the gunshots. But there was nothing, no traffic on the highway. He threw the shotgun away, heard it hit the rocks. Then he sat down in the car.

He calmed. If there was a God, He would see the balance here. He turned the car around in the darkness before he clicked on the lights. He drove back toward Brimstone.

He had the information now, a description of the event, a timetable, hard facts, and he would call the news station in Las Vegas, no, a television station, perhaps both, and he would spread the word, make it impossible for the newsmen not to check this out. The evidence would be everywhere, the proof, the operation in full swing and Roffner would certainly abort it in the glare of that kind of publicity. Monstrous.

He found the Exxon station closed, a floodlight illuminating the telephone booth. He spread his change on the shelf again, picked up the telephone, put in his money. There was no sound. He jiggled the hook, got his money back. Dead. He cursed his ill fortune, scooped up his change, and drove down the street until he spotted the tavern and went inside. A handful of people, working men, a juke box, a clanging pinball machine, and a heavy man standing behind the bar.

"What will it be?" the bartender said.

"I need a telephone."

"We have one but it's out of order," the bartender said. "They let us know it'll be out until tomorrow sometime. They're working on the lines."

Cameron blinked. Of course, the lines would be shut down. Nothing in or out. He wondered if the bartender could see from his face that he had just killed a man. No. Such things did not show. "I'll have a bourbon and water," he said.

His left arm was trembling again. When he was served, he sipped the drink, wondering what would happen if he told the bartender what was going to happen here tomorrow. The man would hear him out, certainly, all the while continuing to swab the polished wood with a damp cloth. He would listen but he certainly would not believe, because this was a place for a venting of personal griefs and stories that made no sense.

He finished the drink, left the money on the counter, went to the men's room. He splashed cold water on his face, examined himself in the mirror. He saw the strain, the tight mouth, the tiredness in the eyes. He took a series of deep breaths, then combed his hair.

Shaw, he thought. An army officer unknown to him. Yet Shaw had risked himself by revealing Roffner's name. It was possible he was another Reeves, another man fed up with the system. He would have to check it out.

He went out into the street and drove the car back to the service station, then drove south to the edge of town, near a trailer park where his parked car would not call attention to itself. He turned off the lights, settled back in the seat to wait.

He slept.

He jerked awake, a dog barking someplace down the block. The luminous hands of his watch were blurred, refused to give him the time until he examined them in the flame of his lighter. Nine-twenty. Twenty minutes after nine.

God, he thought, and he had not been to church since the day he married Annie, and yet now the old superstitions of childhood were rising in him again. No God, no order in what was happening. If the dog had not jarred him awake, he would have slept the night. Coincidence. Nothing more.

Very well, whatever the reason, he had slept, he would accept it. He would scout the gas station and make certain that Shaw either had not come or was no longer there.

He started the car, the old sense of wariness returning. Shaw might indeed be there, but not alone, and he should have stayed awake so he could check the telephone booth long before the time arranged for the meeting. He did not drive directly to the service station but instead drove a pattern through the streets around it. If there were men staked out, he did not see them. He drove past houses with the square pictures of the television sets casting a bluish light over darkened rooms. He saw two couples playing cards in the living room of a small house. He passed an old man walking his dog, some teen-agers sitting on a porch despite the chill of the evening. He saw nothing that alarmed him.

And finally he drove down the main street, praying that there would be no car parked at the service station, no man standing near the telephone booth. But there was. A dark Buick. A man in a uniform standing in the pale wash of the pole light, a tall, spare man who shifted from foot to foot while he waited.

Not fair, Cameron thought as he drove past, turned the corner, parked in the shadows. He would now have to go through it again with no plan in mind, nothing to tie to. He took the pistol out of his pocket, clicked out the magazine and closed it again, too tired to remember the number of shells, only knowing that it was loaded.

This time around the block he pulled the car into the service station, sat with the motor running and the pistol in his lap while the Major turned, his leonine face peering through the darkness. He sauntered toward Cameron's car, cautiously.

"Cameron?" he said, tentatively. He had been drinking. Cameron could smell his breath. Not drunk, no, two or three drinks. There would be no men out there in the darkness. The Major would not be drinking if this was to be an ambush.

"Get into the car, Major," Cameron said.

Shaw opened the door on the passenger side, saw the pistol and glanced away. His voice was disdainful, his words slightly slurred. "There's no need for that," he said. "I'm not armed. I came alone. Where's Wicker?"

"Dead," Cameron said.

Shaw nodded, accepting. He cleared his throat. "I'm on your side in this, Cameron."

"I'm beyond the bullshit, Major."

"You didn't get the computer map of the town by accident when you were running your audit," Shaw said. "I fed it to you. It's true." He took the half pint from his pocket, uncapped it, drank. "It was possible you had the Nixon tape. So I decided to give you the map in the hope you could put two and two together. It was too much to expect that you would. The information was too vague."

"Major Shaw," Cameron said. "If you knew BRIMSTONE was going to happen and you had all the facts, why in the hell didn't you stop it on your own?"

Shaw took another drink and began to talk in a low monotone. He had been in the army long enough to have witnessed the birth and death of dozens of schemes, outlandish operations, new weapons systems, everything from death rays to lethal Frisbees. The computer at Mt. Weather spewed them out by the hundreds. Generally, they were so unrealistic that they collapsed of their own weight.

When this one had not, Shaw sent a letter to a Senator, advising him of a potential scandal involving the prison, thinking that once the Senate had an investigation under way, Roffner would have no choice but to call off the test. Shaw shrugged. "It didn't do any good," he said. "The Senator just used the information for political leverage."

"So what in the hell are you doing here?" Cameron said. "Do you know a way to stop BRIMSTONE now?"

"Grotesque," the Major said, peering at the bottle in the darkness. "I know how savage this is, what a bloody business it's going to be. Yet there's a part of me that's excited by the test, a part of me that wants to see the goddamned thing go off, just to see if it works." He paused. "I owed this to you. I'm not here to stop BRIMSTONE. I got you involved so the least I can do is to get you out of it."

"No," Cameron said. "You're not going to get me *out* of anything. You're going to get me *in*."

"In?"

"You're right at the center of this project. The cruise missile has to be launched from somewhere. There has to be a range control, computers, a whole system. And somewhere along the line, that sytem has to be vulnerable."

"I can't do that. I'm professional army. No, I won't do it."

"The hell you won't," Cameron said. "I've got absolutely nothing left to lose, Major. I've killed a government agent and there are enough charges against me to see me hanged or playing paddleball in some federal penitentiary for the next ten years. As long as there's the slightest chance, I'll take it. Now, I want answers to questions."

The Major did not resist. He went through the whole thing from the beginning, his voice flat, unemotional. The Department of Defense had entered into a joint project with the Law Enforcement Assistance Administration, an agency which in the early seventies had had so much money it could not spend it all. The project called for the construction of a maximum security prison at the edge of the Atomic Energy Commission test range in which felons with life sentences would be trained in the repair and maintenance of military equipment.

The prison was constructed of experimental materials, all under the name of security, with certain sections lead lined, others having walls of concrete three feet thick, all structures laced with radiation-detection equipment, a natural precaution since the prison was being built next to a nuclear range and underground tests were still being considered. The LEAA people knew nothing of the real plan, of course.

"How many people know what's really going to happen?" Cameron said, interrupting.

"I don't know."

"How's the accident going to take place?"

"A systems test will go wrong," Shaw said, matter-of-factly. The vehicle here was a cruise missile, he went on, twenty-eight feet long, propelled by a jet turbofan, with stubby wings that popped out after launch, really a small pilotless aircraft, an intelligent machine designed to launch from a ramp with solid rocket fuel until it was airborne and the engine took over. It would roar along no more than 500 feet above the ground with a velocity close to the speed of sound, a veritable bullet of a missile designed to fly below enemy radar.

As part of a continual training exercise at Nellis Air Force Base, a squadron of F-14 fighter jets would take off the moment the cruise missile was launched, to see if they could intercept it. The interceptors would have pilots, the cruise missile would be guided by TERCOM—terrain contour matching—and the electronic eye of the missile would peer down at ground features to match against the map carried on an on-board computer and the route for which it had been programmed.

"They'll never catch it," Shaw said. "They probably won't even spot it. I've seen these babies work. If you launched from Flagstaff, Arizona, you could program the missile to follow Interstate 40 into Gallup, New Mexico, then turn south and west and follow the highway through the Salt Creek Canyon and hit a particular house in Phoenix, Arizona."

"The accident," Cameron said impatiently, fascinated despite himself.

This vehicle test was not designed for distance, Shaw went on. This missile would be programmed to follow an intricate course over the range, looping back upon itself, following canyons, skimming mountain passes, giving the F-14 jets a good workout. The official test called for the missile to target at the end of the run on a mock group of Russian tanks in the eastern part of the range, where the air force had erected bleachers for the media and selected guests to watch the missile crash into the target area.

"But it will be diverted," Cameron said.

"Yes." Shaw took another drink. "Toward the end of the run it will veer off course and lock onto the prison."

When the electronic eye spotted the prison, the electronic command would be given and this supposedly unarmed neutron bomb would explode, an intense and shattering fireball with the force of a thousand tons of TNT. The area immediately below the blast would be pulverized, a deadly circle with a diameter of 1,200 feet. The men in this area, unless they had proper shelter, would be killed instantly.

But the neutron bomb would have the enhanced radiation of a ten-kiloton hydrogen bomb, a radiation which would spread to a radius of perhaps a mile, and it was this enlarged circle the test was designed to investigate. The prison had been built with shielding devices to offer varying degrees of protection and the test would determine which defenses were effective against neutrons and which were not.

Cameron was filled with the horror of the situation. In his mind's eye, he saw that row of old people on the terrace in the sun, facing the east when the fireball went off, irradiated with lethal particles of energy they could not see. And all around him, in the houses and the trailers, in the few cars on the street, were people who by this time tomorrow night would be dead or condemned to die.

"Jesus Christ," Cameron said. "And what about the rest of these people? Where's their defense?"

Shaw shook his head. "They don't have any."

Cameron rubbed his right hand along his left arm. Despite the night chill, he was sweating. "How much have you had to drink, Major?"

"At this moment I would like to be very drunk," Shaw said. "But the liquor doesn't have any effect on me tonight. A little loss of coordination, maybe. But I'm not drunk."

"Can you get me onto the test site?"

"Possible," Shaw said. "We have a swarm of civilians coming in and I'm in charge of identification. I can get you in. But I'm not sure I can get you out if anything goes wrong."

"We'll take it one step at a time."

"We had better take my car," Shaw said. "Security is familiar with it."

Cameron pulled his car onto one of the spaces near the telephone booth, then took great care in locking it before he realized that in all probability he would not be seeing this car again. He transferred to Shaw's Buick and Shaw began to drive on the road which flanked the prison grounds up the slope.

The questioning began again. "How's the cruise

missile programmed?" Cameron said.

"The on-board computer has been programmed to the target of the Russian tanks," Shaw said. "Sometime before launch, it will be reprogrammed from a computer in Washington."

"Which computer?"

"I don't know."

"How will the reprogramming take place?"

"Teleprocessing. Over the telephone lines."

"Are they vulnerable?"

"No. It's microwave relay. Strong backup systems."

"How can you tell if the reprogramming has taken place?" Cameron said.

"You can't," Shaw said. "All of the monitoring checks at the test site will show up routine."

He fell into silence as they passed the main gate of the prison where a procession of jeeps and army trucks was moving into the compound. "That's the radiation monitoring team," Shaw said. "They've been moving into the prison at regular intervals for the past five years, even when there's nothing to monitor, just to activate the measuring devices. Establishing a routine. All set up for years, just for this one time."

"When will they move out?"

"Long before the explosion. The monitoring will be remote."

"There has to be a simpler way out of this. What happens if you alert everybody at the test range to the whole goddamned business?"

"I've considered that," Shaw said. "But I don't know who already knows the truth and who doesn't. And if I could reach the people who don't know, my guess is that they would approve what's going to happen, consider it a fine idea. This is a military outfit here, after all, dedicated to any new weapons that will make the next war easier to win."

"Then we'll have to concentrate on the computer."

The car followed a winding road around the north side of the granite mountain, past the first red-and-white signs identifying the boundary of the AEC nuclear test range and warning any trespassers that this was a restricted area. Shaw pulled the car onto the shoulder of the road. "What kind of identification do you have on you?"

"A GAO card, driver's license, credit cards." He shook his head. "It won't do. It's possible somebody would recognize the name."

"A fifty-fifty chance," Shaw said.

Wicker, Cameron thought. He checked the inner pocket of his jacket and there was Wicker's identification card Cameron had taken from him in the bar in Missouri. He turned on the dash light, examined the plasticized card, the picture of Wicker's face, not a good likeness, somehow distorted by the flash, no expression at all on the face. Cameron handed the card to Shaw who glanced at the picture and then at Cameron's face.

"We'll go with this," Shaw said. "Maybe you'll pass. They may not ask for confirmation at all but we have to be ready in case they do." He fished his attache case from the back seat, opened it, removed a card and a badge with a blank name space. He lettered Wicker's name on the card, slipped it into the plastic holder on the badge. "Pin this on," he said to Cameron while he filled out an official-looking form, talking while he worked.

"You can still back away from this, you know," he said. "I can get you into Vegas. You can be out of this whole mess by dawn. There are flights out of Vegas for anyplace you can think of. My preference would be Mexico City."

"Are you having second thoughts?"

"A hell of a lot of them," Shaw said. "Death frightens me, especially the possibility of my own. I know what's gone into the planning of this test, Cameron. I know it can't be stopped." He handed Cameron the form. "Sign Wicker's name."

Cameron took the pen and signed. "I'll offer you the same chance you offered me," he said. "You can get out of the car, invent any cover story you like and I'll confirm it."

Shaw thought it over, shook his head. "You wouldn't get ten miles without me. I'll see it through."

Cameron said nothing. Shaw shifted into gear. The car moved on down the road.

Chapter Eleven

"My, God, my God," Ingrid was saying into his ear, gasps of words, some Norwegian, Roffner supposed, and he controlled her with the giant erection planted deep within her. He made her squirm, moving in long, hard, solid strokes while her legs wrapped around his back and her head moved from side to side, that finespun golden hair in disarray, eyes half lidded, mouth slack, puffy from kissing, seeking his mouth with a slippery desperation.

He continued to stir inside of her, a regular rhythm. He knew she had come up here with him in a posture of desire, letting her long black gown slide away in a pretense of passion because she anticipated his weakness and was playing the seductress, even while she kissed him and caressed him into tumescence with soft fingers and a skillful mouth, making her white body available to him.

God, the presumption. She was in her mid-twenties at most and yet she thought he could not see through her, know what she was doing. She could not know the pride he had in himself as a cocksman. He was charged with the excitement of the test in the morning and he would have to be on top of things so that nothing slipped away from him. He would not begin this adventure by allowing her deception to slip past him.

She was moaning now, a rasping thread of breath through the arched neck. Her hands pressed frantically on the small of his back as if to increase his desire and force him to spend himself, the moist softness between her legs grinding against him until he could feel the underlying hardness of her pelvic bone. He began to pull back ever so slightly, each thrust shallower, teasing her, bringing her after him. For that was the proof. If she was faking it, the depth would not matter to her, but as he drew back, she clamored after him, kissing his ear, whispering endearing sexual words, entreaties and commands.

Now he knew he had her, that he had compelled her past herself. He could smell her, a musky odor which would not be faked. He withdrew his penis all the way, held there a long provoking moment and then, signaling no warning, slid into her with all the strength he had. He felt the first convulsive shudder run through her and he withdrew and plunged again, increasing the pace until her body was shaking beneath him, trembling uncontrollably as he penetrated her again and again.

Her legs left his back, spreading as wide as they could. Her arms went around his neck, gluing his mouth to hers, her tongue flicking against his. Beyond control. Caught up. And quite suddenly, her head jerked back against the pillow and she gave a wild moan. He felt the contractions against his penis, a beginning flutter followed by a long, hard series of spasms which seemed to last for minutes.

Then he felt her relax, go limp.

The telephone rang.

He withdrew expertly, raising himself to his knees. He snatched up the telephone, sat cross-legged on the bed. It was Dearborn on the line.

"Sorry to disturb you, General," he said. "But I couldn't reach Major Shaw."

"Shaw's up at the test site. What do you have?"

"Nothing so far. I have the feeling that Cameron drove on north, possibly to Reno. We're covering the area from Brimstone north."

"Get with it. I expect results."

"You'll have them," Dearborn said. "I also intend to ship Wicker's ass back to Washington unless he's operating under direct orders from you."

"He's not," Roffner said. "Do it. When you have the chance, get him out of here." He replaced the telephone. Ingrid was still lying with her legs spread, wide open to him, no deviousness there. She put her hand on his subsiding erection.

"I want you to come inside me," she said. "It will relax you."

"I don't want to be relaxed," he said. "As an intelligence gatherer you should know that. You're a hell of a woman but a lousy agent."

"You know what I do then?" she said. "It's such a silly business, really. The Swedish government gives me money for gossip sometimes, and they take it all so seriously. But I have learned nothing from you that they would be interested in."

"The hell you haven't," he said with a smile. He patted her flank and stood up. "You've passed the word that I'm conducting a weapons test and they are curious as hell."

"No, I—"

"It's not worth denying," he said. "I don't mind.
It serves us both. And tomorrow I'll give you some
information that should bring you a nice price.
The Swedes will leak it to the Russians who will
have no choice except to believe it. So I'll count on
you to pass the word. I want you to stay here, in
the hotel. I'll see you tomorrow, early afternoon."

"You really can't stay any longer?"

"No."

He went into the bathroom, adjusted the nozzle
spray on the shower almost to the point of steam,
then stepped into it, his mind already leaving the
girl and turning to Shaw and Cameron. It was
curious that Shaw had not checked in, but he was
not concerned. For the project had developed its
own momentum, sufficient to carry it to fruition.
The peripheral events were unimportant.

He covered himself with lather and inhaled the
steam, feeling marvelously tuned to his senses.

2

He dozed in the predawn darkness, came awake
when he realized the car was slowing. A light army
truck had appeared as if from nowhere on the
road behind them, a red light flashing. His hand
closed around the pistol on his lap.

"Easy, keep it easy," Shaw said as he brought
the car to a halt. The truck stopped behind them
and Cameron saw four men silhouetted in the
glare of the headlights, four soldiers with black
helmet liners and automatic weapons. He pulled
Shaw's attache case onto his lap, fully awake now,
the pistol at ready.

As one soldier approached his window, Shaw's personality began to change, any visible doubt suppressed, any strain disappearing. The beam of the flashlight illuminated his face; Cameron could not see the features of the soldier at the window but the voice was young, hard.

"Good morning, Major," the soldier said. "May I see your identification, please?"

Shaw handed him the papers. "Has General Roffner arrived yet?"

"No, sir." The flashlight turned to the papers, then the light came through the window. Cameron blinked, momentarily blinded.

"What is your name, sir?"

Cameron tapped the identification badge. "Wicker. I'm with DOD."

"Yes, sir," the soldier said. He looked to Shaw. "We'll radio your clearance into the blockhouse, sir. You can drive on."

The soldier walked back to the truck and Cameron could see it turning around, heading back down the road as the car moved on.

His heart was pounding again now that the danger had passed. He felt light-headed, slightly dizzy.

The car topped a slight rise and the gate was immediately ahead of them, the large warning signs, the coils of barbed wire atop a chain-link fence, electrified. The barrier was up and the guard beckoned them through toward the low concrete building in the distance, washed by floodlights.

And off in the distance, Cameron saw the cruise missile itself, resting in a trough-like ramp, the anodized aluminum skin shining under the work-lights. His first thought was how innocuous it seemed, how small, a shark-like nose swept back to an air intake scoop atop the fuselage, lines and cables snaking from it across the desert to the building.

"It's deceptive," Shaw said, following Cameron's gaze. "Elegantly simple on the outside, but internally one of the most sophisticated weapons in the world."

"Has the neutron device been armed yet?"

"Yes," Shaw said. "We'd better get our signals straight. This place is full of equipment and people, most of them team players devoted to one small section of the test. They're also pretty damned perceptive about what's happening in other sectors. So you follow my lead. We're here to make a final check of the programmed guidance system and that's all."

"I understand." Cameron climbed out of the car and followed Shaw into the building, the pistol back in his pocket. A guard with an automatic weapon stood inside the door. He glanced at their badges, passed them through another room where they received hard hats, and finally they were in a long corridor. Cameron followed Shaw, looking through open doors into rooms full of electronic equipment and technicians and mounted television screens all carrying the same image— the missile and the ramp. Finally, they entered a large room with a window facing the missile itself and a battery of computer terminals and display screens. A cluster of civilians stood in one area, watching rolls of numbers scrolling onto the CRT in front of them. Shaw nodded to them and led the way to a computer terminal at the far side of the

room. He put down his attache case, sat down at
the keyboard.

"The next war will be fought by electrical engineers," he said. He checked his watch. "The new
program from Washington will have been fed in
by now. Where do you want to begin?"

"I don't know. Can you give me a display of the
programmed flight path?"

"Yes." Shaw pressed some keys and the large
screen was suddenly filled with a contour map
and the hard and twisting line which represented
the missile's flight path. For show only, Cameron
realized.

An enlisted man brought coffee and Cameron
listened to Shaw talking with him, the Major's
tone rather remote now as if confronted with the
actuality of the missile and the impossibility of
the task ahead, he had withdrawn to a safer
position, non-involved. Cameron's left hand was
hurting him. His fingers were sweating. He dried
them with a handkerchief. "We sure as hell can't
handle the master program," he said. "So we'll
attack the subroutines. I'm going to need names,
functions. Which subroutine handles the arming
of the neutron warhead, the guidance?"

"I don't know," Shaw said. "There's a
MONITOR subroutine. I heard some technicians
discuss it."

Cameron drank his coffee, closed his eyes,
trying to think, having to force the image of the
dead Wicker out of his mind. The program would
have to allow for either conventional or neutron
detonation. If for any reason it did not hit the
original target, passed it by, the electronic relays
would have to disarm the neutron warhead. It was

logical to assume that the instructions would be contained in MONITOR but whether they were or not he would have to go with it. It was all he had.

He began the tedious routine of punching the keys, calling for a display of the subroutine on the screen, afraid at first that the Washington experts had protected it. The computer responded. The screen filled with the subroutine and his heart sank. The program was in machine language, long rows of data in hexadecimal, combinations of numerals and alphabetic characters, the working language of the computer itself.

"I have to check in," Shaw said absently. "It's routine procedure." He picked up a telephone mounted on the wall. Cameron could not see his face as he talked. Was he changing his mind, getting out from under, calling security to let them know Cameron was here? Cameron's breathing became shallow, forced. He felt a slight pain in the middle of his chest. He closed his eyes, taking deep breaths. The paranoia began to wane. If Shaw was indeed calling for help, there was nothing Cameron could do about it.

But he was not powerless. He forced himself to concentrate on the one area he could control, the rows of numbers and letters on the screen. He could interpret certain parts of the machine language in the subroutine and at the very end of it he saw the instruction, GOTO MPZ. It was like having a road map with no reference points at all, and where MPZ was or what it represented, he did not know.

It seemed logical to assume, however, that the whole center of the missile's control system lay in this subroutine. He punched the terminal keyboard into the edit mode, which would allow him to change the program, and then he inserted the GOTO MPZ instruction toward the beginning of the subroutine. He could be sure of nothing. It was possible that the moment he had shifted the terminal into "edit" Washington had been signaled and even now would be calling the test site to report the violation of computer security.

He did not care. He sat back, trying to make sense of the other parts of the subroutine. He was aware that Shaw had finished his telephone conversation and was frowning at the computer's display screen. Cameron looked at him thoughtfully, reluctant to press the key which would enter the changed program into the missile's on-board computer.

"I've reshuffled the sequence," he said to Shaw. "What do you think?"

"What do you intend it to do?"

"Throw the missile off course," Cameron said. "I want the goddamned thing to lose its direction somewhere out over the range, to fly into a canyon wall, to explode against a mountain. So the question is, will these changes accomplish that?"

"We're going to have to chance it," Shaw said quietly. "We're running out of time."

Cameron nodded. They were out of alternatives. "All right," he said. "We'll give it a try."

He reached out and pressed the button to enter the changed program into the missile's computer.

3

Riding through the brilliant sunshine of a cloudless, calm dawn, Roffner went through the checklist one final time, finding nothing awry, everything on schedule. He tapped his driver on the shoulder.

"Captain Spencer, see if you can get Colonel Dearborn for me."

"Yes, sir," Spencer said. He picked up the mobile telephone while Roffner opened the cold chest in the rear seat, the perquisites of power, of small things never overlooked. He poured a chilled glass half full of milk and thought of Ingrid, smooth-skinned, young. There were disadvantages to young women because they were reference points against which he measured his own mortality, and as he slipped into old age, she would be coming into her prime.

The scientific life was better. It was impersonal, ageless, and his contribution to weaponry would be something on which other men could build. He had received no credit for the gas tests in the New York City subways—indeed that had been mishandled by the investigators, subverted, when all that he had done was to demonstrate to the people of Manhattan how vulnerable they were to an enemy attack. But this test was his; he owned it, had created it, and all the physicists and hardware people had merely contributed to his vision. There was something solid about that thought.

"I have Colonel Dearborn, sir," Spencer said.

Roffner took the telephone. "I've been waiting for a report from you, Colonel."

Dearborn's voice was flat, expressionless. "We've found Wicker's body approximately three miles south of the prison. It appears he was killed by a shotgun blast, close range. He was armed with a small chrome pistol, unfired, probably a reserve pistol. It's my opinion, sir, and only that, that he tried to take Cameron and Cameron shot him. Our team found Wicker so we removed all identification from his body." Dearborn paused, and then, when he got no response: "Are you still there, General? Do we still have a connection?"

"Where in the hell is Cameron and what is he doing?" Roffner said in a sudden release of anger he did not know he had. "Cameron's our primary concern now. He had a car. Where is it?"

"We found it parked at a gas station in Brimestone."

"Did you alert the roadblocks?"

"Yes, sir. No traffic in or out. We think he's in the town."

Roffner calmed himself deliberately, sipped the milk to soothe his burning stomach. There was no percentage in railing against Dearborn who would simply become defensive as a result and move with even greater caution. "What steps are you taking to make certain?"

"It's a hundred miles or better from Brimstone to the test site," Dearborn said. "If he chose to go that direction, then he's either on foot, in which case we'll spot him, or he caught a ride with military traffic. If he managed that, our security patrols will pick him up."

"I want him located," Roffner said.

"I assure you he will be."

"Now, what's your ETA on the Senator's arrival?"

"I'll check." Roffner could hear the rustle of papers. "We have an estimated arrival time of 0830," Dearborn said.

"See that any formalities at Nellis are cut short.

I want him at the test range by 0845."

"Yes, sir. We'll manage that."

"When you locate Cameron, let me know."

"Yes, sir."

When they reached the test site, Roffner did not stop at the command post but instead directed the Captain to drive him to the target site, six miles east. The bleachers had been erected, the folding chairs were being put in place. The air boomed with the loudspeaker tests, snatches of military music. On the flat, less than a thousand feet from the bleachers, the military technicians were completing the wiring of the mock Russian tanks which looked incredibly real and which, on cue, at the proper moment, would erupt with smoke to simulate the effect of an explosion. This was to have been the climax, that big bang of a finish, military show biz, feeding the public desire for spectacular explosions, fire, smoke. It seemed a waste that so much effort would be expended toward an effect which would never happen.

Roffner left the car, put on his sunglasses, chatted with one of the enlisted men lining up the chairs. But Roffner's mind was not involved in the brief conversation; instead, his nose was testing the air—clean, cool, dry—and his eyes were scanning the sky, the wisps of high cirrus clouds. One could sense the right conditions for a test. He knew in his bones that everything would work perfectly today.

He had his driver take him back to the command building where Major Shaw was waiting for him, clipboard in hand. He would have to remind Shaw to shave before the morning briefing. The lean jaw was dark and stubbled. And the Major's eyes were hollowed, dark circles.

"Did you hear about Wicker?" Roffner said.

"Yes," Shaw said.

"Are all the television networks here?"

"Yes. CBS was late, but they checked in about forty-five minutes ago."

Roffner led the way into the media center, a large room equipped with microphones, a dais, television monitors for closed-circuit displays, banks of telephones. He knew many of the boys from the networks. There was a special fraternity of technicians and newscasters who covered the military and he shook hands with them all around, made jokes, noticed that they were set up for tape and film coverage only, nothing here to warrant live coverage. Good. That was the way it should be.

He retired to his private command post, a smaller room with multiple screens providing coverage of the checkpoints of the actual route of the missile. The one key screen, of course, displayed the view from the top of the peak just east of the prison and the remainder of the sets which covered the route between the prison and the bleachers were just window dressing.

He took the clipboard from Shaw and sat down, flipping the pages as Shaw went through the checklist, the systems check, weather, the guest roster, the arrangements lists, the final check of the monitoring equipment from the prison. Roffner was aware of the tons of data which would be accumulated during the next few days, without which the test would be worthless, no more important than the display out there on the desert the civilian observers were supposed to see destroyed.

"You look terrible, Major," Roffner said when the business of the lists was finished. "Did you get any sleep at all last night?"

"None to speak of."

"Let me have one of your cigarettes," Roffner said. He accepted the cigarette, leaned over to allow Shaw to light it for him. "Did you remember the hat for the Senator's grandson?"

"Yes," Shaw said, and he produced a cardboard box and removed from it a hard hat, wrapped in tissue paper. "There was some discussion about this, General, whether or not a ten-year-old boy would be too sophisticated to appreciate the first name stencilled on a hard hat when the crews use last names."

Roffner examined the hard hat, a bright orange which he supposed would be described as Day-Glo red, the letters R-O-B-B-Y stencilled in black.

"There was also discussion about whether this red is close enough to the Red Flag color. They're prepared to stencil another one with the boy's last name if you don't like this one."

"This will do fine," Roffner said. He sat back, his eyes stinging from the cigarette smoke. He observed Shaw's fatigue in the way he moved.

"This test is generating tremendous pressures," Roffner said. "But I think you'll find, when the smoke has cleared, that what we have done here makes sense." He checked his watch. "The Senator will be arriving shortly, but I'll take care of that. I want you to shave, find a way to relax for an hour or so. After the media briefing, you can join us in time for the launch."

"Thank you, sir."

Roffner took the hard hat and went back to the

car. He had Captain Spencer check the ETA of the
Senator's helicopter and found it right on time,
scheduled to land on the helipad near the test site.
By the time he reached the landing pad, he could
hear the chopping sound of the helicopter, the
percussive beating of the blades against the air,
and he left the car and looked for it. He located it
in the southern sky, coming in low, resembling a
hovering insect against the background of the
bare mountains.

He stood well back, watching the dust rise off
the concrete as the helicopter paused over it and
then settled perfectly, the pilot killing the engine
as a team of men in blue coveralls moved out to
open the door for the Senator. Looking at Livermore, Roffner envied his sense of family, something which the General, in his singlemindedness,
had never felt he could afford.

An ideal family, Roffner thought without
derision, Livermore distinguished in his dark-blue
business suit, his hair a silver mane, deboarding
first and then helping his wife, a lovely woman in
her fifties with soft-brown finespun hair and a
gracious smile, off the helicopter. And the grandson, tow-headed, a bright sparkling boy who
extended his hand to shake with Roffner when he
was introduced.

Roffner felt a momentary pang of regret that he
did not have a grandson like this one, not that he
knew of, and if he had progeny at all it was
through the bodies of a dozen half-forgotten
women scattered from Germany to Korea, certainly no continuation of his line as Robby was a
continuation of the Senator's.

He presented the boy with the hard hat and the

lad beamed with pure delight and fastened it onto his head. Roffner conducted them to the car, asking about the flight, aware that Livermore and his wife were relaxed, obviously enjoying themselves. He could see a side to the Senator he had not seen before, for in their last meeting Livermore had shown that he was a conniving son of a bitch who was out to dip his hand in the pork barrel at any cost. Yet here, with his wife, her hand resting on his leg in the car, there was no trace of his Washington personality.

"Robby here is interested in the cruise missile," Livermore said. "He's been looking for a model to put together."

"It's too new for that," Roffner said to the boy. "No models. But you'll have a chance to see it in action."

"What do I call a General?" Robby said. "Do I just call you 'General Roffner'?"

"That's fine," Roffner said with a smile.

"I've never met a General before," Robby said. "I shook hands with the President once, though."

"Then you've met my boss," Roffner said. He pointed through the window. "You'll be able to see the missile in a moment."

The car rounded a curve and there it was, gleaming so brightly silver in the sunlight it almost hurt the eyes to look at it directly.

"We'll attend a briefing in the command post, Senator, and after the launch, you will have plenty of time to get to the target site before it arrives."

They came to the command building and Roffner took them back to the monitoring room and summoned the missile's flight path onto a display screen. He allowed the accommodations staff time enough to get the media people and the visiting dignitaries into the main room, so that when he conducted the Senator and his family into the briefing, they were not entering so much as they were making an entrance. The cameramen were taking pictures, flashbulbs popping. A grand show, Roffner thought, a perfect illusion on a large scale, and there was nobody who did not already know the truth who would suspect it.

The briefing was given by a Colonel who could have been drawn from Special Services, an actor certainly, and as he talked the various display screens around the room began to fill with pictures. Roffner's stomach began to pain him again. It was the price he had to pay for compartmentalizing his thinking, for being able to sit here as a host while the greater part of his mind was back among the checklists.

The Colonel outlined what would happen, made it sound like a game in which the cruise missile would hurtle along a preset course at 500 miles an hour, a course unknown to the pilots of the F-14 jets whose task it was to locate the missile and engage it with rockets and missiles of their own. Except that here, of course, as the missile carried a dummy warhead, the pursuit jets were also unarmed and would destroy the missile by camera, on film which the referees would judge to score direct hits. The missile would run a tortuous course over the AEC range for a full half hour. At the end, with no interference or help from the ground, the cruise missile would find its way to the tank column where the observers here today would have the opportunity to witness an approximation of the missile's explosive effect.

During the presentation, Roffner was aware of the boy's mounting excitement at the films of the missile in action and the motion pictures of the jets which would be in pursuit. A simplified representation of war, yes, reduced to gamesmanship, all precisely orchestrated, and everybody in the room could relate to this, a multi-million-dollar game of hounds and hares.

He glanced at the clock mounted on the wall above the screens. Eleven minutes now to the moment of launch. When the briefing was over, Roffner introduced the Senator and his family to the Colonel who would take them out to view the launch. "You'll have to excuse me now," Roffner said to the Senator. "I have to go to work."

"You've put on an impressive display," Livermore said warmly. "I wish the whole country could be aware of the fine job your boys do."

"Perhaps they will," Roffner said. "I'll be joining you later. I've scheduled a luncheon at Nellis where you'll have an opportunity to meet my team."

"We'll all look forward to that," the Senator said.

Roffner went to meet Shaw at the door. "Did you get any rest, Major?"

"Yes. Thank you, sir."

"We're going to have a full day."

"Yes, sir."

Captain Spencer motioned Roffner to the side of the room, a telephone with a blinking light. "It's General Forbes for you, sir."

Roffner took it, forcing a lightness which he did not feel. Whenever there was a test such as this, there were always bets between commanders.

Forbes was a football fan. He looked on his inter-
ceptors as members of his own particular varsity.
"You calling to back out of the bet, Ralph?"
Roffner said.

"Au contraire," Forbes said. "We think we can
intercept your missile in the first ten minutes of
flight. My boys are confident enough they want to
up the bet another two hundred and fifty dollars."

"You have it," Roffner said. "It's a shame to
take your hard-earned money."

"We'll see."

He severed the connection, checked the clock on
the wall. Three minutes and twenty-six seconds.

"Will there be anything else, sir?" Captain
Spencer said.

"I'll want to go out to the bleachers in about
twenty minutes. Have my car ready."

Roffner moved out of the briefing room into a
small lounge, his stomach paining him. He sat
down, watching Shaw as Shaw anticipated the
General's needs, opening a small refrigerator,
opening a carton of milk, pouring it into a glass.

"You don't look well," Shaw said.

"Nerves," Roffner said. He drank the milk,
closed his eyes for a moment, tried to relax. "I
want you to know that I am not without feelings,
Major. We've had our differences of opinion along
the line about this test, and it may have seemed to
you that I have been a hard-hearted son of a bitch.
But in my heart I know that what's going to
happen will be in the best interests of our
country."

"Yes, sir," Shaw said quietly. "I believe that
too."

It was almost time and the General stood up,

feeling no better but operating on his reserve power. He went into the briefing room, not wanting to share this moment with the crowds in monitoring. He stood at the slot window, clasped his hands behind his back, rocked back and forth on his heels. The missile was gleaming, almost as if the power it carried was shining through the aluminum skin. It seemed to him as if the missile were waiting for him, allowing him a long extra moment to get into position, to observe, for this was his test after all, his moment.

Then, suddenly, there was a bright burst of light, an explosive roar as the solid rocket fuel ignited and the missile leaped away from the trough. He followed it with his eyes long enough to see the fan-jet engine take hold, the stubby wings kick out into position. A silver bird, alert, responsive, full of a life of its own, a shining arc in the bright desert sunlight.

"It's away," he said, almost under his breath.

"Yes," the Major said. "It's away."

Chapter Twelve

It was done. Cameron had watched the launch from a television monitor, the missile leaping away from the ground, and he had witnessed the cheering of the control room. Ah, off in a burst of smoke and flame, a shining blur on the horizon, and he wondered how long it would take for the onboard computer to reach the gap in the programming. Perhaps it would happen as the missile banked for a sharp turn, and he wondered if there would be an electronic confusion in the guidance system, the nose camera relaying pictures for which there was no match. Could a machine be frantic in those moments when there was no control, in the split second before it slammed into a wall or rock?

He sucked in a breath. The test was finished and now all he needed was to find a way out, back to Vegas. He smiled, nodded at a technician as he went by, then picked up a clipboard and pretended to be studying long chains of numbers printed on a piece of paper while he figured out what to do.

He could not stay here, in this room full of technicians, for sooner or later one of them was going to ask him a question and realize that he was faking it, that he had no function. There would be a call to security, the sudden appearance of

armed men who would ask for his credentials, and
that would end it. He sauntered over to a console
near the door, spinning dials, digital readouts on a
panel beneath a television monitor which caught
the missile as it flew by a checkpoint. A roaring
whine, distracting, and he felt slightly breathless
at the monitored flyby over rough terrain, the
sleek cruise missile shooting over the ground,
such a blend of electronics, radar, instantaneous
relays, that it shot up automatically to roar over a
bluff and then tucked itself into the sheltering
configuration of a canyon, moving with such
speed it was difficult to follow it.

The monitor abandoned the picture of the
missile, picked up the view from the nose of the
missile, the ground beneath it passing in a blur as
if the camera were gobbling up the terrain.

He took out a pencil, checked at random the
numbers on the sheet held in the clipboard as if he
was performing a routine duty, then he slipped
out of the door and into the corridor.

There were two security officers at the exit
door, checking the colored badges of the civilians
who had come for the briefing. He could hear the
pattern of the words, the blue badges for bus
number one, red badges for two, yellow for three.
Polite, firm, formidable men. Would they hold him
up if he tried to go out the door? Would they be
able to look at his face and spot the desperation
and know that he was an interloper here?

No time to hold back. Only a half dozen civilians
remaining to be processed through the door. He
took another deep breath and with the clipboard
held firmly in his hand pushed in front of a young
man in a business suit, mumbling apologies,

looking directly into the face of a security Captain holding the bus roster.

"What's going on, Captain?" Cameron said. "You were supposed to stop Dr. Webster and tell him to report to monitoring."

"Who?" the Captain said, unsettled, and the game was working, for in the flurry of words the Captain immediately became defensive. He began to check through the lists of names. "Was he color coded, sir?" he said. "Do you know his bus assignment?"

"How would I know his bus assignment?" Cameron said, unrelenting. "I'll have to check the buses myself. If you see him, tell him we need him in monitoring."

The Captain's eyes flicked down to Cameron's name tag. "Yes, sir, Mr. Wicker."

Cameron went out the door, controlling the incipient panic within him, expecting at any moment to hear a voice call out for him to stop. He decided that if anybody tried to arrest him, he would take the pistol from his pocket and start firing. But no voice called out. He went down the sidewalk to the circle drive where the buses were parked, the passengers in line, loading. For a moment he considered boarding one of the buses and going out to the target site.

He decided against it. The longer he stayed here, the greater the odds he would be caught.

He scanned the horizon to the south, a range of barren mountains, and how many miles would it be to a highway, a settlement? Twenty. Perhaps thirty. Always barriers. In Pennsylvania it had been snow and here it was high desert, dry, rugged, a set-aside target range, thousands of square miles, all uninhabited. He could not walk out of here.

And then he saw the staff car sitting behind the buses, the front plate covered with a canvas shroud, undoubtedly stars beneath that cover. The sun was reflecting off the windshield but he could see the figure of a man behind the wheel. He slipped his hand into his pocket, was reassured by the bulky lump of the pistol. He licked his lips, his mouth dry. He was certain one of the guards was watching him from the gate and he felt a visceral trembling.

He walked back to the driver's window of the car and the features of the driver took shape. Young. Slightly unruly hair. The dryness of the desert. Cameron glanced at his clipboard. "Whose car is this, Captain?"

"It's General Roffner's," the Captain said. "It's a designated vehicle."

Cameron wrote on the clipboard. He wanted to pull the pistol, force the Captain to drive him out of here, for he was not sure how much longer his legs would hold him. No, not the time for it, not in full view of the gate guards. He would have to maneuver the car to a less obvious spot.

"We're running a little behind," Cameron said officiously. "You're to stay in position for another five minutes. If the buses aren't loaded by then, pull up in front of them."

"I'm not supposed to pick up the General for another twenty minutes."

"I don't make the schedules," Cameron said. "What's your speedometer reading?"

The workable diversion of a demand and the Captain dutifully examined the dash. "Seven thousand three six three, point four," he said.

"When you take it back to the motor pool, make sure it's serviced," Cameron said. "We're having too many breakdowns in new vehicles."

He walked back past the buses, still not loaded. He squinted up at the sky, knowing that the cruise missile was out there somewhere. A pair of F-14 jets flew over, low altitude, shaking the ground with their roar. He would wait until the General's car moved in front of the buses and then, very quietly, with no fuss at all, he would slide into the passenger side, pull the pistol, and commandeer the car.

He reached the front of the building. Placing the clipboard under his arm temporarily, he lighted a cigarette and just stood there, highly visible, the cigarette clenched in his teeth, smoking. The best defense, certainly, the stance of authority. And then he saw Major Shaw come out of the front door. He could read trouble in the Major's face, the thin set of his mouth.

"I've been looking for you," Shaw said in a low voice.

Cameron continued to stare straight ahead, methodically sucking the smoke into his lungs. "I'm getting out," he said, and he pulled up the clipboard and wrote another number on it. "In exactly three minutes, I'm going to take the General's car."

"It didn't work," Shaw said, his eyes following the black speck of a bird wheeling in the sky.

"What didn't work?"

"The reprogramming." And Shaw's voice droned on while Cameron tried not to hear, to blot out the words with a force of will because he did not want to hear. But the information came anyway, the technical terms, the discussion of the computer. Aristotelian logic, a binary system to the extreme, and the test was either on or it was off, and the cruise missile either locked onto the prison or it followed its original course to the test site.

"I don't want to hear it," Cameron said through clenched teeth.

"That damn thing is not going to crash," Shaw said. "It's still going to destroy the prison or we've just shifted it back to the original target." Shaw took a moment. He was having difficulty speaking. "The goddamned missile is still armed."

Either the prison would be hit or the spectators at the test site. He felt physical pain: in his wounded hand, in his knees, especially in his head, the area behind his burning eyes. He saw the staff car pulling around the buses, coming into position.

"I've had enough," he said. "More than enough." He took a last pull on his cigarette, dropped it onto the sidewalk and ground it out beneath his heel. The General's car had stopped with the right-hand door no more than five feet from where he stood. The Captain had opened a magazine and was reading, as if to make it easy for him.

He thought of Wicker lying out there on the desert, his own father dead in Las Vegas, Reeves dead in Washington, and if he took the opportunity which now presented itself, then everything that had happened to him would make no sense at all. He stood staring at the car and a rage mounted within him against Shaw for bringing him this information, for not keeping silent, for being so goddamned weak he could not handle it himself. He wanted to hit him squarely in the middle of his face, expend his anger. But he did not.

He had taken this on. He would see it through.

"All right," he said quietly, deliberately. "Where is General Roffner?" And he turned his back on the car.

2

As he stood in the monitoring room, Roffner felt as if his whole life had been lived for this moment, the culmination of all his efforts. The missile was aloft, he could see it in the monitors, a flash of silver, as if it were alive. He checked the electronic panels, altitude, fuel rate, speed. The next wars would be fought like this, from electronic command posts, the sophisticated battles of the engineers. He walked down the room slowly, his hands laced behind his back, pausing to observe a group of engineers watching a screen intently, excited. The ultimate game and they were calculating the trajectory of heat-seeking missiles (hypothetical) fired by the pursuing jets. No contest here. The cruise missile made itself a part of the terrain, threading through shielding canyons with absolute precision.

At the end of the room he found his own team, the unit within a unit, the monitors of BRIMSTONE. They were running continual tests of the measuring devices within the prison itself, waiting for the explosion which throw the needles off the scales, the great and instantaneous flash of radiation which would write its own deadly signature on

multiple tapes. Roffner stood next to Glassic who
sat at a console, absently stroking his beard,
staring through heavy glasses at a single wavering
needle on a dial. He reached out, tapped the dial
with a spatulate fingernail, glared up at Roffner.

"We should have run a new circuit outside the
prison power plant," he said almost accusingly. "I
can't guarantee the reading on this one."

"It will work out all right," Roffner said. "We're
covering the same area with a remote unit."

"It's not the same thing," Glassic said, a mutter
as he turned back to his own equipment.

Roffner felt a brief stab of pain. He had learned
to wait and he did so now and after a moment the
pain disappeared.

"Excuse me, sir," the Major said, and Roffner
turned around to find Shaw standing beside him.

"What is it, Major?"

Shaw looked discomfited, edgy, plainly ill at
ease. "I have some figures that disturb me," he
said, looking around the room to see if anyone was
listening. "We can't talk here. If you'll come with
me, it won't take a minute."

Roffner followed him into a hallway to the small
cubicle of an office which served as a place for the
Range Officer to take care of his paperwork.

The Major opened the office door, stood aside as
Roffner went in. Only when he was inside did he
see the man sitting behind the metal desk, the
pistol in his hand. Roffner heard the door shut
behind him. The Major was standing against it.
And quite suddenly, Roffner knew what was going
on.

"You must be Cameron," Roffner said, no
sense of panic, maintaining a cool non-stressful

demeanor while his mind raced to define the problem and classiy alternative solutions to it. He could not afford to make a mistake.

"That's right," Cameron said. "Sit down, General."

"Nothing can stop the test at this point," Roffner said.

"Sit down."

Roffner eased himself into a metal chair, feeling slightly claustrophobic in the small windowless room with the concrete block walls. "You must know by now, I can't be intimidated."

Cameron cut him off. "You have a problem, General. I've changed the programming on the missile. Now, I think the neutron warhead is disarmed but the Major doesn't."

Roffner shook his head. "I don't believe that."

"You'd better think about it," Cameron said. "Or you're going to have a hell of a lot of dead people on your hands, in the wrong place, where your goddamned measuring devices won't work."

A bluff, of course, Roffner thought, because certainly the Major would have covered all this ground with Cameron. Cameron, he thought, looking at the man, a glorified clerk, a bureaucrat who could not have been expected to get this far and yet had. It would not take much to set him off for he was at the extreme edge of fatigue. Roffner would give him no excuse. He kept his voice low, rational, non-defensive. "Let me understand you," Roffner said. "You're telling me that you've reprogrammed, that the missile will go to the original test site, that the neutron warhead has not been disarmed?"

"Yes, that's what the Major thinks," Cameron said.

Roffner frowned. The computer? Had they actually reached the computer, penetrated the language far enough to affect the program? He licked his lips, looked from Cameron's face to the Major's.

He brought his fingers to his stomach, beginning to massage the pain, lips pursed, thinking. Were they sophisticated enough to have created this perfect dilemma and to have placed him in the center of it? Yes, certainly. He had seen it on the battlefield. If you put an ordinary man through enough hell he either folded or was sharpened by it. Cameron had not folded. "So you want me to abort the test," Roffner said.

"You can't abort it," Shaw said. "You don't have that power. The programming is screwed up, General, believe me. Your first move is to call Nellis and get some F-14's into the air with kill capability. Then you feed them the programmed route. Let them have a clear shot at it."

They were clever, Roffner had to give them that. The part about his inability to abort the test was genius, designed to give the story credibility. "Is that what you would do, Major?" Roffner said. "Then why haven't you done it?"

"I don't have the authority."

"What you mean is that nobody would believe you," Roffner said evenly. "You gentlemen have offered me a hell of a good scenario with the added feature that it has to be accepted blindly. Because there's no way to prove it, one way or the other."

"There's proof," Cameron said. "I bypassed

your MONITOR subroutine. I changed the first instruction in that subroutine to GOTO MPZ. Call Washington. Check it out."

In five minutes the guidance system would lock onto the prison and all the discussion in this room would be academic. He reached out for the telephone and he punched straight through to the computer center at Mt. Pleasant, West Virginia, asked for Reynolds, pictured the man as he would answer the telephone, tall, spare, lanky, pragmatic, the man who had done the highly complex master program in the first place.

But Reynolds' slow voice did not come onto the line. "Smith," the man said, simply, no further identification.

"This is General Roffner. Put Reynolds on the line."

"He's not available at the moment."

"Where is he? Goddamnit, get him on the line."

"Hold on a moment." There was a pause on the line and Roffner could hear discussion. "You'd better give me your extension and let Reynolds call you back."

"This is critical," Roffner said, sweating. "You get him and you get him now. Where is he?"

"He has a bad case of the trots," Smith said. "The toilet on this floor is out of commission and he went upstairs. I'll send someone to get him." He left the line again, came back. "Is there any way I can help until he gets here?"

Roffner closed his eyes, pinched the bridge of his nose, concentrating. "Are you monitoring the test?"

"Yes, sir. We are."

"There's a thought here that we might have a

malfunction in the on-board computer, an inadvertent change in programming."

"If there was any change, the computer would catch it. We would get a red flag here."

"Get Reynolds," Roffner said.

"He's on the way."

Roffner waited and finally he heard Reynolds' deep voice on the line and Roffner outlined the problem, trying to be precise, gearing to match Reynolds' decelerated pace. Reynolds was the best in the business but he spoke with an often excruciating slowness, conversations full of long pauses. Finally, Roffner conveyed to him the changes that Cameron claimed to have made. "Is that bypass possible?" Roffner said.

"Technically, I suppose," Reynolds said. "I can check it out."

"Goddamnit," Roffner said. "This is critical. I need an answer now."

"Ten minutes," Reynolds said. "What's your number? Where are you?"

"No time for that," Roffner said. "What are the odds that we could have an armed warhead and the original target?"

"Let's just say it might be possible. I don't have any way of calculating the odds."

"Then we'll take another tack. If you find such a change, can you correct it?"

"We followed your original instructions," Reynolds said, an almost imperceptible testiness in his voice, and Roffner realized he had run into the man's defensiveness, for Reynolds was launched into a discussion of the original safeguards. Roffner did not try to follow all the logic, the technical terms, the computer mystique, for in the end it came down to a simple truth. Reynolds could do nothing from his end except relay instructions to Roffner who would have to make any changes from here. Finally, with great deliberation, he put the telephone back on the cradle, not through anger but simply because there was nothing left to say.

He looked at Cameron. "There's still no way to confirm or deny."

"I think there is," Cameron said. He reached up, switched on the television monitor on the wall, the picture of a mountain peak, the glimmer of silver as the remote camera picked up the cruise missile as it made its turn. "If we're wrong, the guidance system should be locking onto the form of the prison about now. So have a look, Roffner."

Roffner stared at the screen. The camera shifted slowly, tracking the path of the missile at a great distance, the view widening enough that he could now see the prison itself, the walls, a guard tower. The focus was so accurate he could see a guard in that tower, a large, beefy man leaning on the rail, staring out toward the approaching missile. Roffner's breath caught in his throat. He willed the missile to alter its course, to veer to its right as the TERCOM guidance system took hold. But it did not. In a blur, the missile swept past the prison, the guard watching it go, and in a moment the next camera picked it up. Cameron reached up and switched off the screen.

The telephone rang. Cameron picked it up. The voice on the other end was strained, hushed, bewildered. "This is Colonel Askins. I'm looking for General Roffner."

"You can speak to him in a moment," Cameron

said, his voice clear. "Have all the television crews moved on out to the bleachers?"

"Let me speak to Roffner."

"Answer my question."

"Yes. They've all moved out."

Cameron extended the telephone to Roffner. Roffner took it, cleared his throat. His face was covered with beads of sweat, flesh pale. He had difficulty concentrating. "Yes," he said hoarsely.

"We have a malfunction," Askins said. "We have a flyby on checkpoint seven."

"All right," he said slowly, moving from one word to the next with great deliberation. "Get Reynolds at Mt. Pleasant on an open line. He's tracing the malfunction now. Call General Forbes. Explain the situation."

"That's not advisable," Askins said. "It's an automatic abort. There's no need to involve him."

"We can't be certain," Roffner said. "Tell him we're playing for keeps now." Askins was still talking when Roffner put down the telephone. He removed a handkerchief from his pocket, wiped his face. Heavy sweating. Yet he felt chilled in here.

Cameron stood up stiffly. "How much longer will it take for the missile to reach the target grandstand?"

"Nine minutes," Shaw said.

Cameron sat back down, studying the General whose face was rigid now, then he looked to Shaw again. "I think you had better order the evacuation of the grandstand area," he said. "And once you've done that, have them patch me in with one of the television crews."

Shaw grabbed up the telephone and began to

make the calls, but Cameron could hear the frustration in his voice as he talked to a Lieutenant Anderson in charge of the buses. "I don't give a shit about your schedule, Lieutenant. You get those goddamned buses back there and you begin an immediate evacuation." He severed the connection, called the field number at the bleachers. "Who is this?" he said into the telephone. "This is Major Shaw, Sergeant. You get to Captain Dean and you tell him we have a malfunction. All persons are to evacuate the bleacher area immediately." He was sweating and Cameron could tell that the Sergeant was giving him trouble, protesting the impossibility of the assignment. "I don't care where he is. You do it yourself. Get those people out of there. Any available vehicles. On foot. You do it. Now, get me somebody from one of the television vans. I want to talk to him."

He held the telephone for a long minute, handed it to Cameron. Cameron found a man with a New York accent on the line.

"This is Chylinski."

"I'm calling for General Roffner," Cameron said. "There's only time for me to say this once, so listen carefully. All hell is going to break loose out there very shortly. The missile is armed with a neutron warhead. We need a record of everything that happens there. So pull your van back to a distance of at least two miles. Do you understand?"

"Are you putting me on?" Chylinski said. "Is this a joke?"

"You stay where you are and you'll be one very dead man," Cameron said. "Move it."

He put down the telephone, gestured with the

pistol toward Roffner. "On your feet, General," he said. "It looks like you're going to get your test after all. I want you to be there to see the whole thing."

Roffner shook his head. "Reynolds will find a way to abort it." But he stood up, followed Shaw into the hallway, with Cameron at his back, into the bright sunlight outside the building.

Cameron pulled open the driver's door of the General's car. "Get out, Captain," he said. "Major Shaw's going to drive."

Captain Spencer started to protest but Roffner waved his hand. "Do as he says."

Spencer moved out of the way and Shaw took his place while Cameron opened the back door and sat beside the General. The car jumped ahead, Shaw muttering to himself as he wheeled it around and headed down a graveled road. Too much time consumed, Cameron thought. Five minutes left. Roffner's face was gray.

"It's too bad all your monitoring equipment's in the wrong place," Cameron said. "But you can witness the effects firsthand. It's your project. And they're your people."

Cameron could hear the martial music rising from distant loudspeakers. The car topped a rise and he saw the bleachers and the banners and the tank column sitting off in the hummocky desert.

Surrealistic, yes, down there at the bleachers there were clusters of people waiting patiently in the shade, but the lead bus had blown a tire and two officers were looking at it while the rest of the buses waited in line. No frantic movement. A few people were walking away, up the slope, but it was a warm day and everything was orderly and civilized and the Sousa marches were playing over the loudspeakers. The television and film crews were still in place in front of the grandstand except for one lone van which had moved to the top of the slope. Chylinski had believed. An Air Policeman in a white helmet liner, white gloves, stood waving the few military cars up, one at a time.

On the platform, a Captain stood at the microphone, but whatever he was saying was lost in the blare of the music. Ah, so goddamned orderly. Cameron turned to Roffner. "You get up there on that platform, you son of a bitch," he said. "And if you truly believe that there's no danger, that your scientific safeguards are going to work, then you calm them down, keep them in place until they're incinerated." He waved the pistol. "Get out."

Roffner went out the door, stood for a moment collecting himself, then walked steadily toward the platform. Shaw wheeled the car around the waiting vehicles and Cameron burst out of the door and ran up to a crowd of civilians waiting in line. He grabbed a woman by the arm. "Get into the car," he said.

The woman pulled back slightly. "My husband is—" she began and he immediately moved to the next woman, older, a small boy at her side, and the woman seemed to realize the urgency of what was happening. "Thank you," she said. "Come along, Robby." He moved on, amazed that these people could be so calmly passive. He saw Shaw talking to the people on the other side of the bleachers, having no more luck than he was having. Suddenly, the music stopped and he looked up to see Roffner standing on the platform, at the microphone. His mouth opened as if to speak, closed again.

Cameron was listening past the sigh of the wind. He heard the sound, the vague and almost inaudible whine of the turbojet engine. He could not tell where it was coming from. No time left, none, and he signaled the Major, ran back to the car, his heart pumping. Three women and the boy in the back seat, no more than that, and he jammed the car into gear as the Major climbed in on the passenger side. The car leaped forward, tires throwing up gravel. He drove up the slope.

In the rearview mirror, Cameron saw the wink of light from the west, a flash, something reflecting the sun, so faint at first as to be almost invisible, a speck which shot over the saw-toothed mountains, dipped down to the flat, increasing in size, racing against its own sound, becoming a shape as it drew nearer. Despite the continuing wave of the Air Policeman's arm, summoning the cars, the removal of the people at the bleachers slowed to a standstill.

The television cameras wheeled around to pick up the approaching cruise missile, the people turning to watch. Roffner was still standing there, but he was yelling now, his words lost in the roar of two F-14 jets as they flashed by, impotent, unarmed. The missile drew closer, in its own way dreadfully beautiful, very stable in its path, adjusting to a narrow side arc as its electronic matching device picked up the pattern of the tank column. Seconds away from the tanks, trailing a thin blue exhaust and everybody was watching and nobody turned to run.

The car bounced over the brow of the hill, hit

loose gravel, spun around just as the missile disappeared in a bright, intensely white light of its
own making, a great sphere of light which seemed
to burn away the air. The center tanks in the mock
Rūssian column fragmented, exploded, were gone,
and the fireball lifted up the floor of the desert in a
great column of sand. The car shook with the
shock waves, the earth trembling violently, and
the roar of sound hit at the same time, the rocks
and debris showering the roof, the blowing sand
so thick it silted the windshield.

Slowly, Cameron pushed open the door as if the
devastation required a witness. A woman was
crying in the back seat. He climbed to a rock, dis-
believing, aware that Shaw had joined him. The
whole flat was filled with a haze of smoke and dust
and a large cloud was billowing upward, and
Cameron could only see shapes down below, one
bus turned over on its side, wheels still spinning,
the skeletal outline of the collapsed grandstand, a
few people, just standing in position or wandering
around.

At ground zero, a crater scooped out of the
earth, and incredibly, the tanks positioned at a
distance were littered with rocks and blown dirt
but physically unharmed. The echo of the
explosion persisted, bounced back from the
distant mountains. Only now could Cameron hear
the cries of the survivors.

A jet screamed overhead, keeping its distance.
The radiation, the invisible pall of neutron radiation, and those people down below who had not
been killed in the blast were walking dead, and if
there had been soldiers in those tanks, they would
be dead as well. But around him on the slope he

saw at least a dozen people, perhaps more. The self-reliant ones.

He stood in shock until he heard the muted sounds of anguish and only then did he turn to look at Major Shaw who stood perfectly motionless, his arms dangling at his sides in complete helplessness, the tears streaming down his face. Weeping.

Chapter Thirteen

When Cameron came out of the Las Vegas hospital, he used the rear exit to avoid the camp of reporters at the front, the omnipresent television cameras covering the aftermath of the disaster. The rear parking lot was cluttered with military vehicles, transportation for the teams of medical experts who continued to arrive from all over the country to treat the radiation victims. He half expected to be stopped at any moment by one of the many teams of military policemen he could see around the ambulances, but he was not. He was not reassured. Perhaps the final accounting would be delayed, but it would come.

He saw Connie waiting for him in a rented car. He could read the concern in her face.

"Well, Willie?" she said.

"No radiation," he said, leaning back against the seat. "Not one little goddamned roentgen. The neutron bomb worked perfectly, no widespread damage at all except to those poor damned watchers in the bleachers. Let's get out of here."

She drove away, threading through the military vehicles until she reached the street. "You look like you're dead on your feet. I'm taking you back to the motel."

"I can't sleep, not yet," he said. "Drive down to the post office. I want to pick up the tape."

"It's eight o'clock," she said. "The post office will be closed." It was dark and he had not even noticed. He lighted a cigarette, looked out at the street, the crowds undiminished, the resplendent displays of neon lighting up the sky. Business as usual. Nothing had changed and yet nothing would ever be the same again.

She put her hand on his leg. "Are you hungry?"

"No," he said. "I want a drink, at one of the casinos. I want to be around people."

"I don't want to stay in Las Vegas," she said, shaking her head. "I don't even want to pick up our luggage. I just want to catch a plane and go. Anywhere."

"I'm tired, babe, and I'm numb. I killed one of their men and they can't write that off. I saved a couple of thousand people but inadvertently condemned a bunch of others."

"What really happened out there?" she said. "They haven't released any details."

"Errors," he said simply. "A tragedy of errors." Shaw's face flashed into his mind as he had last seen him in the hospital, gray, heavily sedated. There had been no other way to stop his weeping. "A goddamned massacre," Cameron said at last, and nothing more.

When they pulled up to a casino, Connie turned the car over to valet parking. As she stood beneath the garish light of the portico, she paused to examine the bandage on his left hand. "How's your hand?" she said. "What did they do to it?"

"Gave me some antibiotics for a minor infection," he said. "It's in good shape."

He felt reassured by the noise in the casino, the rattle of the slot machines. The semi-darkness was soothing. He found an empty table at the piano bar and he sat with his back to a rough stone pilaster, cool to the touch. He felt more secure here, the return of the primitive man to the cave, and he thought of the bar in Missouri and tried to remember the shape of the boy who had died in the explosion of the station wagon. Already, the memory was fading. He could remember only general proportions. A sense of vitality, skinny, a child. He thought of Annie and the bars of Washington. She had been a true cave dweller, uncomfortable in sunlight.

He looked up, the face of the waitress young in the candlelight. "What would you like?" she said.

"Bourbon and water for both of us," Connie said protectively. The waitress left, returned with the drinks. He emptied his glass, drank it down.

"Connie, as nearly as I could tell from the talk at the hospital, seventeen people were killed outright."

"I think it's better if you get your mind off it."

"I can't get my mind off it." He ordered another drink. "They still don't know how many people got a fatal dose of radiation. Twenty. Maybe thirty." He tried to bring the scene alive in his mind, to care about what had happened out there, to feel sorrow or rage, anything except the numbness. It was self-protective and he knew it. Major Shaw had taken the other alternative and had been shattered by it.

He saw a man coming across the casino in the semi-darkness, blond-haired, athletic, in his thirties, tailored sports clothes. Cameron tensed slightly. It was one of them and he knew it. Connie touched his arm. "That's Colonel Dearborn," she said.

"You know him?"

"He came to see me this afternoon. No pressure. Questions about when we arrived in Las Vegas."

Dearborn said hello to Connie, then introduced himself to Cameron. "I tried to catch you at the hospital this afternoon," he said. "But apparently I missed you in all the confusion. A terrible thing."

"Yes, a terrible thing," Cameron said wryly. "What do you want, Colonel?"

"Do you mind if I sit down?"

"I mind, but sit down anyway."

"Thank you." Dearborn sat and then signaled the waitress, ordered another round of drinks for Cameron and Connie, a Scotch and water for himself.

"What's your title, Colonel?" Cameron said. "What do you do?"

"I'm in public information. Air Force," Dearborn said, smiling at the waitress as he paid for the drinks. He waited until she was gone, then he tasted the drink without consuming any of it.

"I repeat," Cameron said. "What do you want?"

"General Roffner died this afternoon," Dearborn said. "He was killed indirectly by the explosion, a flying piece of metal." He looked off thoughtfully toward the young man playing the piano. "Senator Livermore also died."

"I'm tired," Cameron said. "So let's cut this short. I know that sooner or later, whether it's by you or some other military son of a bitch, I'm going to be picked up, arraigned, whatever you want to call it. And I'm telling you now, I'm prepared to fight. No more running."

Dearborn looked startled, then blank. "Maybe you know something I don't, Mr. Cameron."

"I don't believe that for a moment." Cameron drank again. "I killed Wicker. He tried to kill me and I shot him."

"Wicker?" Dearborn said, puzzled, as if trying to place the name. "There's obviously a misunderstanding here." He took an envelope out of his pocket, removed a sheet of paper, handed it to Cameron. The light was too dim. Cameron could not read it.

"What does it say?"

"A report from the military police," Dearborn said. "An employee of the Department of Defense named Wicker was scheduled to observe the cruise missile test. He was driving up from Las Vegas, was taken ill, pulled off the road and died of a heart attack. I guess he was unable to summon help. I have a certified copy of the autopsy report, if you'd like to see it. There wasn't any evidence of a gunshot wound. His body was flown back to Washington today. I think his wife decided on an immediate cremation. He didn't have any other relatives."

"So," Cameron said, a sudden exhalation of breath and the whole pattern was beginning to come clear. "I forgot the miraculous powers of the establishment," he said. "The ability to change water into wine. And all the changes in Washington, what goddamned miracle has been worked there?"

"Oh, that," Dearborn said, running the pad of an index finger around the rim of his Scotch glass. "Those charges were cleaned up yesterday. You

simply weren't available to be notified. It was a
combination of bureaucratic foul-ups."

Connie put her hand on Cameron's arm, looked
directly at Dearborn with an intensity which took
Cameron by surprise. "You're saying that at this
minute William is a free man? He can go anywhere he wants, no charges, totally free?"

"Of course," Dearborn said easily. "I don't know
all the details, Mr. Cameron, but from what I hear,
you've been pretty severely hassled. I can
guarantee that is at an end. I don't know what I
can do about an official apology."

"To hell with your apologies," Connie said. "It's
over, Willie, the whole nightmare. Let's go."

"No," he said gently. "It's not nearly over. I
haven't been exposed to the ultimate miracle yet."
He looked at Dearborn. "How will you explain
BRIMSTONE?" he said. "How are you going to
rationalize what happened out there on the
desert?"

"I don't know what BRIMSTONE refers to,"
Dearborn said, his face shining with absolute sin-
cerity. "I've been doing some preliminary investigation of the accident and all the reports aren't in
yet. But it appears that there was a technical
mistake. A neutron warhead was inadvertently
armed. How that happened, we don't know, but
we'll certainly find out. Anyway, General Roffner
learned about the mistake while the cruise missile
was in flgiht, did his best to abort it and when that
couldn't be done, gave his own life in an attempt to
evacuate the people in danger."

"No," Cameron said.

"If you have other information—"

"Jesus Christ," Cameron said, a single feeling

flooding into him, so full that he ached with the power of it, an exuberant sense of indignation, in a new form this time, an anger too large to be satisfied with an attack on a man like Dearborn. "Do you know the trading game, Dearborn? It's excellent conditioning. Raise your left hand off the table. Come on, a fraction of an inch will do it."

Dearborn gave him a quizzical glare, did not move. "I'm not here to play games," he said. "You will come out of this as something of a hero yourself, Mr. Cameron. You saved the life of the Senator's wife, his grandson. They were in your car."

"Wonderful," Cameron said. "Now raise your hand."

Dearborn's hand came off the table, almost reflexively. "I don't see the point."

Cameron laughed, put a ten-dollar bill on the table. "Very good. One exercise of a motor reflex and you get your drinks paid for. And now we try a bigger one." He signaled the waitress, asked her to bring him a telephone and plug it in. "Do you want the Nixon tape?" he said to Dearborn.

"As a curiosity," Dearborn said. "I've heard about the alleged Nixon tape. I doubt that anybody could ever authenticate it."

"There are a couple of minor things I'll trade it for," Cameron said, pushing. "There's a man named Purdy with the General Accounting Office. I want him fired. It's not going to accomplish much to get rid of one entrenched bureaucrat, but let's call it a whim."

Dearborn was obviously uneasy. He raised his glass and this time he drank. "I can see how some officials in government might consider the tape to be valuable," Dearborn said. "They would have a chance to submit it to technical analysis, prove it false, put a disturbing rumor to rest." He paused. "And perhaps I could accept your word that this Purdy is incompetent. But of course we would need evidence to that effect. It might take a little time."

"Colonel," Cameron said, "you have the power to make this trade and both of us know it. Do you want the trade or not?"

Dearborn pursed his lips, stared down at the table. "I can give you a tentative yes."

"Fine, then we'll do it," Cameron said. He had him now, all the pretenses stripped away. He pushed again. "I'll want one additional thing. I want a public admission by the military that my father was murdered."

"I don't know what in the hell you're talking about," Dearborn said, totally unsettled, finding himself in a situation beyond his training.

"Then I take it you don't want the package trade," Cameron said. "It's just as well. That was Wicker's game and it was an insidious one. Once you start trading the small things away, it's too damned easy to start trading the big ones." He picked up the telephone, asked the operator to get him the local Associated Press office. He looked at Dearborn. The Colonel had tensed in his chair, as if he were ready to move. "Now, that is a trade I would make with you," Cameron said. "I'd welcome a bar brawl with you here and now. I might lose, but it would blow your cover sky high."

"Hang it up, Cameron. You're making a mistake."

But the answering voice was there, male, and in the background Cameron could hear typewriters and voices, a convocation of reporters.

"This is William Cameron. You can check around if you don't know the name."

"I recognize the name," the voice said. "What can I do for you, Mr. Cameron?"

"You can provide me with a platform," Cameron said, keeping his eyes on Dearborn who had a dark expression on his face. "Hold on." Cameron checked the matchbook on the table. "I'm at the MGM Grand Hotel, in the piano bar. I'll hold a press conference here in fifteen minutes. I will cover various government murders, the neutron bomb explosion and the missing eighteen and a half minutes of the Nixon tape."

"We'll be there. Fifteen minutes."

Cameron put the telephone down. Dearborn had recovered himself, moving back to the calm demeanor, but the evenness of his voice was a thin veneer. "A great mistake, Mr. Cameron. If you had left this alone, you would have come out of it smelling like a rose. There's nothing you can say that will make any difference at this point. For every statement you make, we'll have at least fifteen credible experts to deny it. We have the paperwork to cover everything."

"Fine," Cameron said. "You do that. But the chances are pretty damned good that there will be more than one Reeves among those witnesses. You expand a lie like this too far and it collapses of its own weight, Dearborn. That's Cameron's first rule of government. And your structure is going to come down with one hell of a crash."

Dearborn shrugged, stood up, left Cameron's

money on the table. "I think we'll be seeing each other again."

"Yes," Cameron said. "I suppose we will." He watched Dearborn making his way out of the casino and then turned to Connie who was looking at him with great admiration. He took her hand in his. "Well, babe," he said. "What do you think?"

"I was wrong," she said. "You really have to make your stand, don't you?"

"There was never any other choice."

She reached out, touched his face, smiled. "You want to give me the odds on this round?" she said.

"It may take some time and it's bound to be bloody, but just offhand I'd say they don't have a chance against the two of us."

"I'm touched by that," she said. "The two of us. That has a very nice ring to it, doesn't it?"

"A damned nice ring," he said, smiling. "Very nice, indeed."

ATTENTION: SCHOOLS AND CORPORATIONS

PINNACLE Books are available at quantity discounts with bulk purchases for educational, business or special promotional use. For further details, please write to: SPECIAL SALES MANAGER, Pinnacle Books, Inc., 1430 Broadway, New York, NY 10018.

WRITE FOR OUR FREE CATALOG

If there is a Pinnacle Book you want—and you cannot find it locally—it is available from us simply by sending the title and price plus 75+ to cover mailing and handling costs to:

> Pinnacle Books, Inc.
> Reader Service Department
> 1430 Broadway
> New York, NY 10018

Please allow 6 weeks for delivery.

_____Check here if you want to receive our catalog regularly.